VOW TO ME

S. WILSON

ISBN: 9798322728412

Cover Designer: A. Rayne

Editor: Belle Manuel

Re-edited: Stacey's Bookcorner Editing Services

NOTE FROM THE AUTHOR

Please note that this is a dark mafia romance containing explicit sexual scenes, graphic violence, blood, death, offensive language, kidnapping, torture and mentions of human trafficking.

To all the badass women being put down by men:
Kick him in the dick and hold your head up high, girl. You've got
this x

CHAPTER ONE

Luca

"Tell me something, sunshine. Either you talk or end up with a crowbar in your ass while we carve our initials into your skin," I say to the piece of shit Colombian strung up like a pig in the middle of the warehouse.

We've been here for seven hours, and it's clear the fucker isn't gonna talk. So far, he's lost all his fingers and eight toes. Unfortunately, he was already missing two, so I couldn't confiscate them like I did the rest. I've also shot him in both of his kneecaps and flayed the skin on his right arm.

All he did was glare at me from where he's tied up, he hasn't made a sound, and it's really starting to piss me off.

Our friend Juan here grew up in the foster system, has never married, and doesn't seem to have a steady girlfriend, so we don't even have any family members we can threaten. We don't hurt women or children but it's always nice to have the threat there to get them talking.

"He's not giving in, bro," my younger brother Marco says from where he stands in the corner, casually leaning against the wall eating a bag of chips.

Marco doesn't enjoy torturing people as much as I do. He isn't squeamish at all, just doesn't find the same excitement in chopping off body parts as I do.

Yeah, I'm a sick bastard, but it's fun!

I sigh, admitting defeat and walk over to the table next to Marco that houses the equipment we use. I pick up a meat cleaver and walk back over, the big fucker knows he's about to die, and judging by the glare he's giving me—rather than begging or whimpering like most men would—I'd say he doesn't really give a shit that his miserable existence is about to come to an end.

I take a deep breath and swing my arm, hitting the spot on his neck just right so I'm left watching as his head drops to the floor at my feet and spraying blood all over the place.

Oops.

"Did you really have to make such a fucking mess?" Marco asks, exasperated.

"I mean, I could have put a bullet between his eyes but where's the fun in that?" I say while sporting a grin. "Besides, it's not like you'll be cleaning the blood off the floor, Marco. Quit your whining."

"Let's just shower and change. We better go see Dad and tell him the ugly fuck wouldn't talk."

Great, we love our father, but he's also the Don of the New York Mafia.

Me, being the eldest son, makes me the heir and his second in command. Marco, the middle child, is a capo and technically the "spare" should I get myself fucked up or killed, and our youngest brother, Enzo, is just a fucking lunatic who likes fucking things up. We tend to send him on missions where we want things blown up or when we want someone to cause some havoc. The kid has a screw loose and enjoys mayhem, so calculated attacks or interrogation aren't exactly his thing. Fuck, he'd probably give in after ten minutes and start playing with their organs.

After we've both showered and changed, I instruct the soldiers placed at the warehouse to clean up the mess inside before we make our way over to the Escalade waiting out front. Normally, I'd drive myself in my Bugatti, however, we've been at war with the Cartel and Bratva for the last eight months, and Dad has ordered us to only travel in bulletproof cars with a driver.

The war between us started last May when Alejandro Muñoz, the head of the Colombian Cartel, made a business deal with Dimitri Novikov, the Pakhan of the Russian Bratva. Their deal fucked us over from both sides, leading to us retaliating and blowing up one of their shipments.

Since then, it's only escalated, and because of their truce, they have the advantage and we're losing men daily.

The Colombian we just tortured for information was one of Muñoz's top men. In the past month, we've had six deals fall through that the Bratva and Cartel shouldn't know about. We know we've got a rat; we just don't know who it is. And if we keep going the way we are, we'll all be dead by the time we find them.

The car stopping shakes me from my thoughts, and I realize we're at the Romano estate, also known as our family home. Me, Marco and Enzo all have our own places now, so it isn't so much a home but a base of operations. Arriving at the gates, the guard gives us a nod to go through and we pull up to the main entrance.

"How pissed do you think he's going to be?" Marco asks as we get out of the car.

There's a stereotype surrounding Mafia Dons, showing them as cold and ruthless towards their family, but our dad is great and always made sure we knew we were loved. He tried his best to give us a real childhood since our mother died while giving birth to Enzo and he became a single parent.

The housekeeper, Beatrice—who's worked for our family since before I was born—lets us in, giving us both a warm smile before telling us that our father is in his office. I give her a nod, and we walk through the entry way and into the office where he's waiting for us.

Taking a seat in front of the desk, I look at our dad and give him the run-down of everything that happened with our friend Juan—explaining how the fucker stayed tight lipped isn't exactly what I enjoy doing considering I'm known as one of the best interrogators in New York, but sometimes some nuts just won't crack. He sits and listens, his hands carefully placed on his lap, his face blank while he takes in the information I'm giving him.

"Well, I hoped you'd have got at least something, but I guess we'll just have to keep trying until we find someone to talk. I'm also keeping certain information within our close circle and feeding false information to the others to see if we can find our rat," Dad says with a sigh.

"The other capos don't know we have a rat. I'm trying to keep it that way. If they start gossiping like a bunch of old ladies, word will get around and then they're going to end up accusing us of not having a handle on things. That's the last thing we need with everything already going on. We've lost forty-two men in the last three months alone, we don't need a rebellion on our hands as well."

"I agree, which is why I've made a deal with Antonio Bianchi," he says, his expression grim. I have a feeling I'm not going to like what he has to say.

I wait patiently, not wanting to be the one to ask what exactly this "deal" with the head of the Chicago Mafia is. We've had a truce with the Chicago outfit for years, but it's very rare that deals are made between us; we usually just exist peacefully and ignore each other.

Marco, who is standing behind me, walks over to the drinks trolley and grabs a bottle of whiskey and three glasses. Clearly, he doesn't like the sound of this either.

Dad sighs. "Bianchi has a lot of spare men. He's agreed to send us an extra forty men to help us while we sort all this out. We've also agreed on gun shipments, seeing as though we've lost our previous deal with the Cartel, we need to set up new contacts. Bianchi agreed to deal with us directly with a fifteen percent discount, he has what we need while we get through the war with these assholes. We need him, we'll all end up dead without him."

"Fifteen percent discount? That's got to be at least eight hundred grand. Why the hell would Bianchi offer us that big of a discount?" Marco asks from behind me.

"And what the fuck do we have that he wants in return?" I add, knowing the answer can't possibly be any good.

"Bianchi never remarried after his wife passed. They only had one child, a daughter. Bianchi is only forty-five—he's got years left in him. He wants to arrange a marriage with his daughter, Isabella, so she can produce an heir for his empire," he says before sighing and rubbing his temples.

"Of course, the men he sends will be given menial jobs, while those doing them at the moment will be promoted. I won't have any fucker feeding information back to Antonio," he adds.

Our family hasn't partaken in arranged marriages in years, but other organizations still use them. A feeling of dread settles in my stomach but I ignore it.

"Right, so we marry off this girl to one of the lower capos, she pops out some kids for him while we get the men that we need to even the odds with the Bratva and Cartel and get cheaper weapons?" I ask hopefully.

He shoots me an apologetic look, and I instantly know my life is fucked. He doesn't need to say the words, but—so there's no fucking confusion—he has to say them out loud and put them into the universe making it real.

"No, Luca, I'm sorry. You'll marry Isabella Bianchi next month. The date is already set, you'll marry the girl on February the twenty-fourth."

Jesus fucking Christ.

"You said Bianchi is forty-five. How old exactly is this daughter of his since I've never even heard of her in our circles? I'm not a fucking cradle robber Dad," I grit out, no way in hell is that happening.

"Of course, you're not, she's twenty-four," he states in a tone that sounds like he's selling me a car, not spending the rest of my life with one woman.

I guess a six-year age gap isn't a big deal. But then again, I'd rather not get married at all.

Fuck my life.

Once we're finished in the office and I'm back in the car, I decide I need a drink to drown out my thoughts. I pull my phone out my pocket and pull up Alec's contact, knowing he'll be down to meet me for a drink. The line rings a couple of times before he answers.

"Look who's calling me at this time of night. What can I do for you, sweetheart?" he cheers mockingly into my ear.

"Shut the fuck up," I groan. "I need you to meet me for a drink," I say in a somber tone.

"Shit man, you good?"

"No, I'm so far from being good it'd be comical if this shit wasn't happening to me. Meet me at Arcane in twenty," I say before hanging up the phone, knowing he'll be there. He always is when I need him.

Alec Cane has been my best friend since freshman year of college. We were paired together in a group project and I hated him at first, I thought he was just another entitled asshole with a stick up his ass, turns out he isn't so bad after all, he won me over with his carefree attitude and happy go lucky personality. But the thing about Alec is, he's always there to lend a helping hand, whether I need his help when it comes to business, or if it's personal shit I'm dealing with, the man would drop everything and show up.

I walk into Arcane and head up to the VIP section where I know he'll be waiting for me. I chose to meet him at the club his brother owns rather than one of my family's clubs because I don't think I can deal with seeing anyone from the Cosa Nostra right now. Work has already taken up too much of my life today.

I reach the top of the stairs and spot Alec sat at one of the far tables, knowing he chose that spot to give us more privacy and I head over to him.

"What the hell is going on Luc? It's not often you grace me with your presence on a Saturday night," he drawls.

I swallow past the lump in my throat, not wanting to voice my issue. I shake my head, *just say it you asshole.*

"Ah you know, wanted to catch up, see how you are, see how business has been, invite you to my upcoming wedding... the usual," I say with a fake ass grin.

He bursts out into hysterical laughter, thinking I'm joking. But when I don't join in, he realizes I'm being deadly serious. Any humor fades from his face and he stares at me with wide eyes and a slack jaw. He's looking at me as if I've grown another head, as if I'm crazy. Maybe I am, I sure do feel like I'm losing my mind.

"What in the ever-loving *fuck* are you talking about?"

"I'm talking about getting married, me, in one month. Mark the date in your calendar, I expect to see you there," I say with a grimace before going into detail, explaining the deal my father made and how I'll soon have some docile little woman attached to me.

I take a swig of the whiskey that Alec had waiting for me, before swallowing the rest of the liquid, I drain the glass and look him in the eye. "I'm gonna need you to find out everything you can on the Bianchi's and anyone close to them. I need to know what the fuck I'm getting myself into."

CHAPTER TWO

Izzy

From the outside looking in, my life is perfect. To everyone around me, I'm the picture-perfect Mafia princess. The one who spends her time reading books in the library, dresses respectfully and is always dolled up to the max, never having a hair out of place. A real life doll. I attend galas in lavish gowns and I'm always polite. I have men protecting me everywhere I go, always fucking protected.

My father thinks he's shielded me from the horrors of our world, little does he know his pretty little princess can shoot a gun better than most of his men. I could kill a man in seventy-two different ways and not break a sweat. He doesn't know that I've been training in self-defense and have been having weapons training since I was twelve.

I've always known one day I would be sold to the highest bidder, and like fuck am I going to marry a man without knowing how to protect myself if he turns out to be the world's biggest asshole.

So, when Margaretta, our family's housekeeper came into the library at two o'clock on a Wednesday afternoon, informing me that my father would like to see me in his study right away—when

I'm usually told to stay out of his way and I only normally see him on Sundays—I knew my time was up.

"New York is struggling. They're at war with the Russians and Colombians and need a weapons deal, and I'm sending some of our men to help out. In exchange, you are to marry their underboss and the Don's son, Luca Romano. They've lost over forty men in the last couple of months, they're getting hit left and right. I've agreed to give them what they need and in return you'll marry Luca, you will produce heirs, so that I have someone to take over when I retire," my father says while giving me a look that says there is no argument.

I sit quietly, waiting to see if he has anything to add. Apparently, I was right, and he wasn't done because he continues, "I told Romano he must have a rat. They're working on figuring out who it is, but you will need to be careful. I'd rather you not end up dead." Oh, how charming, father dearest. "Congratulations Isabella, you're engaged to be married. The wedding will take place three Saturdays from now. I suggest you use this time to prepare and pack your things for New York, keep an eye on your husband and forward me any information I may find useful," he says with finality, clearly dismissing me.

I give him a nod, remaining silent because anything I have to say right now will end with me being backhanded by my loving father, and leave his study going back to the library to sit and think about how the fuck I'm going to deal with this.

I've heard about the Romano's, everyone in Chicago has. They're known to not harm women and children because it's been instilled within them from birth, so at least I know my dear husband isn't going to attempt to force himself on me.

However, if he thinks he's going to get a pretty little docile wife then he can suck a bag of dicks. I'm not about to sit at home and play housewife for him.

I'm honestly surprised they've agreed to the deal. The Romano's haven't agreed to an arranged marriage in decades, so clearly, they're royally fucked in the war they're currently in, otherwise there's no way in hell they would agree to my father's deal. I guess I'm going to have to prove to my husband that I'm a motherfucking queen. No more pretending to be a pretty little princess for me.

I don't have an issue with relocating to New York, the so-called friends that I have here are all shallow and superficial. I use them to keep up appearances of seeming like the usual spoilt daddy's girl.

In all honesty, I've never been able to be myself here. It may be good to move to a different state and start over. I'll be able to be myself from the beginning, now that I won't be under my father's control, so I suppose there is an upside to marrying the Romano heir.

After a couple of weeks of planning, I pack up the belongings I'd like to keep. Which, admittedly, is not much at all. A few outfits, my laptop and some jewelry my mom bought me when I was younger are the only things I can't part with.

I 've spent the last nine days in New York, hiding in plain sight. I told my father that I wanted to come here early to visit my friend and find myself a wedding dress. It's three days until the wedding, I still haven't bought a dress, and I also don't have a friend who lives in New York. But hey, what Daddy doesn't know won't hurt him.

In actuality, I've spent my time here getting to know the layout of the city, I've spent time in the clubs owned by and frequented by the Mafia, the Cartel and the Bratva. I've been in disguise, of course, and gotten myself up to date on this war that everyone is so worried about.

Turns out the Italians used to be in business with both the Cartel and the Bratva, until around nine months ago when the Colombians and the Russians made a deal to cut out the Italians, ending their business and fucking them over at the same time. From there it escalated to sabotaging shipments, shooting up places, deals being made and attempting to hit the top members of each organization. To say it's a shit show would be an understatement.

Typical men, measuring their dick sizes.

What I have deduced is that the New York outfit definitely has a rat, and I've spent the last four days surveying Alejandro Muñoz and manipulating his men into talking to figure out who it is.

I'm in Bailar, the club that's owned by the Cartel. I'm wearing a black wig to cover my dirty blonde hair, a short leather skirt and a red cropped top. I doubt anyone in here would recognize me even without a disguise unless they're also keeping up to date on the

Chicago outfit, but I figured it's better to be safe than sorry. I don't need some asshole blowing my cover before I get what I came here for.

I've spent the night flirting with Muñoz, dancing and grinding up against him, plying him with drinks while I pretended to drink mine. I'd rather get my information the old-fashioned way, with loose lips, rather than torture it out of him. I'm not ready for anyone to know I'm in town yet.

Eventually, he invited me up to the VIP section where we now sit with his men, him joking and bragging about what he's been up to with the Romano's.

"*Mierda*, we took out eight of their men in one hit," he laughs, boasting about how he shot up one of the Romano's establishments last week and I barely contain my eye roll.

"How do you do it Alejandro? Surely, they see someone like you coming?" I purr in a seductive voice and flutter my eyelashes while inwardly rolling my eyes. How this shit has been working on him all night I have no idea. He's like a kid in a candy store the second I bat my eyes at him.

Pathetic.

He pulls me onto his lap, and I can't help but shiver in disgust. Luckily, he takes that as a good sign, thinking I'm turned on, and not in fact itching to stab him in the hand that rests on my hip for touching me.

"It's quite funny really, *muñeca*. Two idiot sons of one of their capos started buying drugs from me and ended up with a debt they couldn't pay, so their papa has to pay me back, doesn't he?" he says with a grin.

"Romano, *el cabron*, has no idea his *amigo* Amate is the reason he's losing so many men," he says with a smirk.

Ah, keep smirking sweetheart, you've just given me everything I need, I think to myself while giving him a sweet smile and gazing up at him like he hung the moon. Fuck, I wish I could be the one to put this asshole down, but I know how this life works, it needs to be Salvatore Romano or one of his sons if they're going to keep their house in order.

I spend another twenty minutes on his lap—not wanting to leave too soon and make him suspicious—before I excuse myself to the bathroom and make a quick exit through the back door of the club.

So, it turns out this Amate and his sons are the reason for so many Cosa Nostra deaths. Seems like I've got some more work to do if I'm going to find them before I tie the knot.

And *fuck*, I know just what to get my darling husband as a wedding gift. I'm done being underestimated. I need to show Luca Romano that I'm not just some sort of broodmare or a pretty trophy wife that'll stand for being shown off around his men.

After all... doesn't every man need a woman to put him in his place?

CHAPTER THREE

Luca

"I'm so happy for you man, look at you wearing your tux, getting all dolled up for your little princess," Enzo laughs from the armchair.

We're in my penthouse getting ready for this fucking wedding. I tried for weeks to find an alternative, so I don't have to go through with this deal, but the Russians and Colombians are closing in on us.

We're no closer to finding our rat and if it carries on this way our father is gonna blow a gasket and make himself ill, landing himself in early retirement, and there's no way I'm becoming Don right now at the ripe old age of thirty.

So, alas, I'm getting ready to meet my bride to be, at the fucking altar. Antonio Bianchi must have kept his little girl behind lock and key, or at least off of social media, away from the press and away from any cameras because I haven't even seen her face.

All I know from the digging Alec did on her is that she's twenty-four and has a degree in computer science that she completed remotely. What the fuck she plans on doing with computer science I don't know. The weird thing is that he couldn't find anything else on her, and considering his occupation, that's a red flag if there ever was one.

I dug around with some contacts I have in Chicago and found out that she's the epitome of spoilt Mafia princesses; spending her days at home, or out shopping while spending her daddy's money, spending her time with equally spoilt socialites, and drinking the day away while out for brunch with her friends. I don't really give a fuck what she does with herself as long as she doesn't annoy the fuck out of me, stays out of my way and she upholds her vows.

I may not love the woman—or even know her—but to me, marriage is a lifelong commitment. I won't have her fucking around with other men. Same as I won't fuck other women.

It's simply a matter of respect. If a man so much as looks at my wife for a second too long, I'll put a bullet between his eyes, and if someone thinks they can touch her? Yeah, I'll dig out their fucking intestines and use it as a noose before hanging him from the Empire State Building for all of New York to see. Let that be a warning of what happens when someone touches what's mine.

Huh, maybe I'll do that anyway. Could be fun.

"He's not paying us any attention, Enzo. He's lost in his own little world dreaming up a white picket fence and a minivan," Marco adds with a chuckle. Clearly, they're both enjoying my demise.

"Go fuck yourselves. I hope Dad makes some more deals and gets you both married off."

They both snort, knowing that that's highly unlikely. Lucky bastards.

They might piss me off, but I know that both of them would step up and do exactly what I'm doing right now if the family needed them too. My brothers and I have always had each other's backs.

Enzo is the wild card out of the three of us, he's either chill as fuck or quite literally blowing shit up—there is no in-between. Whereas Marco is the serious one, the planner, he does nothing without thinking about everything methodically and he never lacks a plan. And finally, I'm the one everyone comes to for help, I'm the fixer out of the three of us, as shown by this sham of a wedding.

Growing up without our mom taught us to appreciate the family we have. I'd take a bullet for the both of them, just like they would for me. Before Mama died—and before Enzo was born—she would read me and Marco bedtime stories to get us to fall asleep, sometimes she made them up too.

I always remember her telling me a story about a prince that saved a princess from a dragon. The dragon had kept the princess locked up in a tower, only letting her out when it served its own needs, or something along those lines. My point is, after that story, Mama told us that one day, we might be the prince that saves our very own princess. She told us not to be afraid of the dragon, and that sometimes you have to become one yourself in order to survive in our world. She taught us to not fear darkness, but to embrace it, and that maybe one day, we might have our own happily ever after.

I can't help but wonder if she'd be disappointed in what we're doing today, because this sure as hell isn't the start of a happily ever after for me. Then again, I never believed it would happen for me anyways, but at least I'll be able to save the princess.

I take a deep breath, trying to calm myself from raging at the fact I'm basically being forced to marry a complete stranger. Over the last couple of weeks, I debated reaching out to her. I thought it might be a good idea to meet her at least once before she becomes my wife. However, Marco pointed out that I'll be better off going into this indifferent, rather than giving her false hope of us having a happy and loving marriage.

"Seriously, brother, we can probably find a different way to get ahead of the other organizations without you going through with this, there's still time," Marco says from where he stands at the kitchen island, nursing a glass of whiskey.

"You know as well as I do that if we back out now, not only will we be at war with the Cartel and Bratva, but we'll be adding the Chicago outfit to that list as well. There's no fucking time," I sigh.

Speaking of time, I check my watch and cringe. Fuck. I need to be at the altar in thirty minutes.

I look out over the crowd. They're mostly familiar faces, with a few I don't know from Chicago. Both of my brothers are on my left, snickering to themselves about who the fuck knows what, probably gossiping away to each other and using me as a punchline to their jokes—the usual. I'm past caring at this point, ready to get this over with so I can go home and drown myself in a bottle of whiskey.

On the other hand, I'm dreading getting home, knowing it will no longer be my sanctuary and instead my space will be taken up by some random woman. I don't even let my hook-ups into my home, no woman has ever stepped through the threshold for as long as I've lived there.

I wonder what she expects of tonight, will she want to consummate the marriage? Her father needs heirs, so I'll have to fuck her at some point.

Fuck, what if she's a virgin?

I'm not a nice man, I'm not gentle or into love making or whatever the fuck women expect when they lose their virginity. What does she do with her days? I hope to fuck she doesn't expect to come in and redecorate my space, or move my things, or—

My thought process is cut off as the orchestra starts playing and I turn just in time to see Bianchi come into view, he walks a couple of steps and then his daughter joins him at his side. I take in her long, white silk dress, noticing the curves of her body. She's not stick thin like I expected—most Mafia princesses only eat salad and won't eat anything over three hundred calories.

No, she's got curves in all the right places. My gaze travels higher to see her full breasts, and then I get to her long blonde hair, which of course is perfectly styled. Suddenly Bianchi is handing his daughter off to me, as she steps up next to me I see her face for the first time and, well, *fuck*. I have to make an effort to keep my expression indifferent, I don't want her getting the wrong idea before we've even exchanged rings.

I stare straight into her chocolate brown eyes, getting lost in them. She's got long, thick lashes and rosy cheeks and goddamn, she has to be the most beautiful woman I've seen in my life. Still, just because she's gorgeous doesn't mean I'm about to like the woman, she could have the personality as prickly as a cactus for all I know. And I hope she doesn't expect me to end up falling in love with her, because I sure as shit do *not* do all that emotional stuff. She's also tiny, like really fucking small. I tower over the girl.

My brain isn't even registering the vows we're repeating back to each other while we stare at each other. She doesn't seem particularly happy, but she's not scared either. She's not afraid to meet my gaze as most people are. No, the little spitfire holds eye contact, where half the men I know would end up looking away.

Finally, the rings are exchanged, and the priest kindly says, "You may now kiss the bride."

Yeah... no. If I'm ever going to kiss the woman, the first time sure as hell isn't going to be in front of three hundred people. I give her a quick, chaste kiss on her cheek before turning and extending my hand out to her, ready to escort her back down the aisle.

CHAPTER FOUR

Izzy

My new husband is hot, probably a complete asshole, but he's hot. Thick brown hair that's styled perfectly, not a hair out of place, piercing brown eyes and a sharp jawline. Not to mention that he's built like an Adonis and could be on the cover of GQ magazine. I already knew he was handsome from the research I'd done on him, but pictures really did not do him justice.

He's the type of man who can get any girl he wants, as though he could just click his fingers and panties would start dropping all around him. He must be at least 6'3, so compared to my 5'4, the man towers over me. Like seriously, if I took off my heels, we'd look fucking ridiculous stood next to each other. And his muscles? I've never seen a man fill out a suit the way he does. Luca seems like the type of man who doesn't leave the house unless he's perfectly put together, wearing a three piece suit and polished shoes. Whereas I'd be perfectly happy lounging around in oversized sweats and messy hair. We're complete opposites.

He extends a tattooed hand out to me, and I place my hand in his before he escorts me inside to meet the photographer. The wedding is being held at his family's estate. The home itself is beautiful, they really have gone all out, decorating the garden in white roses and peonies. There's a tent set up for the reception which is more like a work of art. They've tried really hard to sell this charade, especially since they've invited every important and influential person in New York. But it is what it is, a business event.

We pose for the photographer, who continually has to tell Luca to move closer to me, to smile, and to overall seem happy to be here. It's clear he's not happy to be doing any of this, but these pictures will end up in the paper, announcing our nuptials, and they can't be looking as though he's secretly got a gun to him just to snap a few shots.

"You need to work on your acting skills," I gripe as we make our way over to the reception where our guests are waiting. This is the first time I've spoken to him other than my vows, and if the scowl he's wearing is anything to go by, I'm guessing he'd have rather I stayed silent. He shakes his head and stops walking, turning to face me fully.

"Look, you and I both know this wedding shouldn't be happening, I just didn't want you to get any ideas about how this marriage is going to be. I'm not going to end up falling in love with you, Isabella, and I think it's best we get this out the way now before you start coming up with notions of true love and fairytales. You seem like a good girl, I didn't want to lead you on into thinking this is more than what it is—a business deal," he says.

I bite the inside of my cheek to stop from laughing, he really thinks I'm cooking up ideas of this shit? Jesus Christ, he really does think I'm a spoilt little girl like most Mafia daughters. Then again, I haven't given him anything to make him think differently.

Deciding to have a little fun and run with it, I pout my lips and tug my eyebrows down into a frown.

"I didn't expect true love, I'm not naïve enough to think a man like you could ever love a girl like me, Luca. But it's our wedding day, and people will be expecting us to be head over heels in love, they'll be expecting you to look like a man who just couldn't wait to make me his wife. We can talk about the rest later, but for now, for tonight, we should at least act as though we're not complete strangers, don't you think?" I say with a sweet smile.

He gives me a reluctant nod, takes my hand in his and gives me a show stopping smile, showcasing his dimples before continuing towards the tent. "Show time, princess," he mutters as we enter the reception and starts to greet our guests.

We parade around the room, listening to the guests tell us what lovely kids we'd make and how it was such a gorgeous ceremony. *Insert eye roll here.* My father is here somewhere, probably cozying up to the city officials or with a woman who's far too young and far too pretty for him.

Finally, after twenty minutes of Luca showing me off like a prized cow, we sit down for dinner, joining his dad and brothers at the table. Luckily, they had the foresight to *not* sit my father with us as well.

Once Luca helps me into my seat, I adjust my dress before refocusing my attention to the table, only to see two sets of eyes on me. His brothers, Marco and Enzo, are both staring at me as if they can see into my soul. I give them a smile, not averting my gaze. If there's one thing I've learned when it comes to men like them is they enjoy inflicting fear, and like fuck am I going to let them intimidate me.

"So, where are you guys planning on going for your honeymoon? Maybe a nice little romantic getaway in the Bahamas? No, no... Hawaii?" Enzo grins. I can already tell he's the carefree joker out of the three brothers.

"We're not going anywhere," Luca grunts from beside me making Marco roll his eyes. Their appearances are all similar, yet Marco is the one who looks the most like Salvatore. Their hair is darker than Luca and Enzo's, and their faces are both round, whereas Enzo and Luca both have sharp jawlines. Luca and Enzo both have brown eyes, whereas Salvatore and Marcos are green.

"Please ignore my idiot sons, Isabella, they have no manners. I'm Salvatore, it's nice to officially meet you, welcome to the family," their dad says while giving me a warm smile. I can immediately tell he's the complete opposite of my father, his welcome seems genuine, and he actually seems to care about his children.

Huh, I wonder what it's like to have a dad who genuinely gives a shit about you.

"Thank you, it's nice to meet you too. Please, call me Izzy," I say, returning his smile.

The rest of the evening continues, me and Luca cut the cake, which was awkward as hell, we have our first dance, also awkward as hell. The only part of the night I enjoyed was the fact that our wedding song was also my mother's favorite song. God, I wish she was here today, she always told me stories of how her mother helped her get ready for her wedding to my father. How they laughed and cried when they were getting ready, she always said she would love to be the one to plan my wedding one day.

My mama died when I was eleven, she was shot by one of my father's rivals at the time. She was only thirty-four, she had so much fucking life left in her. She was a pure soul, one that didn't deserve the life that she was handed.

After we went around the guests, saying our goodbyes and thanking them for coming, Luca asked me to wait in the car while he spoke to his friend Alex or Alec? Something like that. I'm standing leaning against the car, staring up at the night sky and wondering if Mama can see me, is she here with me today? Is she upset with my father for doing this to me? What does she think of who he has become?

He hasn't always been like this, not completely at least. There were times when I was younger that he really was a semi-decent dad. He loved my mother more than life itself, and part of him died when she did, turning him into the man he is today. I'm sure he'd rather she was still here instead of me. Hell, there's days when I wish the same.

"I miss you," I whisper up into the sky.

"Talking to yourself?" Luca's voice sounds from in-front of me, making me jolt, it's not often I'm caught off guard.

I clear my throat before getting into the car. He closes my door behind me before rounding the car and getting in the other side. I'd asked the driver to give me a moment alone so he's already in the driver's seat ready to leave.

"There's somewhere we need to go before you take me home," I say, knowing he won't like that I'm making demands, I'm sure he'll be able to appreciate it when he gets there though. Though he probably won't like that fact I've been able to do what he hasn't.

"And where, exactly, do we need to go princess?" Luca asks in a cocky tone and with a raised brow.

Princess, fucking *princess.* I'm about to show my husband I'm the exact fucking opposite of a princess.

"Well, to give you your wedding gift of course," I say with a saccharine smile.

This is going to be so fucking fun.

CHAPTER FIVE

Luca

I have no fucking idea what is going on right now. After my lovely bride announced that she wanted to take me somewhere, to give me a wedding present of all things, she gave the driver the address of where she wanted to go. We've been driving for forty minutes and we're in the middle of nowhere. Literally. The. Middle. Of. Fucking. Nowhere.

This has been one of the longest days of my life. I hate having to deal with people on the best of days, never mind walking around listening to how cute our kids will be and asking if Isabella is expecting due to our apparent quick union. What a fucking shit show. If it was up to me, we would have just eloped, had my two brothers as witnesses, signed the papers and got the hell out of there.

But no, I'm the goddamn heir of the New York Mafia, so of course I had to put up with all the pomp and circumstance that was my wedding. All the while wishing someone would just put me out of my misery in the form of a bullet between the eyes, or maybe a nice knife across my throat?

Isabella played her part well, acting thoroughly in love with me and never once complained, which I'm thankful for. She had been nothing but accommodating while I paraded her around to anyone of importance to boost our network. That was until she decided she needed to drag me out into the middle of nowhere after we've just spent hours around a bunch of assholes and while I want nothing more than to go home.

Christ, where the fuck are we going? I'd ask but I'd rather not open up a conversation. Don't want my wife thinking she can get all chatty on me. To be honest, she probably thinks I want to spend the night inside her and is just trying to delay it. Not that that would happen, not that she isn't my type, because she's fucking stunning. But because I feel like we need to get to know one another a little better first, set some boundaries and expectations.

What a fucking weird situation we're in.

Finally, we're reaching our destination, which appears to be a cabin in the middle of butt-fuck nowhere. Wonderful. My wife gets out the car and I sit for an extra second, dreading what sort of gift she thought to have got me.

And also, why the fuck is the "gift" all the way out here? I'd be worried she brought me out here to attempt to kill me, but she didn't object to the other two cars full of guards that have been following us, and I don't really think she's stupid enough to make an attempt on my life. I sigh, better follow the little princess into her cabin.

Isabella leads me through the cabin, passing a small sitting room consisting of a fireplace and two armchairs, down a corridor and to a door at the end of the hall. She opens the door and descends the stairs, flipping a light switch on at the same time. It's utterly ridiculous, me following her into a basement while she's dressed in a fucking wedding gown.

As I get to the bottom of the stairs, I turn and my jaw drops. In the middle of the room are three men, each tied to their own beams. The first is Marcello, a capo who's been Cosa Nostra and one of my dad's closest friends for twenty years. The other two are his twin twenty-year-old sons, Angelo and Lucian. I take a look at my wife, wondering why in the ever-loving fuck she has three of my men tied up in a random basement.

"Happy wedding day, my dear husband," she says with a smile. "I caught you some rats."

What the fuck?

"Explain, Isabella," I spit out through clenched teeth.

"Well, you see, I heard about your little problem, so I decided to do some digging. Turns out Marcello here has been feeding information to his *amigo* Muñoz in exchange for writing off the debt twin one and twin two have got themselves into. Turns out your boys here have gotten themselves a little drug problem and racked up a debt amounting to eighty thousand dollars, which kept increasing weekly as they were unable to pay. Therefore, their daddy here stepped in to help by giving times and places you and your family were and where you were making deals and having shipments come in."

"You're trying to tell me that you not only figured out who our rats were, but that you managed to bring them here? On your own?" What the fuck is happening right now?

"Yes, that's exactly what I'm telling you. I decided to come to New York a little early, take in some sights, and do a little exploring. I picked up a lot in a short amount of time, don't you think?" she says in that sweet voice of hers, her eyes twinkling with mischief before she steps towards me and wipes the smile off her face, a blank mask in its place.

"I need you to know something, Luca. You called me "princess" earlier tonight, I'm far fucking from it. I'm not going to be some docile little wife cooking your dinner and birthing your offspring. I did this, so you know not to underestimate me. In return, I hope you treat me with respect. You're on my good side, husband," she says and pulls a gun from a pocket in her wedding dress.

Has she been carrying that all day? And since when did wedding dresses have fucking pockets? And fuck, why is my dick so hard from seeing her handle a weapon?

"I don't like it when people get on my bad side."

She aims the gun at Angelo, and shoots him between the eyes without blinking, and without showing an ounce of remorse. Instead, just staring at his body with a blank expression, seeming completely relaxed.

Great, I've married a sociopath.

Marcello's and Lucians screams fill the room as she tucks the gun back in her pocket while I stand and stare at her, unable to comprehend what the fuck is happening.

"You have three cars upstairs and plenty of guards, I'll have someone take me to your penthouse. My feet are killing me after being in heels all day. I'll see you at home, darling," she says, smiling at me as she walks towards the stairs.

"Oh, and please call me Izzy. Isabella just seems so... impersonal. You're my husband now, after all. Enjoy playing with them." She smirks before gracefully walking away.

And then I'm staring at her retreating form, wondering what in the goddamn hell just happened, and wondering who the fuck I married. She's right about one thing though, she's certainly no princess, she's a fucking queen. Psychotic, but a motherfucking queen, nonetheless.

CHAPTER SIX

Luca

As soon as I left the cabin, I called an urgent meeting with Dad, Marco and Enzo. So here I am, sat facing my father at his desk at eleven o'clock at night—my wedding night, no less. And to think I was worried about *Izzy* wanting to consummate the marriage tonight.

"If you're here to complain about the marriage, you're too fucking late Luca. Not sure if you noticed earlier today when you stood at the altar, but you're already married," my dad says sternly while giving me look that says he wants to throttle me.

Sighing, I decide to just lay it all out there. "Marcello Amate is our rat, his sons racked up a debt with Muñoz and therefore in exchange for writing off their debt, Marcello has been giving the Colombians information on all our dealings and our whereabouts. Angelo is now dead. Marcello and Lucian are tied up in the basement of a cabin an hour's drive from here but should be getting moved as we speak."

"How the fuck did you do all of this while also getting married? You left your wedding reception three hours ago! And how the fuck did you figure out it was the Amate's?" he asks, dumbfounded.

I grind my jaw and explain how my pretty little wife isn't so innocent after all. After she left the cabin, I interrogated Marcello into telling me exactly what he'd been telling Muñoz, and also how he ended up in the basement. Turns out my wife has some skills, considering she took down all three of them, tied them up and managed to get them into the back of a fucking rental, before driving them to the cabin, dragging them down to the basement and tying them up. Without help.

When she first told me what she did I was convinced she had to have had help, turns out she did not. She even told them she'd kept them awake so that they knew she was alone, and that they'd been caught and taken down by a little woman. It's a good tactic on her part, feeding into their views of misogyny, bet that hurt their fragile egos. She's a fucking spitfire, that one.

"So, what? You just killed Angelo in front of her? Please don't tell me you ruined her wedding dress; she'll likely tie you up in a basement like she did with them," Marco says, making me realize I skimped out on that detail.

"Oh no, I forgot to mention that part. My sociopathic wife whipped a Glock out of a pocket in her wedding dress, shot him between the eyes and then insisted I call her *Izzy* before walking away as if the whole thing never happened," I say dryly.

Once I'm finished, I'm left with Dad, Marco and Enzo all staring at me, slack jawed and fucking incredulous that my wildcat wife managed to hold three grown men hostage, and not only that, but find the rats we've been trying to find for the past three months, in a few days, no less *and* kill a man without any hesitation. The whole thing is surreal, absurd, it's utterly fucking ridiculous.

Enzo is first to crack, breaking out into hysterical laughter, with tears streaming down his face while Marco snickers next to him, and my father just sighs and gazes up at the ceiling. I'm waiting to see his reaction the most, who the fuck knows how he'll react, it could go one of a few ways.

Finally, he looks at me, right in the eye. "I'll leave you boys to take care of them, and keep that woman close, Luca. Not because we shouldn't trust her, but because we need to earn her trust. Having her on our side can only lead to good things. Oh, and be prepared, because you're fucked, son," he states with a smug grin.

"Prepared for what?"

"Be prepared to fall in love with her," he says as if it's obvious. "It won't take long. You can only hope she ends up loving you in return."

Well, fuck.

That was an unexpected turn of events. I half expected Dad to warn me to be careful, not to trust her, to keep an eye on her. Not fucking tell me to be prepared to fall in love. I don't even know what love feels like, I'm pretty sure I'm not capable of it, but I give him a nod to appease him before turning around and walking my ass straight out the door, with both my brothers hot on my heels.

I'm tired as fuck, and all I want to do is go home to bed. But Izzy's now at my apartment, doing who knows what, and I really do not want to get into anything with her tonight. The woman is kind of scary, I get the feeling she'd happily chop my balls off and feed them to me if I pissed her off enough.

We decided to deal with the Amate's tonight, figuring it would look better to our men if we dealt with the situation straight away, and me being the one to do it on my wedding night shows I'm not fucking around when it comes to the *famiglia*. So, we made a plan for me to deal with Marcello, and I left Lucian for my brothers to fight over. Marco, of course, was indifferent, choosing to let Enzo deal with him just to shut him up.

Before I left the cabin to meet my family, I instructed my men to move Marcello and Lucian to one of our warehouses in the city and to dispose of Angelo. Which of course they did without hesitation, even though they must be wondering why, considering we kept a tight lid on the fact that we had a rat.

So here we are, in the middle of the warehouse, with both *stronzos* stung up to the metal barred wall, and with thirty of our men standing on the sidelines. We invited some of our men so they can witness their deaths and get word around about what happens if you go against us, we can't have them thinking they can double cross us and get away with it.

I'm going first, so I take a step towards Marcello.

"Was it worth it? You know you're about to die, so was it worth betraying your family?" I sneer. He stays still, his features set in stone, but I can see the flicker of fear in his eyes and like hell if I don't thrive on it.

"I did what I did, Luca. Let's just get this over with, surely you want to get home to your new *puttana*."

Rage simmers up inside me, how fucking dare he call my wife a whore? But I give him a nod, and while he tries to stay nonchalant, I see his shoulders drop slightly in relief, probably thinking I'll just shoot him to hurry this show up.

That's not how this is gonna go, sorry man.

I chuckle and walk over to the workbench and look at my pretty little utensils, deciding what to use today. I see the pliers, shears, and a small mason jar. An idea flickers in my mind and excitement bubbles up in my veins.

After picking up what I need and handing it to Marco, I stroll over to Marcello and grab a blade from my ankle sheath before cutting his shirt open in one quick motion, making him audibly gulp.

"You think you can betray us, then call my wife a whore?" I seethe, letting the rage show on my face.

"I-I'm sorry," he sputters.

"No more talking for you," I snap and motion for Marco to pass me what I need.

With my hand on his jaw, keeping his mouth open, I grab his tongue with the pliers. He starts thrashing around but I keep a steady hold and using the shears I chop it off before motioning for Marco to open the mason jar.

I grin when he holds it out for me before dropping the tongue inside.

"Good." I nod to myself. "Now to get started." The sheer terror in his eyes, realizing I'm only just getting started and that I'm not at all going to keep this quick, sends a thrill through me.

Fuck, I love this shit.

I spend the next hour removing fingers, strategically slicing him open in places that won't let him bleed out too soon and carving off pieces off his skin. All the while our men continue to watch, making sure they keep their expressions stoic.

Marco stands to my left with a look of boredom on his face while Enzo has spent the last hour barring his teeth at a crying Lucian like a wild dog, fucking maniac that he is. Marcello has passed out a couple of times, but Marco gave him a shot of adrenaline, ensuring he stays awake for what's about to happen next.

Finally, we're down to the last stages. I intentionally kept his chest and torso free from torture for my plan to work. Grabbing a small knife, I start carving off a strip of skin from his chest, the flesh I'm carving spans from just below his belly button up to his breastbone and is about an inch wide. After detaching the skin, I motion for Marco to pass me the mason jar again.

I wrap the skin around the top of the jar and tie it together.

"Uh, Luca, what the hell are you doing?" Marco asks in confusion, wondering why the hell I'm bothering putting his tongue in a jar in the first place, never mind using his skin as a bow to top it off when we already have our men here to showcase Marcellos' demise.

"My wife is the reason he's here, it's only fair she gets something for her hard work. After all, I owe her a wedding gift, and that gift needed a pretty little bow," I say with a grin and Enzo barks out a laugh as Marco cringes, probably imagining her reaction. I know she killed Angelo earlier without a second thought, but who knows how she'll react to my gift. *Ah well, fuck it.*

I'm trying to show her I don't see her as a princess like I implied earlier. Surely, she'll appreciate that, right?

Once I finish admiring my handiwork, I step back up to Marcello and stare into his empty eyes. Seems he checked out a while ago and is barely hanging on.

"Let this be a lesson not to turn on us," I announce to the room before taking my knife and slitting the bastard's throat.

"Fucking finally, can I play with mine now?" Enzo whines and I give him a nod. That crazy bastard could be here all night playing with his newest toy, or he could be here for five minutes after accidentally killing him.

I do a slow spin around the room, giving each man a *don't fuck with us look* before picking up Izzy's gift and strolling out of the room.

I've had enough excitement for one day, I think I'll give her it in the morning.

CHAPTER SEVEN

Izzy

L ast night, after one of Luca's guards escorted me up to the apartment, I took the time to look around. I now apparently live in a three-bedroom penthouse apartment, right in the heart of the city. Luckily, the décor consists of black, white and gray. I don't know what I would have done otherwise, I was never one of those girls who liked girly girl things, I'd rather decorate the walls with blood than flowery wallpaper.

After giving myself a nice little tour around my new home, I found myself a guest room furthest away from my husband's bedroom. I'm aware we'll have to consummate the marriage at some point, and I'm pretty sure he's not the type of man to force himself on a woman, but I'd rather get to know him before I fuck him.

This whole situation is ridiculous, why we're still buying into the antiquated ways our ancestors ran business I really don't know. My children certainly won't be subjected to an arranged marriage if I have anything to say about it, and I'd stab Luca through the hand if he ever tried to force them.

I've just woken up and I'm aware of his presence before I even open my eyes. I stay still and control my breathing while I wonder just how long my sneaky husband has been watching me sleep.

Giving in, I open my eyes to glare at him. I'm not a morning person, the least he could have done is brought coffee.

"Do you always enjoy watching women sleep?" I ask.

He's sat on the corner of the bed, the opposite side to where I'm sleeping, dressed in grey sweatpants and a black t shirt that showcases the tattoos covering both his arms, I couldn't see them yesterday because his suit jacket covered them, but if I had to guess, I'd say he's covered in them. His hair is ruffled, so it's clear he's not long since gotten out of bed. His eyes are staring into mine as if they hold the answers to the universe.

"Not particularly, but I'm also not used to having a woman in my house. Who knows, I might just become a creeper now that you're here," he deadpans.

I roll my eyes before I roll onto my back and stare up at the ceiling. "I'd rather you didn't, I'll have to start sleeping with knives under my pillow. If I accidentally stab myself in my sleep, I'll happily kill you in yours," I say and turn my head to face him. His eyes lock on mine, and I hold his gaze, it's as if he's challenging me to look away. *Keep trying sweetie, it isn't gonna happen.*

"Get up, wife. We need to have a chat," he says before getting up and strolling out the room without a backwards glance.

Fucking wonderful, I can't wait!

I check the time on my phone and see it's only six a.m. *What the fuck is wrong with him!?*

Sighing, I hoist myself out of bed and grab my toiletry bag from my suitcase, I'll have to unpack at some point, but that can wait until later.

After using the bathroom and washing my face, I don't bother getting dressed. Hope he doesn't have an issue with me wearing my pajamas around the house because like fuck am I getting dressed at this time of morning. I make my way through the apartment and into the kitchen. I stay silent while I make my coffee, keeping my back to him, then I take a seat opposite him at the kitchen island, coffee mug clasped in my hand, I wait patiently for him to start.

"From everything your father told us, we assumed you were a sheltered Mafia princess. I was expecting an airhead socialite afraid of her own shadow who would spend all of my money on shit you don't need. Clearly, that's not the case. Care to explain why Bianchi told me you were a spoilt little girl?" he asks, I'm not sure whether he's impressed with me or pissed that I'm not a brat, who the fuck knows?

"Honestly?" I ask, looking at him. He gives me a nod, so I continue, "Daddy dearest thinks I'm the perfect princess, who spends her days reading and cooking, preparing myself to be a good housewife and pop out as many kids as my husband wishes. He thinks I'm weak, with no means to defend myself and probably sees me as more of a nuisance. He's underestimated me my whole life."

He cocks his head to the side, pinning me with his gaze.

"Why would he think that? Clearly, you're capable of taking care of yourself, you've obviously trained hard if you were able to take down three men twice your size. Why would you make him think differently? And how did you manage to train without him noticing while living under his roof?" he asks.

"Before Mama died, she sat me down and explained that one day I'd be traded as part of a deal. She told me that while my father would try and choose a good match for me, sometimes things aren't always as they seem. One of the guards who was issued with protecting me was my mother's friend's son. He started training me in martial arts at the age of twelve. At thirteen, he started teaching me how to stay silent, move around without being seen or heard, and he taught me the basics in hacking in case I ever needed to escape and wipe any traces of myself on security cameras. At fifteen, he started my weapons training, how to shoot, the best places to slice and stab a man, knife throwing and more. The lessons stopped last year when he died while out doing a job for my father," I say, taking a deep breath.

I'll always be thankful to Alessi for my lessons, he was always like a big brother to me. When he died, I looked into it to make sure my father hadn't found out what he was doing and set him up, but there was nothing that pointed towards it being foul play.

"I knew that if my father found out what Alessi was teaching me, he'd see it as a threat to him with me being his only heir. So, while he thought that I was out at a salon getting my hair done or out getting a fucking pedicure or some shit, I was actually training."

He stares at me with compassion in his gaze, I hate it. "I'm sorry you had to live like that, Izzy. I promise that I'll never lay a hand on you, I'll never force you to do anything you don't want to do.

You will have choices here, it may take some getting used to for the both of us but I'm sure we can make this work. The only thing I'll ask is that you take guards with you when you leave the apartment, especially now while we're at war. I won't compromise on your safety, even though I know you can take care of yourself. Another thing that I absolutely will not tolerate is you being with other men. I know we didn't marry for love, but I won't have my wife sleeping with other men, the same as I won't be sleeping with other women."

I stare at him for a beat, he plans on being faithful? That's a given for a woman, but it's unheard of in Chicago for the men not to take mistresses. It seems the Romano family really does have values when it comes to family.

Staring into his eyes, I can see the truth written all over his face. He really is going into this as if it were a real marriage.

"I'll agree to being faithful as long as you do the same. I'll also agree to any security precautions you see fit while you're still at war with the Colombians and Russians, but once the dust is settled, I'd like you to reconsider me having a guard twenty-four-seven," I say, I'd rather not have anyone following me around at all, but figure it's better to compromise. Look at me being all mature in this marriage.

He stands before nodding. "You have a deal, once we have everything figured out with the other organizations, we can chat about getting rid of your detail, or at least relaxing it," he says, and I whisper my thanks.

"I wanted to show you how much I appreciated your wedding gift," he says with a sly smile before reaching into a bag on the counter. *Where the hell did that come from?*

He sets a jar on the counter, but it's too far away for me to see what it is. When all I do is gape at him, he slides it closer to me.

Wait, is that? *What the fuck!*

The man has "gifted" me a tongue in a fucking jar.

And is that... flesh positioned to look like a bow?

"I'll leave you to settle in, I need to get ready for the day and get to work. I'll see you tonight, *mia regina*," he says with a smirk before coming to stand in front of me and pressing a kiss to my forehead while I'm still staring at the jar.

And then he's gone, leaving me to sit and stare at a jar containing a fucking human tongue, who I'm guessing belonged to Marcello or one of his sons.

Weird turn of events aside, it turns out my husband may not be a total and complete asshole after all. Still, I'd rather not have this shit in the house.

Unsure of what the fuck I'm supposed to do with it, I leave it where it is and retreat to my room, intent of going back to sleep, but not before Luca barges in uninvited once again and putting his number into my phone in case I happen to need anything.

What a strange morning.

CHAPTER EIGHT

Luca

After giving Izzy my number—something you'd have expected us to exchange before we exchanged our vows—and making a hasty exit from my... sorry, *our* apartment, I instruct the driver to take me to Cane Security's offices.

Alec runs a multimillion-dollar security and tech company that specializes in providing security to celebrities and highly influential people.

He's known as the biggest billionaire playboy in New York. What most don't know is that Alec happens to be one of the best hackers our country has ever known. Alec likes to try to only use his skills for legal means where he can, but with the war happening between the organizations, he agreed to help me out and try to find where Novikov is hiding since our tech guy isn't having much luck.

Novikov hasn't been spotted in seven weeks. We know that the fucker is still alive, and we suspect he's hiding out in one of his safe houses while he has his men fight on his behalf, what we don't know is which out of his eighteen safe houses he's hidden away in.

I walk into Alec's office and give my men a nod to let them know they can leave. Alec's sitting behind his desk with a huge grin on his face, he's dressed like me in a Tom Ford suit, his short brown hair is mussed up. Clearly, he's been running his hands through his hair like he usually does when he's stressed.

"Wipe that fucking grin off your face," I growl at him.

"My, my, look at you, reaping the benefits of marital bliss, you're positively glowing." He beams. "How is your wife, Luca? Did you have a good wedding night?" I know he's fishing for details, wondering if I've fucked her or not.

I sigh and close my eyes.

You can't stab your best friend. You can't stab your best friend. You can't fucking stab your best friend.

I open my eyes to glare at him. "Don't fucking speak about my wife," I spit, I may not exactly know the woman, but she's my wife and I won't have anyone talking about her, or our *non-existent* sex life.

Alec just smirks, knowing he's hit a nerve. "Aw, you're getting all protective already, is there a reason you didn't introduce me to her yesterday?" he laughs.

I guess he picked up on the fact that I purposely avoided him whenever Izzy was at my side. I love the man like a brother, but I never know what's going to come out of the idiot's mouth. So, I figured it was best to leave introductions until I got to know her a little better.

"Shut the fuck up and just tell me what you've found," I sigh, shaking my head.

For the next twenty minutes, I listen to him drone on in detail, about the Russian soldiers' phones he hacked and what information he's gathered. All the while I'm actually deep in thought about Izzy, and how it went this morning when I went to check if she was awake and found her sleeping.

She was so relaxed, her blonde hair a halo around her head making her look like an angel sent just to torture me. I was so fucking hard just from watching her sleep, I've never been so attracted to a woman in my life. It's unnerving. What I wouldn't do to have a taste of her full lips, hear her moans in my ear or her whispering dirty words to me before I fuck her so hard, she screams my name. The woman might be a little crazy, but she also has this aura of innocence around her that draws me in like a moth to a motherfucking flame. Even when she had just woken up, she was the most exquisite creature I've ever laid my eyes on, all I could think about was climbing on top of her and slamming myself inside her.

Jesus Christ, I'm getting hard thinking about her again.

I need to stop thinking about this shit, if we're going to have a somewhat normal marriage, then I need to take things slow. Also, I have no idea how the woman feels about me, she doesn't show a single emotion on her face unless it's planned. It's fucking infuriating.

My phone buzzes in my pocket, pulling me from my thoughts of fucking my little queen.

Unknown

> Hey husband, I need to go to the mall for a few things, can you let my new bodyguards know they need to babysit me, please?

Pleased she's asked me, rather than just gone off on her own—which I half expected her to do if I'm honest, she seems the type—I text Tomasso to let him know that him and his team need to take Izzy to wherever she needs to go and that if even a single hair on her head is out of place by the time she gets home, I'll slice their fucking necks from ear to ear before I leave them in an unmarked grave. Positive I got my point across; I save Izzy's contact and text her back.

> Hey Wife, Tomasso and his team are waiting in the lobby for you whenever you're ready, make sure you stay with them, please. And it's not babysitting, they can count themselves lucky they get to keep the queen of the Romano empire safe.

My Wife

> Thank fuck, I've graduated from princess!
> Thanks Luca.

She graduated from princess the minute I realized she could probably castrate me in my sleep before I even had the chance to stop her. I chuckle to myself, earning a glare from Alec.

"Dude! Are you listening or writing fucking love poems?" Shit, I should probably be listening.

I shake my head. "Sorry man, you were saying?"

He sighs, finally getting to the point. "Moral of the story, Novikov is hiding in a house in Queens. I've checked out his security and he has around twenty men stationed in and around the property. I'll be able to disable all of the alarm systems if you let me know when you're hitting him." He stands, rounds the desk and claps me on the shoulder. "Be fucking careful, I've just attended your wedding, that's enough of a fancy event for me, I don't need to be going to your funeral as well," he says, and I stand, ready to get the fuck out of here.

"Are you worried about me, sweetheart?" I ask, teasing him and he sends me a glare. "I'll be good, don't worry. Thanks for your help," I add before patting his back and strolling out the door.

Alec has no idea just how much I appreciate him; I'd have probably ended up in the ground years ago if it wasn't for him. I'm not sure exactly what the fuck he really does on that computer of his, but there's been countless times when he's informed us of shit going down in our world, including a couple of hits that had been put out on me.

Luckily, he saw them in time, did his special kind of magic removing them from the site and gave me a heads up, letting me get to the fuckers who thought they could get rid of me first.

The driver opens my door and I get into the car while sending a text to the group chat that I have with my brothers and Dad. We have a hit to plan.

CHAPTER NINE

Luca

Walking into Di Nuovo, one of the restaurants owned by our family that we usually use to conduct business, I nod to the servers and make my way into the back room where I know Marco and my father are waiting for me.

I decided it's probably in everyone's best interests to leave Enzo out of the planning. That crazy little shit would probably go off on his own and blow the place up, himself along with it.

I step into the private room and see Dad and Marco sitting at the table each drinking a glass of whiskey. I don't look much like our father, I got most of my mother's genes, but Marco is an exact replica of him when he was his age. And to see them both sat next to each other, both taking a drink at the same time, wearing what could very well be identical suits is eerie, and rather fucking comical, if you ask me.

I take a seat opposite them, and we start getting into details on how many men we'll need for our mission. Alec gave me a copy of blueprints for the home Novikov is holed up in. We decide it's best to take four teams, three of the teams will enter from a different entrance and each take out as many of the men as possible while the fourth team guards the perimeter to make sure Novikov doesn't try and escape.

Slimy bastard that he is, it wouldn't be a surprise if he tries to run. Any man who decides to hide out somewhere while having other men fight his battles for him is a fucking pussy.

"I had a meeting with Sergei Andrev yesterday," Dad says after we finalize the details, I immediately tense. What the fuck was he doing meeting with Novikov's second in command? And why did I not know about it? He usually keeps me up to date on every-fucking-thing so for me to not know about it means it wasn't planned.

"What do you mean you had a meeting with Andrev yesterday?" Marco balks at him with wide eyes, voicing my thoughts. We shoot each other a *what the fuck* look before turning back to Dad and waiting for him to explain.

"Andrev is done being Novikov's little bitch. Apparently, Novikov is wanting to get into trafficking, which you both know I do not tolerate, and apparently Andrev doesn't either. He said something about his sister, I investigated it, and it turns out she was killed a few years ago when she was picked up by traffickers back in Moscow," he says with a grimace. "The girl was only fifteen, picked up right off the street before being sold to some perverted fuck in Boston. She died a few days later," he says, and I shake my head, what sort of sick bastard buys a fifteen-year-old girl?

"Andrev has the backing of over half of their organization, they were just waiting for the right time to overthrow him. We made a deal, we take out Novikov and Andrev takes over, once he does, he cuts their alliance with the Colombians and we resume our old deal, and we get an extra five percent cut off the top of any business we do together."

"Makes sense, it's not like we can take out the Russians completely, we need to keep the balance between us, and this way it leaves the Colombians vulnerable with them no longer having the Russians on their side," I add while they both nod, agreeing with me.

Me and Marco stay for a while longer, chatting about inconsequential nonsense, when he asks how Izzy reacted to the gift that I made for her.

"I'm not really sure, she just kind of stared at me like I'd lost my head. I can't figure her out, man. One minute she's this perfectly manicured Mafia princess, the next she's this scary as shit badass and I'm one wrong move from having my balls removed," I say with a sigh.

"Just take things slow and see what happens, she's clearly been taking care of herself for a while, just try to get to know her. She'll warm up to you eventually," he says, while I wonder whether her warming up to me is a good thing or not.

After a while, we say our goodbyes. We've decided to carry out the hit on Novikov next week.

On my way out of the restaurant I stop and speak to Matteo, the manager, and tell him I'll need a table reserved for tonight, deciding to take Marco's advice. I want to get to know Izzy more and I figure taking her out to dinner is probably a good way to start,

I'm pretty sure this will be the first time I've ever taken a woman out for a meal; I don't do dates.

Exiting the restaurant, I pull out my phone and send her a text.

Can I take you out for dinner tonight?

My Wife

Sure, what time?

I'll pick you up at 8.

CHAPTER TEN

Izzy

After I left the mall, where I went to pick up some new hard drives because I'm not saving shit to the cloud where anyone with two brain cells can access anything they like, I came back to the apartment to do some work.

I work for an online organization who specializes in stopping sex traffickers and rescuing their victims. The organization has special operatives who go to locations to save those who have been taken and take out the traffickers. The organization is in no way legal, but it's not as if the cops do shit to stop them, so we take it into our own hands.

I'm not a physical part of operations, my hacking abilities allow me to trace the sales of women and children online and trace them back to the sellers and buyers. I also help set up the missions, erasing traffic cameras so the operatives stay out of sight, formulating the best routes for them to take and overall, just using my computer skills to help them.

After a few hours of work and unpacking my things in my new home, I hop in the shower and start getting ready for dinner with Luca.

To say I was surprised by his text is an understatement. I half expected us to live in uncomfortable silence and awkward small talk, not for him to take me out for dinner. I style my hair down with loose curls and apply minimal eye makeup with a red lip before choosing a black satin dress paired with gold heels. The dress comes to around mid-thigh, it's classy yet sexy and in no way scandalous, considering I have no idea where we're going, I figured it was a safe choice.

I glance down at my left hand and see my wedding ring. It's hard to believe I'm actually married. I've always known this would happen, but it's different to it actually happening. *It could be worse*, Luca seems respectable enough, and *Jesus Christ, he looks good in a suit.* When he asked for my number this morning, I had to stop myself from blatantly ogling him. It took all my strength to not maul him right then and there.

I'm not allowing myself to get too comfortable, though. For all I know, this could all be an act and he could turn out to be a monster, like one I'd always imagined marrying.

After taking the elevator down to the lobby, I walk through and spot Luca waiting near the entrance. He's still in the same suit from this morning and I can sense the moment he sees me, his gaze lights my skin on fire and has my senses in overdrive.

Holy fuck, I don't think I've ever been this attracted to a man before.

As I reach him, he looks me over once more before his eyes meet mine.

"*Bellisma*," he breathes. "You're beautiful, Izzy."

"Thank you," I say, giving him a shy smile.

No man has ever pulled this reaction from me. I'm not fucking shy.

What the hell is wrong with me?

He takes my hand and leads me out to the car that's waiting, he nods to the driver before he opens my door for me and waits for me to get in before closing it and rounding the other side where the driver opens the door for him. We make the short ride to the restaurant in comfortable silence, where I gaze out the window at the busy city.

Before long, we're pulling up in front of an Italian restaurant. If I had to guess, I'd say this was one of his family's restaurants. That becomes clear when the manager ushers us to our seats and greets Luca as though they're well acquainted. Luca makes sure my back is facing the wall, another security precaution from him.

I've noticed my safety is a top priority to him. It's nice to have someone take care of me, considering the only person who was there for me after Mama died was Alessi, and since he died, I've been alone. Even if he is only doing it to prove a point to his men and any staff members, the point being that he's a happily married man, I can live with that if he's going to continue to put my safety first. I'll take any—albeit small—wins I can get in this marriage.

"I invited you out to dinner because I figured we're better off getting to know each other, and it might make living together easier if we can get along without any threats," Luca says, his lips tipping up into a small smile.

"What do you want to know?"

"What is it you plan on doing with your days now you're in a new city? Do you know anyone in the city? Do you plan on stabbing me at any point..." I chuckle. "Because if you could just give me a heads up, that would be great. I like to let my guard down at home. I'm not used to having a woman in my space, never mind a woman who could probably dismember me without flinching," he continues, making me laugh.

I take a second to really look at him. He has a small smile on his face, making those dimples of his more prominent. *Those goddamn dimples.* His eyes are twinkling with mischief and there's no coldness or hardness there that I've seen him have with others, even with his own brothers, his facial expressions are never this expressive, that I've seen anyway.

"I know *you* in the city," I say, raising my brow. "But no, I don't know anyone else here, and I plan on spending my days working. I work from my laptop, so I can work from anywhere. And no, dear husband, I don't plan on stabbing you, that is unless you give me a reason too," I say and shoot him a flirty grin.

Damn, seems like I'm now a woman who flirts without an agenda. What the fuck is he doing to me?!

We spend the next hour chatting while eating the best Alfredo I've had since my mama was alive. We talk about how we grew up; Luca tells me about his brothers and about what his mom was like before she died. It sounds like Don Romano tried to give his boys a normal childhood, unlike most other heads of criminal organizations. I enjoy talking to him, it feels easy, like the conversation just flows with no effort whatsoever. Normally, I'd keep chatter to a minimum, that tends to happen when you hate most human interaction, I'd rather sit in front of a screen and work with numbers than ask my neighbor how her granddaughters dog is feeling after its recent trip to the vets or what-the-fuck-ever normal people talk about.

After dessert, Luca pays the bill and stands up to pull out my chair, just as I start to stand, there's a deafening sound of gunshots, along with glass shattering and screams.

Luca immediately grabs me and throws me to the floor with him on top of me, covering my body with his, once again looking out for my safety. It's unnecessary but appreciated all the same.

As he gets up, I manage to get myself into a sitting position as he flips the table next to us so we're out of the line of fire and pulls his Glock from his waistband beneath his suit jacket.

"Stay here," he orders and goes to pass me a gun, but I shake my head and pull my own from the garter belt attached to my thigh. By now the place has emptied of patrons who must have run out the back patio doors and Luca's men are shooting towards the roof of the building opposite us. Luca moves with precision, positioning himself so that he's not in the line of fire as he observes what's going on around him, processing what the best plan of action to get us out of here alive is.

Luca starts barking at his men, ordering a group of them to find the shooters while telling the rest of them to surround me. Within seconds, I have a horde of men circling me, ready to take a bullet meant for me.

If only Mama could have been surrounded when she was attacked, I think to myself before shaking my head and focusing on what's going on around me. Now is not the fucking time to be thinking about this shit.

The shots continue, so loud my eardrums rattle from the sound. From the precision of the shots and the angle coming in, I'd say it was a premeditated attack, probably a sniper, and not some careless drive-by shooting.

Eventually, the shooting stops and after a couple of seconds, Luca's phone rings. One of his men joins me near the wall holding a piece of material, he starts wrapping it around my arm where I must have cut myself on the glass from the shattered windows. I'm about to tell this mystery guard that it's fine when I turn my head and my gaze locks with Luca's.

CHAPTER ELEVEN

Luca

S eeing Tomasso's ID on my phone, I answer. "What?" I bark at him through the speaker.

"Uh, boss, we were waiting outside as instructed while you were having dinner when the shooting started, we approached the building the shots were coming from with the group you sent to check things out, by the time we got to where they were we spotted three shooters, but they ran before we could do anything. I managed to shoot one of them in the leg, but he still managed to get away. They were Russian."

"Fuck," I sigh. "Thanks man," I say before ending the call and turning to face Izzy, it's only then that I realize she's stood against the wall with one of my men wrapping what seems to be some sort of makeshift bandage around her arm. I walk over to her and take her arm from Gianni, undoing the material to see she got cut from the glass after the windows shattered.

"It's fine," she says. She's right, it isn't a deep cut, but that doesn't stop the blind rage I feel simmering up deep inside me that those Russian assholes made my wife fucking bleed.

I close my eyes and take a deep breath to try and control my anger. "Come on, let's go home so I can clean and wrap it properly," I say softly while taking hold of her hand and beginning to walk through the destroyed restaurant to get to the car.

Needing to make sure Izzy really is okay, I pause my steps and run my eyes up and down her body again, checking for additional injuries. I feel slightly better when I don't see any, but I still sweep her up in my arms and carry her out to the car, bridal style, I might add. *Oh, the irony.*

My men are positioned all around us, shielding us in case someone decides to start firing shots at us again, this shit is happening far too often for my liking. This war needs to end, and soon, because what if next time it's not just a small cut, what if next time she gets seriously hurt?

"Was carrying me really necessary?" Izzy huffs when I position her inside the car.

"Just let me help you woman," I groan as I put on her seatbelt. She just shakes her head at me and gives me an inquisitive glance.

Yeah, I have no fucking idea what I'm doing, baby. Don't look at me for answers, you won't find any.

During the drive back to the apartment, I give my Dad a call to let him know what happened and that we're okay. Luckily, no one was hit during all the chaos—it's the first hit in a while that we haven't lost anyone. I can't wait to put a bullet between Novikov's eyes next week. The fact that my wife got hurt makes me want it so much more, I don't give a fuck what the rest of the family say, that fucker made my wife bleed, it's only fair I get to take his blood in return.

Once we exit the elevator to the penthouse, I immediately sense someone else in the apartment. My security is so good there's less than a handful of people who would make it up here without ending up in an early grave, so I know it's probably one of my brothers, specifically the idiot who wouldn't think to not just show up here now that I'm married. I know Marco would never just turn up here so that leaves the delinquent brother.

We turn the corner into the sitting room to see Enzo sprawled out on the armchair watching some cooking show on the tv and eating an apple. *Fucking hell.*

"What the fuck are you doing here, Enzo?" I growl.

He glances up from where he's sitting to smirk at me. "Hey, bro," he says before turning to Izzy. "Hey, sis, I've come for some womanly advice," he states as though that's the most normal thing in the world, while I'm absolutely baffled that my emotionally unattached, psychotic brother has just turned up at my house to ask my wife of two days—who he barely knows and has only met once—for dating advice.

God help the poor girl that's caught his eye, she has no idea what she's in for.

CHAPTER TWELVE

Izzy

Luca leaves to find a first aid kit, which is completely unnecessary for the scratch on my arm, but whatever. There was no use arguing when he, very clearly, doesn't like the fact that I lost even a single drop of blood because of the Russian assholes who shot up the place. Now I'm left sitting alone in a room with his brother Enzo, who's closer to my age than he is Luca's, and apparently wants some womanly advice. Well, this should be fun.

"So, you're a woman, right?" he says, completely serious.

I bark out a laugh. "Yes, I'm a woman."

He looks at me for a beat, empty eyes staring at me. "I need help, I met a woman at a club but didn't get her name, the asshole owner wouldn't show me the security feed so I could see her face again no matter what I offered him, and I'm really close to trying to fucking sketch her just to see her again." *Okaaaay, this isn't where I thought this was going.*

"So, I was hoping that if I describe what she was wearing, you can tell me the type of girl she is, then from that you might know where I can find her or where she goes so I can see her again."

I blink at him, then blink again. Surely, he did not just say that? *Jesus fucking Christ.*

I bite my cheek to stop from laughing at him. From what I can gather, Enzo doesn't handle his emotions normally, or act like a human whatsoever, clearly.

And I thought I was lacking in that area, this dude's on another level.

So, for him to be so fixated on a woman probably isn't good for her, and the fact that he thinks I'll be able to know all about her from what she was wearing? *Cazzo.*

I debate for a second on whether or not I should actually help him, on one hand, I really do feel for this girl, knowing she's about to become entangled with a man so unhinged he probably belongs in a mental facility. On the other hand, who the fuck knows what he'll resort to if I don't help him. Knowing it's a lose-lose situation, I decide to just go for it and hope like hell it works out for this girl.

I sigh before getting up to grab my laptop, I sit back on the couch. "Okay, so what club were you at? And where inside the club did you see her? And when was it?" I ask, but before he can answer, Luca comes back into the room. He starts to open his mouth, as if going to tell Enzo to leave but I shush him and turn back to his brother.

"We were at spotlights on Friday, and she was standing at the center of the bar. Why? What exactly can you do with that thing?" he says while waving at my laptop and clearly underestimating me.

I work my magic and hack into the club's cameras within seconds and then spend a few minutes checking the footage. I finally see Enzo on the screen staring as a small brown-haired girl sat at the bar, he's looking at her as though he wants to swallow her whole.

Guess that's the girl. She seems *far* too sweet and innocent for the likes of Enzo, but I'm not about to get into that right now.

I zoom in and transfer her image over to the facial recognition software I built, it's so accurate that if a person exists, they're on the fucking database. I can find anyone, even with a partial shot of their face. Within minutes I'm sending her name, address, work address, phone number and social security number to Enzo, along with her social media handles and eight photos attached, including one of him eye fucking her in the club. His phone buzzes and he checks the screen.

"How in the ever-loving-fuck did you do that? It hasn't been five minutes and you've got everything on her? What the fuck, Isabella! They're some skills you've got," he says to me, clearly shocked, before turning to Luca. "Careful with that one bro, she's scary," he says in absolute seriousness. Then before I even know what's happening, he's across the room and pulling me off the sofa, wrapping his arms around me and pulling me into a hug where he squeezes me so hard that I can barely breathe.

"I suggest you get your fucking hands off my wife," Luca barks.

Enzo gives me a smirk, then lets me go, but not before giving me a kiss on the forehead making Luca growl at him.

Huh, I guess he doesn't like his little brother touching me.

"You're the best sister in the world!" Enzo exclaims before turning around and walking out without a backwards glance and I can hear him chucking as he walks away.

The whole exchange was weird, but at least my new brother-in-law seems to like me, even if he's a special brand of crazy. I shoot Luca a confused look and he sighs and shakes his head in a *what can you do* gesture, before tilting his head to stare at me as if he's trying to get inside my head.

"How did you get that information so quickly?" he asks and I shrug my shoulders.

"I've been hacking for years; I've gotten pretty good," I say and smirk at him. He gives me another look as though he doesn't quite know whether to believe me or not, then he grabs my arm and sits me back on the sofa before tending to the cut.

"Fuck, Izzy, I'm sorry you got hurt. We should have just stayed here and ordered something for dinner. You wouldn't be bleeding if it wasn't for me, I'm so sorry," he says, distressed, his eyes are full of guilt and I want nothing more than to wipe it away.

He's gentle as he takes his time to clean and dress the wound on my arm and I find myself thinking about how strange this is.

How can he be the ruthless Mafia heir that he is to the rest of the world, yet he's sweet and caring with me? It doesn't make sense. For all of my twenty-four years, every man I've known has either been one or the other. My father, while he would be "loving" sometimes, was only ever putting on an act. Alessi, he was always sweet to me, he did everything he could to make me feel safe, he was more marshmallow than mafioso, which is exactly why my father made him my security detail, saving the harder men for himself.

I'm so fucking confused. At first, I thought maybe Luca was putting on an act like my father would, but the look in his eyes is genuine, he really does care. Why does that make my stomach flutter? Is that fucking *butterflies?* Oh god, I think it is. Either that or I'm losing my mind.

Hello, insanity.

"I'm fine Luca, it's barely a scratch," I say while I grab his hand and squeeze. It's meant to be a comforting gesture, but his touch burns, it's like every time his skin touches mine there's a fire that lights me up inside and I never want it to end. Which also makes me wonder how it'd feel to touch him in other places, or what he tastes like, or—

Fuck, this isn't good. Stop it Izzy!

I let go of his hand and thank him for taking care of my arm before saying goodnight and making a hasty exit to my room.

My body is coursing from adrenaline, whether it's from Luca's touch or almost getting shot, I'm not sure. But my insides are buzzing, my panties are soaked, and I feel as though I'm about to combust. I go to my nightstand and grab my vibrator, ready to fuck the feeling away myself.

CHAPTER THIRTEEN

Luca

I sit in confused silence, wondering what the fuck just happened. I must have pissed Izzy off somehow for her to fly out of the room like a bat out of hell.

Seriously, she couldn't get away from me quick enough. Was she pissed about my reaction to Enzo hugging her? It didn't seem like it at the time, or maybe she's pissed that she got hurt. I know she's been around the Cosa Nostra her whole life, but it can be difficult at times, maybe she's not used to being that close to the chaos and mayhem my life brings?

For the first time in my life, I'm unsure of what to do. I've never done the girlfriend thing, the most serious relationship I've had is a fuck buddy that I used for a quick fuck when the need arose. Should I talk to her? Give her some space? Ignore it all together?

Fuck, I sound like a little bitch.

I debate for a moment on whether or not I should call Marco or Alec to see what they think, then think better of it. I'd only be opening myself up to abuse from those two fuckers if I hit them up for dating advice, I'd never hear the end of it.

Hell, back when we were in freshman year of college, Alec made the unfortunate mistake of asking me for advice about a girl he was seeing. At the time, we were both idiot teenagers who did nothing but chase tail and fuck around.

Anyway, Alec made the mistake of asking me for advice, and rather than being helpful, I tore into him for weeks about how he couldn't land the girl. He effectively learned his lesson, never making the same mistake again, and if I was to ask him for advice? Forget it, he'd go on about it for months just to be a dick.

And if I was to call Marco for advice? Knowing him he'd snort into the phone before hanging up on me. Useless asshole.

Fuck it, I'm just gonna talk to her. What's the worst that could happen? I don't think she'd actually stab her own husband, right?

I stand and walk through the apartment towards her bedroom. Reaching her door, I raise my hand to knock on the wood just as the faint sound of buzzing comes from her room. Blood instantly rushes south to my dick. Fuck, is she getting herself off? Just as I think it, I hear her gasp and then let out a breathy moan.

Holy fucking fuck.

My dick is as hard as steel and throbbing painfully, I reach down and squeeze myself to relieve some of the pressure. I've never been so hard in my life, all from just hearing Izzy playing with herself through the door.

"Oh fuck, yesss." I hear her breathe and let out a raspy moan before she moans, "Fuck... fuck, Luca."

Jesus Christ, my name has never sounded so good.

I need to get out of here before I walk in there and make her fantasies a reality. *Talk about crossing boundaries.*

I stalk back across the apartment as quickly as I possibly can towards my bedroom. I enter my room, close my door and start shrugging out of my clothes as I walk into the bathroom. Once I'm naked I walk straight into the shower and turn it on to the coldest it'll go and hope my dick will deflate enough for me to be able to sleep.

I can still hear those sexy little moans, her moaning my name in that lust-filled, raspy voice of hers is playing on repeat in my head. *Fuck it,* I think as I wrap my hand around my dick and start slowing pumping myself.

I imagine Izzy in front of me on her knees, begging me to fuck her face right before she parts those red painted full lips of hers and I slide my cock through.

"Fucking hell," I growl as I imagine sliding to the back of her throat. I fuck my fist faster, imagining fucking her face while she chokes on my cock, pretty tears streaming down her face.

Fuuuckk.

I have to grab on to the wall to stop my knees from buckling. I bet she tastes so damn sweet; I could make her scream my name while I feast on her like it's my last goddamn meal before slamming myself inside her. The image is so real and so vivid inside my head that the next thing I know is I'm coming harder than I have ever come before, all over the shower floor.

Once my breathing calms down, I stand for a few minutes, wondering how the hell a woman I've known for less than three days has me so worked up, never in my life have I fantasized about fucking a specific woman in so much detail. Normally I'd just imagine fucking a woman from behind. They wouldn't have a face to identify them. Like I said, I don't do attachments.

On the bright side, at least now I know why she couldn't get away from me quick enough, I smirk to myself but then a realization has the smirk dropping from my face and if I were to look in the mirror, I'd probably see a horrified expression in its place.

Dad was right, if Izzy is affecting me this much after only a few days of knowing her, then I really am fucked.

CHAPTER FOURTEEN

Izzy

The days pass in a blur of work and narrowly avoiding my husband and whenever it's been impossible to avoid him, we either sit in silence or make small talk. It isn't exactly awkward, but things could definitely be better. I'm sure he thinks he's done something wrong to make me avoid him, but, if I'm being honest, I can't even be in the same room as him wondering what it'd feel like to have his body on top of mine while he fucks me six ways to Sunday. *Focus Izzy, you have work to do.*

I've spent today working from the kitchen island, needing a change from the dining room. I'm tracking the lead of a buyer who posted on a site known to be frequented by traffickers. I was tipped off by the creator of the organization, Hurricane. They contacted me two years ago when they started Freethem. They're a good hacker and had the basics for the site down, but they needed help to set the algorithms right. I'm good at what I do, it was only supposed to be a one-off contract, but once I saw what they were doing I wanted to help, growing up in the Mafia, you see a lot of shit.

Before I agreed to the job, I did a little research, wanting to make sure that they were legit. It turns out that he's a big shot CEO here in New York, and I'm pretty sure I saw him in an article for New York's most eligible bachelors.

Luckily, my father doesn't deal in sex trafficking, but that doesn't mean it wasn't happening in and around Chicago. I felt like my family takes enough lives and spills enough blood, this could be my way of giving back and doing something good, I like to think I'm making a difference.

I haven't seen Luca since last night, which is probably a good thing as all I've thought about all day is how I got myself off last week to thoughts of him fucking me on the kitchen counter and I don't think I'd be able to look at him without blushing. I need to get a hold on myself, the longer I go on like this, the more likely I am to end up begging him for his dick.

For fuck's sake, Izzy. Just stop. You need to focus! I reprimand myself and busy myself with work, I'll try anything to keep my mind from spiraling to dirty thoughts of my handsome husband.

I hear the elevator ping and out walks Luca. *Think of the devil and he shall appear.* I shake my head and chuckle to myself before focusing back on my laptop.

"Something funny?" he asks from the other side of the island and my head snaps up. His eyes darken as he takes in what I'm wearing. Shit, I didn't think earlier when I changed. I'm wearing a flimsy camisole with no bra and to make matters worse, the longer he stares at me the harder my nipples get.

Realizing he's still waiting for an answer, I clear my throat. "Uh, no. Just busy with work, what are you doing here? Your back earlier than usual," I state, and he nods.

"What is it you do on that thing all day, anyway? Are you an influencer or something?" he asks.

I roll my lips to hide my smile, he really needs to let go of that Mafia princess mentality he's got going on.

"I'm a software engineer and I work with a company creating software for their operations while I also help them find their missing... shipments," I say dryly.

I'm not entirely sure why I don't just tell him what I'm doing, I know his family don't deal with sex traffickers so he'd probably try and help where he could, but I've always kept what I do a secret from the world. I guess old habits die hard. The look on his face is hilarious, he's completely stunned, it's like he expected me to be some ditzy little girl and instead he's left with one of the world's highest skilled computer nerds.

He seems as though he's about to say something, but his phone buzzes. After checking the text, he says, "Needed to come back and get ready, we're hitting Novikov tonight," before disappearing into his room.

Thirty minutes later, I'm still working at the island when he comes out of his room dressed in full tactical gear. *Fuck, now I'll be having fantasies of him wearing that get-up and keeping me prisoner.*

"I'm texting you a list of take-out places that are good in the area in case you want to order something for dinner. I won't be back until late, so I'll grab something when I get in," he says while typing away on his phone.

"Thank you," I whisper before clearing my throat and wishing him good luck tonight. He thanks me and walks towards the elevator. He makes it a few steps before stilling, seemingly lost in thought.

He turns around and gazes at me through darkened eyes for a beat. "Fuck it," he murmurs and quickly stalks towards me, I'm so shocked and confused and don't know what the fuck is happening or how to react that the next thing I know his hands are cradling my face and he's slamming his lips on mine.

I freeze for a second before I can gather myself and kiss him back, his tongue teases my bottom lip with a languid stroke and I open for him, letting him take the kiss deeper as I wrap my arms around his neck. The world fades away and we lose ourselves in each other. I open my legs where I'm sitting on the stool and tug on his hair, he steps closer and his hard body presses into mine, making us both groan in unison.

"Fuck, baby. You're my new favorite flavor," he rasps between kisses, making me whimper into his mouth.

All I can feel is his body heating mine, he tastes like cold winter nights and smells like cedarwood and citrus. His hands roam from my face down my body to where he stops at my hips and squeezes them. I'm so lost in his kiss that when he finally steps back we're both panting. I have to take a moment to gather myself before I open my eyes. I feel dizzy, I'm a shaking mess of hormones and lust. His kisses are like a shock to the system, and I need a moment to reboot.

By the time I steady my breathing and pry my eyes open, he's gone.

CHAPTER FIFTEEN

Luca

Walking away from that kiss with Izzy was one of the hardest things I've ever done. I left before she even had a chance to open her eyes because I knew I'd see the same lust reflected back in hers that were in mine and seeing that isn't something I'd be able to walk away from. I'd end up dropping to my knees right there and begging her to let me worship her like the queen she is.

Kissing her set my fucking soul on fire, as soon as my lips met hers, I felt like I was finally home. I don't know how to describe the feeling of her body pressed to mine, just that no matter how close I could get, it wasn't enough. All thoughts of tonight left my head and it was just her and me, nothing and no one else existed, I could lose myself in that woman and not give a damn about real life if it's like that every time.

Fuck, get your head right, man. Now is not the time of this shit.

I'm thinking like a horny fourteen-year-old boy who's never kissed a girl before.

I shake my head to dispel my lustful thoughts and focus on my dad's voice, we're driving through Queens towards Novikov's safe house. "Luca, you're with me and group A, we're going in through the front. Marco, you're with team B going through the back patio and Enzo you're with team C going through the side entrance while the rest of our men are positioned around the perimeter in case any of those fuckheads think they can get away."

We drive up the gravel driveway of our destination. Our men are already here, scattered around out of sight.

"Enter on my count, and *for fuck's sake* do not get shot. I do *not* want to bury one of my sons, so stay alive and Luca, you're married now—let's not make the girl a widow a week after the wedding. Kill anyone who isn't one of ours," he growls as the car comes to a stop and before adding, "Novikov belongs to Luca, he owes him a debt." Damn right he does after last week. We all exit the car and split up into our groups. We're all wearing headsets so we're able to communicate with each other.

"On three. One, two, three!" Dad says and we all make our way into the house. One man comes rushing towards me, he's just flipping the safety off his gun when I land a bullet into his neck and he drops to the floor. Two more men come around the corner, they're too close to get a decent shot so I throw a punch to the one on the right and put a bullet between his eyes as he falls to the floor just as one of our men grabs the one on the left and slices his throat from ear to ear.

I can hear the commotion of the other teams through my earpiece, but I drown it out while I make my way up the stairs and into the bedroom. We knew Novikov was likely to hide in his panic room, but rather than having Alec disable it completely, we thought it would be fun to keep it active and instead I'm using the code to enter. *Ha! Let the little fuck face think he's got a shot at surviving.*

I walk through the closet and enter the code into the reader on the back panel, the door unlocks, and I kick it open to see Novikov reach for his gun on the table.

Seriously? Your house is being attacked and you leave your gun out of reach?

Fucking amateur.

How he's survived this long is one of the world's biggest mysteries, like on those god-awful tv shows I've noticed Izzy likes to watch about crop circles and shit. Great, I'm thinking about her again, this is why I've never bothered with a girlfriend, they're fucking distractions.

I shoot Novikov in the shoulder, not wanting this to be over too quickly, and he manages to get a shot off at the same time that just narrowly misses me. "Get fucked, Italian piece of shit!" he shouts.

Oh no, he hurt my feelings. I narrow my eyes at him and cock my head before donning a wide, maniacal grin.

"Good to see you, Dimitri," I sneer as I step closer and fire off another shot to his right hand and making him drop his gun, so he doesn't get any more ideas about shooting me. "You've been a pain in our asses for months, but that's finally coming to an end, did you know that your best friend, and second in command, was planning on overthrowing you? It seems even he's had enough of your shit."

"Fuck you, you're lying," he growls, and I just laugh. I grab a knife from my ankle strap and throw it at him, hitting him in his left eye. His knees buckle so he's kneeling before me. "That's right, sunshine, kneel for me," I laugh.

Fuck, this is so much fun.

"Did you know your attack at Di Nuovo's caused my wife to bleed? The sweetheart that she is kept trying to reassure me that she was fine, but I don't like that she lost even a drop of blood because of you," I say and use pressure to drag my knife over his arm in the same place Izzy was hurt, granted his cut is a lot deeper than hers was.

His cries and whimpers fill the room, but it's not enough. I kick him in the chest, so he falls backwards, and I kneel over him, so my legs are pinning his arms in place. He's bucking his body, trying to throw me off but it's useless, he's not going anywhere. I reach to my ankle and take another knife from the strap before using it to cut right up his shirt and exposing his bare torso to me and carve the words "we're coming for you next" into his skin as a little love letter to Muñoz. He's sobbing and gasping for breath but I'm not ready to put the sick fuck out of his misery just yet.

"I hear you're interested in the sex trafficking business," I grit out through clenched teeth. "What would you have done if you could get your hands on an innocent woman or child that's been snatched off the street? Would you have violated her? Raped her? Kept her as your little pet? Do you prefer them older, or are you a sick fuck that likes them underage?" I spit.

I really hate assholes who think they can prey on innocent women and children, it's the twenty first century for fuck's sake, the flesh trade should have ended with the fucking slaves. Thinking about what he could have done to an innocent woman makes me think of Izzy. What would this bastard do if he could get his hands on my wife? Rage like I've never felt before bubbles up inside me from the very depths of my soul and I have to take deep breaths to calm myself down. I can't just go flying off the handle because of hypothetical scenarios I've drummed up in my head.

My wife seems to be fucking with my thoughts more and more as the days pass. There was a time when I would be laser focused on the task at hand, now everything in my life revolves around her. I keep finding myself distracted to thoughts of her, and not only sexual. I find myself wondering if she's eaten, or what she's doing, how she's feeling in a new city. It's weird, and the worst part? I don't entirely hate it.

I shift backwards and use my knife to cut open his trousers and reach around to my back pocket and take out the set of pliers. I use the pliers to get a grip on his small, flaccid dick and slice it off with my knife with a wince before grabbing his jaw, so he opens his mouth and shoving it in. Don't get me wrong, I live for this shit, but cutting off someone's dick? This is by far the most gruesome thing I've done, but going after his manhood seems like poetic justice to me.

I close his jaw and place my hand over his nose and mouth, giving him a death that he's deserving of, choking to death on his own cock. I may be used to blood and violence, but this is on a rather different level, I have to hold my breath to stop myself from gagging.

"Luca, are you done fucking around? Where are you?" I hear Marco say through my earpiece, only now realizing that everyone has just had a front row seat to me killing the piece of shit beneath me since they can hear me through their earpieces.

"I'm good, we're coming out now," I answer him and take a deep breath before standing.

I grab Novikov by his ankles and drag him from the room—it'd be too much work dragging him down the stairs—so I just give his body a kick, he bounces down the stairs and lands at the bottom with a thud.

Huh, that was fun, maybe I should have kept him alive a bit longer, I think to myself and chuckle. When I reach him, I grab hold of his ankles once again and make my way out to the driveway where I dump him for everyone to see.

"It's about time," Dad says with a smirk before instructing Enzo to do his part next through the earpiece. A few seconds later there's a loud boom and the sounds of windows shattering before the whole house is lit up. *Ah, an Enzo special.* I stand and watch the house burn from the inside out while the rest of the men are tending to those wounded, luckily there were only a few injured, and they all seem pretty minor. We managed to kill every one of Novikov's men without losing any of our own.

As I watch the flames dance around the night sky, I sigh and let out a breath of relief.

Finally. One down, one to go.

We pile back into our respective vehicles and make the drive back into the city. Now that the chaos has died down, I'm back to thinking about the kiss I shared with Izzy before I left. Fuck, I wanted to take it further, so much so that I don't think I've ever been so desperate for something in my life. I check the time on my phone and see it's only eleven thirty, she might still be awake, I hope like fuck that she is.

I wonder what she thinks about what happened. I know for a fact that she's attracted to me, especially after I heard her calling out my name while she brought herself to orgasm. But fantasizing about something and actually doing it are two *very* different things.

Will she want to take things further? Or would she rather just keep things how they are now, platonically living together while ignoring the sexual tension. I guess there's only one way to find out. Fuck it, I'll talk to her about it in the morning.

We finally reach my building where I say my goodbyes to my father and brothers. "Good work tonight, son. Take the day tomorrow and I'll see you on Saturday at the Mayor's gala," Dad says with a smirk. *Fuck me,* another goddamn event to keep up appearances, he knows there's nothing I hate more than sucking up to the city officials but shit like that is what keeps us the fuck out of jail. It's unbelievable really, how many respected politicians and other influential assholes are dirty as shit. I give him a reluctant nod and make my way up to the apartment.

Adrenaline is still coursing through my veins as I step off the elevator. I head towards my room but make a split-second decision and head towards the guest room that Izzy's staying in. Stopping in front of her room, I raise my fist and bang on the door, deciding I'd rather have my answer tonight.

CHAPTER SIXTEEN

Izzy

I'm woken up to the sound of banging on my bedroom door. I wipe my hand over my face, moving the hair from my eyes to orient myself before hurrying to open the door. I'm just reaching for the handle as the door flies open and I see Luca standing there still decked out in black cargo pants and a black, long sleeve t-shirt, the only differences from earlier this evening are that he's no longer got his weapons strapped to him and he now seems to be covered in blood.

"Hey, are you okay? How did it g—" I don't even finish my sentence before he's pressing his lips to mine in an all-consuming kiss. His hands grab my hips, and he walks me backwards towards the bed. His tongue teases mine in a slow, teasing rhythm before he presses his mouth to mine harder, kissing me with everything he has and pouring every emotion he's feeling into me.

My world tilts on its axis and the next thing I know I'm laid out in the middle of the bed and Luca is climbing up on top of me. His hard body is pressed to mine. In the back of my mind, I'm acutely aware that he's soaked in another man's blood and probably covering me and my bed in it too, but do I care? Not even a little bit.

"Tell me to stop," he pants, and I shake my head, unable to form words I'm so fucking turned on.

"No, don't stop or no, stop. I need to hear the words, baby," he says while peppering my neck with kisses before he lifts up to stare down at me.

"Don't you dare stop!" I growl at him while writhing beneath him. He chuckles and stares at me for a moment before slamming his mouth back down on mine. His tongue battles mine for control and I give in, letting him set the pace. I lift my hips to grind myself against his pelvis, I can feel his erection through his pants, so I keep grinding, making him groan into my mouth before he pulls back and starts kissing my neck. He makes his way down my body, pulling up my camisole so he can see my breasts.

"Jesus Christ, your beautiful, Iz," he rasps just as he captures my nipple between his teeth, making me moan and arch my back, pushing my breast further into him. He swaps between licking and pinching both nipples, biting them slightly and leaving me a shaky, wet mess. Just as I'm about to demand more, he starts making his way lower, kissing my stomach as he pulls off my sleep shorts and settling himself between my legs.

"Fuck, baby, you're something else," he says in awe and pressing a delicate kiss to my clit before he digs in and feasts on me like a starving man. His tongue laps at my clit in a punishing rhythm as he slowly inserts a finger inside me. "Oh God... Luca," I moan, and he groans in response.

"You taste fucking delicious, baby," he rasps before adding another finger and working them faster, his tongue continues its fast pace on my clit and *fuck*, I'm so close.

"Fuck, baby, the sounds you make, your taste, your body. *Christ woman*, you'll be the death of me," he groans and the sound of him groaning in pleasure from my taste makes me even wetter as his pretty, dirty words send a buzzing sensation through me.

"You like that, huh, dirty girl? You like driving me wild, walking around the apartment in your little shorts, your see through little tops where I can see your nipples poking through, begging me to taste them?"

I grab a handful of his hair and pull on it as he curls his fingers inside me, hitting the spot that I needed him to as I buck my hips up and down, grinding on his face while I chant unintelligible nonsense, I don't even know what I'm trying to say at this point.

"Fuck, Iz. I need you to come for me, come all over my face while screaming my name, fucking *please*, baby," he begs.

And I do, I come screaming his name and drenching his face in my release.

Fuck me, that has got to be the most intense orgasm I've ever had. Luca kisses his way back up my body while I come down from the high of my orgasm, he presses a sweet kiss to my lips before getting up.

I think he's about to leave the room, but instead he picks me up bridal style and walks to the bathroom. He turns on the shower, sets me down on the floor and guides me into the shower before stripping off his clothes and stepping in beside me.

This is the first time I've seen Luca without his clothes on, his broad chest is covered in intricate tattoos, blending well with the tribal themed tattoos that cover both of his arms and damn, he's got a six pack. His body is an honest to God work of art.

Christ, why does he have to look like that?

Luca makes quick work of scrubbing his body as I do the same, deciding I'm not in the mood to deal with the nest that is situated on the top of my head, I forgo washing my hair, deciding that's tomorrow's issue. I step out of the shower and before I can grab a towel, Luca's already wrapping one around me and patting me dry. I go to reach for him, wanting to reciprocate the mind-blowing orgasm he gave me, but he swats my hand away and shakes his head.

"Not tonight. Just let me take care of you, Iz," he says so gently it almost brings tears to my eyes; I've been on my own for so long I can't remember the last time someone wanted to take care of me. I give him a shaky nod and he picks me up again, carrying me through the apartment and into his room.

He sets me on the bed and tilts his head in a *move over* gesture. I scoot over as he climbs into the bed beside me, then he loops his arm under my neck and around my back before he pulls me to his chest, tucking my head under his chin and stroking up and down my back with a featherlight touch.

We lay in comfortable silence, neither of us feeling the need to talk. Luca keeps a tight hold on me, as if he thinks that if he loosens his grip for even a second, I'll disappear, never to be seen again. I've never felt so cherished in all my life. I've never been one to snuggle, a couple of the men I've been with in the past may have tried, but that was quickly shut down. It feels different with Luca, as if I belong here in his arms.

For the first time in my life, I'm relaxed while lying in bed. I'm not thinking about the horrors of our world, I'm not wondering what he's thinking or what the hell we're doing, I'm simply just living for this moment, safely tucked up with my husband surrounding me like a barrier to the thoughts that would usually consume me and terrorize me at night.

For the first time in my life, I'm safe.

"Goodnight, *mia regina,*" he whispers as I'm drifting to sleep and presses a soft kiss into my hair.

CHAPTER SEVENTEEN

Luca

F ucking Izzy with my mouth has got to be one of the most erotic things I've ever encountered. She's like a goddamn drug that's so intoxicating you'd happily die for just one more hit. She tasted so sweet, and her raspy little moans nearly made me come right there in my pants. Jesus Christ, I'd never been so turned on in all my life.

No woman has ever had that much of an effect on me, a bomb could have gone off and I still wouldn't have been able to pull myself away from her pretty pink pussy. I'd have happily been blown to pieces as long as I did it while feasting on her. And fuck, when she pulled on my hair while crying out for more? It's an honest to God miracle I didn't blow my load, which would have been embarrassing as fuck. Luckily, I managed to control myself.

I know she was confused about why I wouldn't let her touch me, and if I'm being honest, it killed me to turn her away, but I wanted last night to be focused on her. It took all my strength to not bend her over and fuck her while we showered. Especially after I'd just felt her pussy clamp down on my fingers, knowing she'd squeeze the fucking life out of my cock and seeing her soaking wet in the shower, washing her tits, water dripping from them and begging me to give them another taste? Her swollen pussy on display, begging me to take her right there? Or when she turned around, and I got a full view of that perfect, full, plump ass that begged me to lean over and give it a sharp slap? Fucking torture. *Jesus, I could come from just thinking about it.*

I barely slept all night, too preoccupied staring down at Izzy's angelic face while she clung to me in her sleep. I never thought a woman would be able to capture my attention the way she has. I'm not sure whether it's because I know that I'm married to her and I'll have to spend my life with her, or whether it's just her. To be truthful, she had me mesmerized from the second I laid eyes on her when she walked down that aisle.

The woman has managed to worm her way inside me, and I don't think I'll ever get her out, and I honestly don't think I would want to. It feels as though she was made just for me, as though my soul recognizes hers, like we're both two halves of a whole, destined to complete each other. She's quickly becoming the most important person in my life, which is strange since I've known her for such a short amount of time.

I've just woken up, and she's still lying in the same position she was in last night when she fell asleep. As I peer down at her, I try to imagine what life has been like for her.

I know her father is an asshole who basically sold her off like cattle, but it sounds as though she's had it rough growing up. She lost her mom when she was eleven, and since then it seems as though the only person she's been able to rely on was her bodyguard, the one who trained her into the pretty little killing machine that she is. She told me about how Alessi died last year and I can't imagine the pain that that caused her, knowing that from then on, she was on her own.

Girls growing up in the Mafia have it hard as it is, I can't imagine how much worse it was for my girl. *Yeah, I'm embracing this shit, she's my girl.*

When we lost our mom, at least me and my brothers still had each other, along with our dad too. We had each other to lean on and support each other. I never realized how truly lucky I've been to have a loving family until Izzy shared her story with me. My little queen has been alone for so long.

Well, she's not alone anymore. Fuck that, she has me now and I'll burn the city to ashes to keep her safe and happy.

Izzy's head burrows further into my chest before she realizes that I'm not actually a pillow and her eyes flutter open, a crease forming on her brow as she wakes up and sees she's still sprawled out on top of me and not in her own bed.

Fuck, she's so goddamn adorable.

My heart squeezes in my chest and my breath stills as her eyes meet mine. Her lips tip up in a shy smile before her eyes dart to the clock on the nightstand.

"Luca, what the hell! It's ten in the morning, what the fuck are you still doing here?" she blurts with wide eyes and a look of horror, making me chuckle.

She's right to be shocked, I don't think I've stayed in bed this late in the morning since I was a kid. Christ, I'm normally out of the house by eight most days. I don't normally see her in the mornings, other than the first morning she was here.

"Dad gave me the day off after everything that happened last night. Don't worry, I've been comfortable right where I am with you clinging to me like a koala," I say, and she gives me a wide smile that lights up her whole face. She's so fucking beautiful, that smile alone could bring me to my knees.

"How did it go? You didn't exactly answer my question when I asked you last night," she says with a laugh and sits up to peer down at me, naked breasts on display with the blanket pooled around her waist.

I shake my head, avert my eyes from her tits to her face and tell her everything that happened last night, in excruciating detail, not leaving anything out. Most women would be horrified hearing the details of what I did to Novikov, not my wife though. No, Izzy's sat with a shit eating grin on her face, absolutely enthralled with me detailing the gruesome scene, speaking up to ask questions like she can't get enough, the little psycho that she is.

After I get up to make Izzy a coffee—because she really isn't much of a morning person—we lay in bed for another hour, talking about everything and nothing. It's so easy to talk to her. I normally hate small talk, but with Izzy conversation just flows, and we can just sit in comfortable silence, things never becoming awkward. I'm starting to think we actually have a shot at having a normal marriage. I also tell Izzy about the gala we're expected at tomorrow night, and she's about as thrilled about the evening as I am.

It turns out Izzy didn't bring much with her, only a few outfits and some personal things she didn't want to leave at her family's estate, so we decide to make some lunch before we go shopping to buy her a dress.

After showering—separately, much to my dismay—and getting dressed, we eat lunch before heading to a boutique owned by one of my men's wives. I called ahead to make sure we could have some privacy, I don't need anyone other than the staff there ogling my wife. Fuck, if it could just be me and her alone and no staff to interfere, I'd be a very happy man. But unfortunately, I have no idea what she'll need or want when it comes to shopping, so I'll just have to deal with sharing her.

Izzy looks hot as fuck wearing skintight black denim jeans that showcase her full, round ass and a red sweater that's tight around her tits. How the simplest of outfits can be such a goddamn turn on, I really don't know. I'm struggling to keep my attention away from her sexy as fuck body long enough to hold a conversation with her.

We walk into LaRosa, the high-end store that specializes in designer brands and formal wear. The walls are covered in roses, the place is decorated in different shades of pink, with the walls lined with different gowns, each wall is coordinated by color. Izzy turns to me making screwing her face up and giving me a look of disgust.

"Not good enough for you, princess?" I ask, slightly offended by her reaction. She snorts, yes, fucking *snorts* and shakes her head.

"The clothes are fine, but the place is decorated like a fucking florist. Seriously, why are places like this always covered in pink and all the girly shit? It's making my eyes bleed, Luca!" she says dramatically in a hushed whisper, making me belt out a laugh. I shake my head at her, she really isn't like any woman I've ever known.

A sales assistant comes to greet us, eyeing us hungrily as if she knows she's about to make a hefty commission and guides us to the private dressing room while offering us champagne. I turn to Izzy in question, but she just rolls her eyes at me as if she's already had enough of the woman and politely declines before telling the assistant what her size and preferences are.

Izzy only tries on three dresses before she's decided she's had enough. She decides on the second dress, an emerald green silk dress that reaches the floor. It fits her curves perfectly and has a slit up one side, showcasing her legs, making me want to reach out and slide my hand up her leg and into her panties. The dress isn't too low cut, but it still gives a good view of her perky tits, making me think I'm gonna end up causing a blood bath in the middle of the gala if any men think they can look at what belongs to me. She's a goddamn dream, made with the purpose of driving me wild. My cocks throbbing painfully from just the sight of her.

Fuck, this husband thing is going to be a challenge, she's too damn sexy for her own good.

I expected this shopping trip to be like those scenes in movies where the man sits in a chair, a high pile of clothes strewn over his lap whole the woman tries on dress after dress while complaining about the color or fit—turns out I couldn't be more wrong.

I can't believe I was convinced that I was getting a spoilt socialite for a wife. Izzy is the complete opposite from what I expected. If anything, she's anticipating this event even less than I am, which proves she's perfect for me.

She's a psychotic little spitfire that matches my crazy, wrapped up in the body of a goddess. She's half angel, half succubus. She's fucking mine.

CHAPTER EIGHTEEN

Izzy

Once we get home from the boutique from hell—which we ended up being in and out of within twenty minutes—Luca changes and heads down to the gym while I set myself up at the dining table to get some work done. Spending this morning in bed with Luca was surreal, I never thought it possible that we could gel together so well, we talked about our childhoods and what it was like for him growing up with two younger brothers.

When I was younger, I always wanted a little sister. However, in hindsight, it's probably for the best that I was an only child. It's better that way, at least my father didn't have any more children for him to force his control over, the way he did with me.

Hearing Luca talk about what he and his brothers got up to when they were younger makes me think about the kids that we'll have one day.

Obviously, they'll have to grow up in la Cosa Nostra, but I want to give them the kind of childhood the Romano's had. I've never really thought about having kids before, it was always just a faraway fact that one day I would have to produce an heir for my father, because that's the only thing I was good for.

I grew up listening to my father complain about me being a girl. He once called me a selfish little bitch for being born a girl, because of course it was my fault. As if I somehow took control and decided my own fate.

I spend the next hour tracing leads and sending the data to Hurricane about some whispers I found on a site about a shipment of girls coming into New York next month. It makes me feel sick that there's people out there who will just sell these girls and I'm eternally grateful for the life I've lived, even if sometimes I do wish it was different, easier, normal.

I'm just about to get up to stretch my legs when my phone rings on the table. Looking at the caller ID I see that it's my father calling. I roll my eyes before picking up the phone and answering.

"Hi, Papa," I say into the speaker.

"Isabella, you've been in New York for a while now. Surely, you've got something to tell me?" he grunts.

What? No how are you? How's married life? Are you happy with the man I sold you to? At least he's consistent in being a dick.

"Something like what, Papa?" I say, playing dumb. There's not a chance in hell I'm telling him anything about what Luca or the rest of the family have been up to.

"You know exactly what I mean, Isabella. Surely you know something? It's always good to keep some blackmail material. Honestly, it's a wonder you've made it this far in life," he says and I have to hold in a snort. I've made it this far in life because I fought tooth and nail every single day while putting up with him being a controlling and demanding asshole.

"Luca and I don't talk about his work, or anything even remotely related to it. I'm sorry, but I don't know anything. I have to go," I say before hanging up the phone with a huff.

I'm not exactly sure what on God's green earth makes the man think I'd help him, considering he's done nothing but belittle me my whole life, but his brain seems to work differently to others. To him, I'm just a pawn, and that doesn't stop now that he's sold me off. No, he now thinks he can use me to spy on the New York outfit. Hopefully, if I keep dodging his questions, he'll eventually give up. I'm done being his little puppet.

Deciding to be open with Luca, I make my way down to the gym, where I find him sat on the bench lifting weights. He's facing away from me, only wearing a pair of loose-fitting shorts. I can see the muscles on his back rippling with each rep. The tattoos on his back glistening from sweat. He's so fucking hot, my core tightens, and my panties grow wetter for every second I stand here staring at him.

How can one man turn me on so much? I've never once gotten wet from the sight of a man alone. Hell, in the past, the men I've been with have had to work me up to get me ready for them. Whereas Luca could just glance in my direction with his heated eyes, cocky smirk and I'd be gushing, ready to take his dick, no work necessary.

I clear my throat, announcing my presence and making him turn his head to look at me.

CHAPTER NINETEEN

Luca

I turn my head to see Izzy standing near the door to the gym. She's still wearing the jeans and sweater from earlier, only now she's barefoot and her hair is piled up on top of her head in a messy bun and she's removed any makeup from her face. She's stunning.

I came down to the gym to try and work off some of my sexual frustration. I knew if I stayed anywhere near Izzy, I'd end up begging her on my knees to let me fuck her, so I removed myself from the situation to let her get some work done.

"Iz, are you okay? What're you doing in here?" I ask, knowing she was planning on working for a few more hours. I spin my body to face hers and her eyes darken as she takes in my naked torso.

Fuck, I can't take it when she looks at me like that.

"I... Uh, I just wanted to tell you about the phone call I had with my father."

Intrigued, I give her a nod to continue.

"I thought you might like to know that he's digging for information, wanting me to pry into your dealings, he wants some blackmail material. Not sure what for, but I figured you and your family would want to know what he's up to, I told him we don't talk about any of your business."

"Don't worry about him, Izzy. He won't find anything on us, just keep telling him we don't speak about it and hopefully he'll stop asking, he probably just wants dirt on us in case we try to cross him in the future," I say wanting to reassure her. She's had to deal with that asshole her whole life, and even now, after he's gave her away as part of a business deal, he's still trying to use her.

My blood heats as anger wells up inside me. She deserves so much more than him, she deserves the world. How the fuck can he think that she'd ever do anything for him again after he willingly offered her up to us without an ounce of remorse? Hell, she's even too precious for the likes of me, not that I'll be giving her up.

I stand, intending to walk over to her, but by the time I can take a step forward, she's already advancing on me. I still, waiting to see what she'll do. She reaches me in three quick strides and before I can ask her what she's doing, she drops to her knees right there in front of me.

She peers up at me from under her lashes for a second before she grabs hold of my shorts, yanking them and my boxers down in one quick tug and leaving my hard cock bobbing in front of her face. Her eyes widen while taking me in. I noticed last night while in the shower she kept her gaze averted, never once taking a peek at what I was packing.

My breathing is starting to grow heavier just as she gently wraps her fingers around the base and tests the weight of me in her palm. Ever so slowly, she leans forward and licks the tip, making me groan.

"Fuck, baby, you're killing me here," I pant.

She shoots me a seductive smile and slowly takes me into her mouth while swirling her tongue around my tip. She starts off with a slow, torturous rhythm, making me want nothing more than to grab hold of her and fuck her mouth, but I refrain, letting her take control and set the pace.

I lace my fingers through her hair and give her a soft tug, making her moan around my shaft, the vibrations pulling another groan from me. She has her hand wrapped around my base, working me with her hand and her mouth at the same time. Her other hand slowly moves down her body, where she makes quick work of undoing her jeans and putting her hand down her panties. *Oh fuck, she's getting herself off at the same time.*

"Christ, baby, that's it. Fuck your hand while I fuck your mouth," I rasp as I start to take control of her movements, fucking her mouth quicker and making her take me deeper.

"Open your throat for me, *mia regina.*" I push all the way in, hitting the back of her throat and making her gag. Tears well up in her eyes as I start thrusting my hips quicker, her hand working herself faster while she lets go of my cock and she uses her other hand to hold onto my thigh to steady herself.

"Holy fuck, your mouth feels so fucking good. You look so pretty taking my cock with tears streaming down your face, baby," I groan, and she shudders at my praise.

My girl likes being complemented? *Good to know.*

Tingles start forming at the base of my spine. Not wanting it to be over yet, I pull out of her mouth and let her catch her breath for a second before I reach down and grasp her under her arms and pull her up so she's standing.

I slam my mouth down on hers, pulling her into a frantic kiss as I reach into her panties, finding her drenched. I break the kiss and start peppering kisses on her neck.

"You're fucking soaked, Iz. Choking on my dick really gets you wet, huh?" I say with a chuckle before quickly pulling off her jeans.

Reaching down, I grab her thighs and lift her up, she wraps her legs around my waist and runs her fingers through my hair while I walk us towards the mirrored wall. She pulls my head down and brings her lips back to mine just as I push her against the wall and move my hands backwards, squeezing a handful of her ass.

"Full disclosure, I started the pill a week before I came to New York, so if you're doing this to get me pregnant, it won't work," she says, pulling away from the kiss.

What the fuck? Does she seriously think I'm only fucking her to get her pregnant?

"Look at me, Izzy," I bark, and she tips her head up to meet my eyes, the sadness in her eyes makes me want to rip my own goddamn heart out and hand it to her. Jesus, I'd sell my fucking soul to the devil to never see that expression on her face ever again. This girl is tearing me up inside.

She can rip me to goddamn pieces so long as she never leaves.

"I need you to listen to me, baby, okay? I am not only fucking you to get you pregnant. Hell, you could decide you never want kids and I'd be okay with that, the only thing I give a shit about is you and making sure you're happy. You don't have to do this, Izzy,

I only want this if it's something that you want. I don't want you to regret this," I say, desperation clear in my voice and I hold my breath while I wait for an answer.

"Show me how you fuck, Luca. Please, I need to feel you inside me."

Thank fuck.

I pull back and line myself up with her entrance, I search her eyes for a second, making sure she's absolutely sure she wants to do this. She gives me a steely look of determination before I slam forward, making her cry out. I still, giving her a moment to get used to my size, she's so fucking tight, I have to clench my jaw to stop myself from railing into her.

"Jesus, Izzy, you feel so goddamn good, how are you so fucking tight?" I ask breathlessly as I pull her sweater over her head and quickly unclasp her bra, throwing it to the floor.

"Luca, you need to move, dammit! Please, please fuck me," she begs. Fuck, I could get used to hearing her beg.

I slowly pull back before thrusting back into her and bringing her mouth to mine. She moans into my mouth, and I start fucking her harder.

"You're taking me so well, little queen. You're such a good girl for me," I pant, continuing with punishing thrusts. I've never felt so connected to someone; I've never felt so free.

"Oh my god, Luca! So good... so fucking good," she whimpers as her walls start to tighten around me. She's so wet that I can feel her juices soaking my balls. *Christ, I'm not gonna last much longer.*

I pull out and drop her to her feet in one quick motion before I spin her around. I push her head down, bending her forward before I enter her again. Grabbing her hair in my fist, I pull her head up so she's facing the mirror. "Look in the mirror while I fuck you, wife. I want you to watch while I make you come on my cock for the first time," I grunt while slamming into her like a man possessed. "I'll never get enough of you, Izzy, I'll fuck you every day for the rest of my goddamn life."

"Oh my God, Luca. So... good," she whimpers the last word.

"Fuck, baby, be a good girl and come for me, I need to feel you coming all over my dick," I grit out through clenched teeth, while I reach my hand to her front and roll her clit between my fingers. It's been far too long of me fucking my fist to the thought of fucking her, yet this has been one thousand times better than I ever could have imagined. I feel my balls tighten and I know this isn't going to last for much longer.

Her walls pulse, her pussy clamps around my dick, strangling the life out of me and she screams my name as she comes, drenching me even further. Her hot, wet heat making it impossible to hold on, and I roar my release right along with her, filling her with my cum.

I turn us both around before sliding down the wall and sitting on the gym floor, holding her to my chest as we both fight to catch our breaths. I peck a soft kiss to her forehead, savoring the feeling of her naked in my arms. That has got to be the best sex I've ever had in my life. The whole thing was like an out of body experience. Fuck, I really don't think it could ever get any better than that.

Izzy's breathing eventually evens out, and I glance down to see that she's fast asleep in my arms, snuggling into me. It's then that I realize I never want to go back to life without her, she's fucking sunshine, lighting up my whole life.

I want to wake up with her in my arms every morning and go to sleep peppering kisses in her hair every night. I want to bottle up all of her smiles. I want to be her shoulder to lean on. I want to be the one she tells all of her secrets to. I want to be her savior, her hero, her dark knight and her future. I want her to be mine, always. And more than anything else, I want to be *hers*, too.

CHAPTER TWENTY

Izzy

I must have fallen asleep at some point because the next thing I know, I'm waking up to Luca peppering kisses along my jaw while he wraps his arms around me and lifts me up from his bed. He must have put me to bed once I fell asleep in his arms in the gym.

"Time to wake up, baby, we need to clean you up," he whispers softly in my ear, and I let out a grunt of acknowledgement as he carries me into the bathroom and sets me down in the shower, since we're both still naked from earlier, before pulling on my hair tie to let my hair loose from its messy bun.

Unlike last time, Luca doesn't let me wash myself—no, he takes the loofah, squirts some of the soap that smells uniquely like him and begins slowly washing me, he remains gentle as he washes my arms, chest and back.

Once he's finished making sure my upper body is clean, he drops to his knees and begins washing my legs, slowly inching his way upwards.

"Mmm, I could get used to seeing you on your knees," I murmur.

"I'd drop to my knees and worship you anytime you like, baby. I'll treat you like the queen you are, always," he says while staring up at me with such an intense look in his eyes that it almost makes me want to break eye contact with him.

He slowly inches his mouth forward and presses a light kiss to my bikini line before he starts washing away our combined releases.

"I can't wait to taste this pussy again, baby. Can't wait to feel you squeezing my fingers while you let out those sexy little mewls of yours. I'd love nothing more to bend you over again right here in the shower and fuck you so hard you see God," he says, painting a picture in my mind and making my insides turn to lava. "But you're sore, Iz, and I never want to hurt you, ever. We're just going to have to wait, and trust me, baby, when you've recovered, I'll make it my goddamn mission to fuck you so hard you see shooting stars and I'll make it so you can't sit down for a week. I'll make you remember what it's like to have me inside you every time you take a step, reminding you that you're *mine*," he rasps as he stands. He reaches his full height and I take the loofah from him, but before I can wash him like he did me, he turns me around and pulls me backwards, so the shower spray soaks my hair.

After thoroughly washing and conditioning my hair, Luca quickly washes himself before he turns the shower off and wraps a towel around me. He leaves me to dry myself off, just as I'm about to head back to my room to get dressed he throws a pair of his boxers and dress shirt at me.

I turn to him and raise my eyebrow, he gives me a pointed look in return that says *just put the clothes on*. Deciding this is not a hill I want to die on, I quickly dress, and we head into the lounge where Luca sets up the show I've been watching.

After we've ordered some takeout and eaten dinner, I keep over-thinking everything Luca said to me while we we're in the gym, specifically about us having kids.

I can't understand why he would say that when he *needs* to have kids. That's how it works in our world, so why would he say something like that? I was ready to have sex with him either way, so why would he make a declaration like that when he knew he didn't need too? And why—

"What are you thinking about so hard over there? What's going on in that pretty little head, baby?" he asks, interrupting my inner ramblings. I move my body to face his and he wraps an arm around my legs, placing them on his lap, gently stroking my ankle.

"Did you mean what you said in the gym?" I ask while nervously biting my lip.

"Trust me, Izzy, I never say things I don't mean, but what exactly are you referring to?"

"You said that if I didn't want to have kids, we didn't have to have them. But you and I both know that we *need* to have kids. You need to carry on your family name and the whole reason my father prop—"

"Fuck your father, Izzy," he grunts, interrupting me. "If you don't want to have kids then we won't have any. Simple. As. That. You don't need to worry about what anyone else wants but yourself. Marco, or—God help us all—Enzo can carry on the family name, there's no law that states the next in line *has* to be my heir. And as for your piece of shit father? Fuck him. You're not under his thumb anymore, baby, you're not under his roof and you're not his to control any longer. You're my wife now, you're fucking mine and I'll always protect what is mine. So, if you want kids? Great, we'll have as many as you like. You don't want to have any? That's fine, we'll be the cool aunt and uncle to our nieces or nephews. You don't need to worry about what any other fucker wants ever again. The only people who matter are me and you, you got that?" He finishes his rant and pulls me over and maneuvers me so I'm sitting on his lap.

Holy shit, how can one man be so perfect?

He really would go back on the deal he made with his father, which would cause backlash for not only him, but for his family too, all to make me happy. When I envisioned getting married, I imagined marrying a man who would start trying to get me pregnant as soon as possible, and if I happened to have a daughter like Mama? Well then, I figured I'd just have to keep having children until one of them was a boy. The only reason my parents didn't have any more kids was because there were complications while Mama was pregnant with me. At one point, my father nearly lost us both. They both decided that it wasn't a safe option for them to try and have any more kids.

But what about what Luca wants? Would he really miss out on being a father because I decided I didn't want to have children? Or would he decide that the alliance he has with my father wouldn't be worth it, considering he would be starting conflict anyway if I did decide I didn't want them, he could just divorce me and marry a woman who would happily give him whatever he wanted.

And why the hell does that make my chest grow tighter and my throat close up? Why does the thought of him marrying another woman make me feel rage bubbling inside me, trying to claw itself out? And why the hell—when all I've ever wanted was to be able to avoid a marriage that helps my father—do I want to do anything it takes to keep Luca as mine?

"What about you? Do you want kids?" I ask, trying to organize my thoughts.

"Honestly? I've never really cared whether I have them or not. I never envisioned getting married, but here we are. I'd happily raise a baby with you, Izzy, but I don't mind either way," he says gently and gives me a small smile.

He's been sitting patiently this entire time, giving me space to think over everything he's put out on the table.

Who would have thought the big, bad, Mafia heir Luca Romano, could be as patient as a saint?

Not me, that's for sure.

"I know you'll have always pictured having children for the sake of your father, but what about for yourself? Did you grow up thinking about having kids one day? The white picket fence? Did you have boyfriends you wanted all that stuff with?" Luca asks, and I can tell by the dip in his eyebrow he doesn't like picturing me with these "boyfriends".

"Is this your way of asking about my past? Because you could have just asked me directly," I say dryly while raising my eyebrow at him to which he just stares blankly at me, as if not wanting to verbally voice his question.

Ugh, men.

"To answer your unasked question, no, there aren't any boyfriends back home waiting for me, I haven't had a boyfriend since freshman year of high school and that relationship only lasted a month. I don't keep boyfriends," I state, hoping to be done with this conversation, as inquisitive as I am about his past, I really hope he keeps it to himself. Otherwise, I'll end up sharpening my knives and going hunting.

"Why not?" he asks.

"Because the men in my life always disappointed me. The only man I could ever trust was Alessi, but he ended up leaving me anyway. I never wanted to become attached to someone for them to turn right around and hurt me. I can't get my heart broken if my heart was never involved to begin with," I say with a shy smile and I shrug my shoulder awkwardly. This just got far too deep for my liking.

What is it about my husband that makes me want to confess all my thoughts, secrets, sins and what-the-fuck-ever-else that comes to mind?

"I'm never going to be one of those men, Izzy. If you ever decide to let me into that guarded heart of yours, I'll never leave, and I'd rather die than hurt you. I may not be able to promise you romance or all that flowery shit girls like guys to give them, but I can promise you that," he says with a smile, making me snort like the motherfucking lady that I am.

I lean up and press a kiss to his lips which he immediately accepts, cupping my jaw and taking the kiss deeper. I pour everything into the kiss, all of my fear, my gratitude and my thankfulness that this is the man I ended up marrying. He's a goddamn dream, a rare light shining through my darkness.

He's everything I never knew I needed and everything I could ever want wrapped up in a sinfully handsome package.

"We need to stop, baby. If we keep going then I won't be able to control myself, you're too sore for all the things I want to do to you," he groans as he pulls back from me. He wraps his arms around me, and I rest my head on his shoulder, snuggling into him before turning my attention back to the show we were watching.

And that's how we spend the rest of our evening, cuddled up on the couch watching some show that's so bad, it ends up being funny. We laugh and we talk and just enjoy each other's company. I don't know what will happen next for us, but I'll happily sit back and find out.

I start drifting off to sleep, still perched on his lap. Luca must realize because suddenly he stands, still holding on to me and walks me to his room.

It's an unspoken agreement that I'll be staying in this room now too, I guess. He places me on the bed and climbs in beside me.

"I don't know what the hell I'm doing here, Izzy. You never asked earlier, but this is the first relationship I've been in. We may not be conventional, but we are *everything*, and I'll do whatever it takes to prove that to you," Luca whispers to me from behind, where he's spooning me as I drift off into sleep.

I don't think it will take much work for him to prove anything to me, because I think I already know.

CHAPTER TWENTY-ONE
Luca

I wake up to find Izzy snuggled into my side, we must have moved at some point during the night because she's now draped over me, as if she's trying to burrow herself into me. *She already has,* I think to myself.

It takes far too much effort to pull myself out of bed and away from the sleeping woman who occupies not only my bed, but my head and heart too. Unfortunately, I have shit to do today, and lounging around with my new wife isn't on the to-do list, as much as I wish it was.

Yesterday felt like a dream, *she's a fucking dream.* Not once have I ever spent a day with a woman the way I did yesterday with Izzy, it wasn't about sex or anything trivial like that, like it probably would have been in the past. I just wanted to spend time with her, watch her, breathe the same air as her.

I meant every single word I said to her, if she decided she didn't want to have kids, I'd happily go to war with her father if it came to that, and I know my family would too. We may need Antonio's shipments, but we could always make a deal with someone else if we needed to. My family would support me in whatever I wanted; they'd do anything it takes to make me happy.

And Izzy is what makes me happy.

I get ready for the day, dressing in a suit as usual and make the drive to my father's estate so we can prepare for a meeting with Andrev. Dad texted me last night to let me know we had a meeting with the new head of the Bratva later today and asked me to come see him beforehand for breakfast and to catch up on business. I may have only taken one day off, but the Mafia stops for no one, not even me.

Reaching his home, I let myself in and make my way to the kitchen, where Dad is sat at the kitchen island with a coffee and today's paper.

"Morning, old man," I quip, and he curses me under his breath.

"You're later than I imagined you would be, I figured you'd be itching to get out of your apartment after spending the whole day with your wife yesterday," he says with a smirk.

Asshole.

"Keeping tabs on me?"

"Yup," he says, emphasizing the "P" and shrugging. "I keep tabs on all my sons. Speaking of which, you need to have a chat with Enzo and see what the fuck he's doing following some girl around all day." He pats me on the back as I take a seat beside him, and Beatrice sets a coffee down in front of me. I thank her before turning to my dad.

"There is no fucking talking to him, you should know that by now. Christ, he let himself into my apartment to ask my wife for dating advice. He's finally lost it."

He just stares at me, a look of disbelief covering his face. Clearly, that was one thing he didn't know. Fuck, now that's a rare event, not much gets past our father.

"Just talk to him and make sure he's not going to hurt the girl," he grunts. "How are things between you and Izzy?"

I stare up at the ceiling, trying to decide how much I should divulge. My dad is probably the best person to talk to about this, my brothers and Alec have never had a serious relationship with a woman, so they would be as clueless as I am. Whereas my dad loved my ma with everything he had.

"Honestly? I've known her for a week, and she's fucking embedded herself deep inside me. She can be batshit crazy at times, but then she's also the sweetest person I've ever met. I spent the whole day at home with her yesterday. The. Whole. Day. I can't remember the last time I just stayed home and did nothing. I could have happily stayed home this morning, she's on my mind constantly and I feel like I can't breathe when she's not around me. She's messing with my head. What the goddamn hell is wrong with me?" I finish my rambling and turn to look at my dad, who's sat with a shit eating grin that takes up his whole face, his eyes twinkling with delight.

"Well, son, I think it's safe to say you're in love with your wife," he says with a laugh.

"I can't be in love with her, I've known the woman for one fucking week!" I roar.

"That shit doesn't matter, Luca. I loved your mother from the second I laid my eyes on her," he says with a wistful smile. "Tell me something, if you were in a room with two dozen other people, would you be able to sense her? Do you always need to be touching her? If she's in pain, do you feel it too? What would you do if she was in danger? If she was hurt? What do you feel when you imagine your life without her?"

I think back to the shooting at the restaurant and not only the rage that I felt that she was hurt, but the worry too. I think about my constant need to take care of her, about how I need to always have her in my arms, about how I'd burn the fucking city to ashes after painting it with blood if she was in danger, and if I think about her not being in my life anymore? I can't, it's too painful, just the thought alone makes me feel as though my soul is ripping in two, my throat closes, and I struggle to take a breath.

Oh fuck, he's right. I'm so fucking in love with that woman. I've had these feelings since pretty much the beginning I just didn't know what they were.

"Fuck, you're right. I love her."

He laughs at my obvious demise and drops the subject. We eat breakfast while discussing today's meeting, tonight's gala and anything but my new revelation. Once that's done I say goodbye to Dad and Beatrice.

I make my way over to Enzo's to have the chat I promised Dad I'd have with him. I called ahead to make sure he's not out lurking in some alleyway watching the girl he's so obsessed with, and, apparently, I'll have to make the visit quick because she starts work soon.

Enzo's sitting on the floor of his apartment staring out of the window at the city when I arrive. He's so lost in thought he doesn't see me approaching as I sit down on the floor next to him. I've never seen him like this before, it's worrying.

"What's up, man," he says and turns to me with a lost look in his eyes.

Fuck, this is bad.

Enzo is the joker, the one who never has a thing in the world to worry about, because he usually just doesn't care. Enzo's mind works differently, he's never once formed an emotional attachment. Sure, he likes me, Marco and our father well enough, he'd take a bullet for us. But he's not one for love, for friends, for *feelings*.

"What's going on? What happened?"

"Nothing's going on, just feeling different lately, I guess."

"Well, Dad sent me to make sure you're not gonna hurt this chick you keep following around. Is she the reason you're feeling different?" I say softly, not wanting to make him skittish. I feel like he should come with an "approach with caution" warning.

"Hurt her? Are you fucking crazy!" he roars, making me rear back. "I'd never hurt her, she's a fucking angel sent from above, I've been watching her to make sure she's safe! She walks alone! At night! I need to protect her, and I do it from the shadows because I don't want to taint her light with the fucking dark cloud that lives within me, I'd rip my own goddamn heart out, sell my soul, and tear myself to pieces before I ever let Robyn get hurt. Jesus!" he exclaims before standing and storming out of the apartment.

I'm not sure what the fuck just happened, or what sort of spell this *Robyn* girl has put over my brother, but at least I don't have to worry about him hurting her. What I am worried about is *her* hurting *him*.

We've just finished up with the meeting with Andrev, where we discussed our new alliance and how our deals are going to go in the future. The meeting took longer than expected, I had to text Izzy halfway through to let her know I'd be late and that I'd meet her down in the lobby again.

Andrev met us at one of our warehouses as a show of good faith, which was fucking ballsy of him, but also lucky for me because I keep a stash of suits and tux's here for times like today.

I quickly shower and change before heading to my Bugatti to go pick up Izzy. Now that Novikov is no longer a threat, and we only have the Columbians gunning for us we decided we'd be okay to ditch the drivers.

Muñoz may be a sly piece of shit, but he's not stupid enough to try something right now while we've got men from Chicago and the Russians on our side.

I drive through the city, dreading tonight's event. Everyone who's anyone will be there, Muñoz will no doubt be there too. We have an agreement that even when shit is going down in the underworld, we don't bring it to places like tonight's gala. Not only would we end up arrested if something happened during an event like this, but we do a lot of business with the officials of the city, and they need to keep that quiet from anyone who we're not in business with—never a good look being in the pockets of a criminal organization. Though to most of the public were perfectly civilized businessmen.

So, that means I won't be able to throttle him on sight tonight, I'll also have to keep an eye on my crazy little wife and make sure she doesn't get any bright ideas about stabbing the fucker either.

I pull up outside our building, hand my keys over to the valet and make my way into the building to meet Izzy. Just as I'm approaching the elevator, the doors open, and my wife steps out.

Even though I've already seen her wearing the dress she bought for tonight, she still takes my breath away,

Fuck, she's a vision. She has on light makeup—never one to overdo it—and has her long blonde hair styled in waves, similar to how she wore it for the wedding. She looks like an angel. Except I know she's not, she's my little demon begging me to take a ride down to hell with her.

She's gorgeous, and I run my eyes up and down her body again, taking in the shape of her curves that I can't wait to strip bare and—wait a second.

"Please, for the love of fuck, tell me you're wearing panties under that dress," I growl as I pull her into me and dip my lips down to hers.

CHAPTER TWENTY-TWO

Izzy

L uca pulls me into a kiss that has my brain short-circuiting and has my insides electrifying. Any previous thoughts of him wearing a tux gone, all that's left is the way his body feels against mine, his taste, how his tongue teases mine and how his intoxicating scent makes me dizzy with lust.

I pull back, needing to catch my breath and clear my head before I end up doing something like dropping to my knees right here, or begging him to fuck me up against the elevator door for the whole lobby to see.

"Well?" he asks with a raised brow. Did he ask a question?

"Well, what?" I ask, trying to recall whatever he said before that kiss.

"Tell me you're wearing panties under that dress, baby."

Oh, *that.*

"I couldn't wear anything under the dress. The dress is cut too low on my back for me to wear a bra, and if I wore panties, you'd be able to see the outline. So no, husband, I'm not wearing a single thing under this dress," I say with a smirk.

Luca cuts me a glare before looking up to the ceiling and mumbling something about driving instead of keeping the driver.

After a couple of seconds, he brings his gaze back to mine, and the heat in his eyes is so intense I have to grab on to his arm to stop myself from swaying. *Fuck, it's gonna be a long night.*

I'm already thinking about all the dirty things I want him to do to me once we get home from this godforsaken event.

"Fuck, if we weren't already late, I'd drag you back upstairs and fuck the defiance right out of you, little queen." He loops his arm around mine and escorts me out of the building and into the car. Once again, he straps me in and closes the door before getting in himself, only this time we're not driven by a driver.

No, Luca is behind the wheel of the Bugatti—which is a stunningly beautiful car—and starts the engine, pulling out into traffic. What is it about this man, that he can do the most basic of things, like *driving,* and it turns me into a needy, squirming, messy puddle of hormones.

I rub my thighs together, trying to reduce the ache in my core and he peers at me from the corner of his eye, smirks and places a hand on my thigh to still me, the cocky fucker knows *exactly* what he's doing to me.

We make the short drive to the venue the gala's being held at. Pulling up outside, Luca throws the keys to the valet and comes to open my door. He offers me his hand and helps me out of the car before we walk inside, his hand on the small of my back, guiding me.

I don't even know if he's conscious of the fact that he can't keep his hands off me, but whenever he's near, he always touches me somewhere. Not even in a sexual way, he'll just place a hand on my thigh, run his hand across my shoulder, play with my hair, whatever he can do to make sure I'm still there. It's as though he's worried that I'll disappear.

Trust me, I'm not going anywhere.

We enter a large ballroom, decked out in pretentious decorations that are more suited for a sweet sixteen than an annual event held by the mayor of New York. It's like he's having a pissing contest, showcasing how much money he's spent on tonight, but rather than looking good, it's as though the event planner just went around the store and picked out the most expensive items, no matter that they're fucking awful and clash with each other.

I hate events like these, I had to attend them all the time as the heir to the Chicago outfit, even though I'd never personally take it over—with me being a woman—but I was forced to attend all the same.

Luca steers me over to a table in the far corner where his father sits with a fake ass smile on his face. That is, until he sees me and Luca walking over to him, and his smile turns from fake to genuine in seconds and he stands.

Salvatore gives Luca a nod as we reach him before he turns to me and kisses my cheek.

"Izzy, it's good to see you sweetheart, you look lovely. I hope my son is treating you well?" he says with sincerity and warmth in his tone.

"Thank you, it's good to see you. We've been getting to know each other," I laugh, not knowing what the hell to say and he grins at me.

We take our seats just as Marco joins us. Apparently, Enzo had something he needed to do tonight and couldn't make it. I'm guessing that's code for *stalking*, but hey, to each their own. I chat a little with Marco, he seems quiet and reserved, not one to initiate conversation and happy to keep the chatting to a minimum, which I'm grateful for.

For all the training I had for this type of thing growing up, I've always been terrible at filling the awkward silences and making small talk. If I'm honest, I'd rather cut my goddamn tongue out than talk about the weather. Maybe I could put it in a jar like my gift from Luca?

"I'm hosting a family dinner for my birthday in three weeks, I expect to see you all there. Enzo too, so make sure he comes," Salvatore announces while shooting a pointed glance at Luca.

The evening progresses slowly while me and Luca walk around the room, chatting to the attendees.

We're about to walk over to the bar when I hear a male voice that I don't recognize from behind me.

"Isabella Romano, oh how I have been *dying* to meet you," the voice says, and I turn to see a man the same height as Luca with light brown messy hair, he's not quite as built as Luca is, yet he's handsome in his own right.

And that's when I recognize him. I've researched him, I've worked with him every day for the past two years. But *how the fuck* does he know who I am? I know for a fact that there is no way he'd be able to link my online persona—Scorpion—to myself. There's no way in hell, I'm too good, too skilled, too paranoid to ever let that happen.

Luca must read the confusion on my face and see it as something different because he sighs.

"Izzy, this is Alec Cane, businessman, billionaire bachelor of New York, and my asshole best friend."

My asshole best friend.

How the *fuck* did I miss something like that?

I quickly mask my shock and offer Alec a smile while trying to calm my racing pulse.

"Nice to meet you, *asshole best friend.*"

"Best friend is right, love. Me and you are gonna be besties," he says with a grin, making Luca slap him on the back of his head and Alec laughs.

"Like fuck you are!" Luca growls, which only makes him laugh harder. I can tell from the way they act with each other that they're close.

Hell, Luca probably had Alec investigate me before we got married, and he clearly didn't find much as neither of them have mentioned my online presence.

"Oh fuck, it's so easy to mess with you, man."

Shaking his head, Luca takes my hand and leads me to the bar to escape his friend who just follows.

Luca and Alec start talking about something in hushed whispers, not purposefully excluding me, just trying to avoid being heard by anyone else stood at the bar. I rise on my toes and whisper to Luca that I'm going to use the bathroom. He gives me a nod and kisses my temple before letting my hand go.

I walk through the room, narrowly dodging people in an attempt to avoid anyone stopping me to chat. Apparently, being the woman who managed to wear down the elusive Luca Romano in such a short amount of time is no small feat, and women around the room have been bursting at the seams to know what "tricks" I used on him.

No tricks here, honeys. Just a good old contractual agreement between our fathers.

We've been getting along well, and Luca is everything I didn't know I needed. It's comfortable, but I have no delusions of us actually falling in love.

CHAPTER TWENTY-THREE

Luca

I watch Izzy's hips sway as she walks away, the silk material of her dress clinging to her curves that beg me to grab onto them and never let go. The evening has been a nightmare, all I want to do is get home and sink my cock into my wife's hot, wet, cunt while she cries out and begs for more. I shake my head, trying to clear my mind of the unadulterated lust that I keep getting lost in and I watch Izzy until she's out of my view.

When I can no longer see her, I turn back to Alec to resume our conversation, except he's staring at me with wide eyes and a look of utter shock on his face.

"What's wrong?" I ask and glance around me to see what his problem is.

"*Dude*, I've been keeping it together until now, but would you care to explain what the ever-loving fuck has happened to you? Are you sick? Are you being blackmailed? Have you just lost your fucking mind? I'm worried man," he says, utterly bewildered. That makes two of us.

"What the fuck are you talking about?"

"Oh *Jesus*," he says with a burst of laughter. What the fuck is wrong with him?

"You realize you're in love with your wife, right?"

Oh, *that.*

"Yes, I'm aware. My father made me realize that this morning," I grumble, not wanting to have this conversation with the king of non-commitment.

"Oh goodie, just making sure you were aware. I'm loving this. Big, bad, scary, Luca Romano has been turned into a fluffy marshmallow, is this the part when you start waxing poetic, telling me to find myself a woman and settle down, that it'll be good for me? Have you fucked her yet?"

"Fuck off," I growl.

"I'll take that as a yes, then. You know..." He continues but I'm not paying attention. Izzy has been gone for at least ten minutes, I'd expect any of the other women in this place to take that long to use the bathroom, but not Izzy.

Izzy isn't high maintenance, she's not the type to stand in front of the mirror gossiping or whatever the hell those women do, so where the fuck is my wife?

Something's wrong.

I walk away from Alec, where he's still in the middle of rambling about my love life and make my way towards the women's bathroom to find Izzy.

I swear, if something has happened to her, or if someone's hurt her, I'm g—

I turn the corner to the hall where the bathrooms are and find Izzy clutching the strap of her dress, and as if that wasn't a bad enough sight, I see red when I see who the man is that's stood next to her, attempting to help her with the strap.

"What the fuck is this?" I bark.

"You should keep a closer eye on your little wife, Luca. I found her here, fighting with her dress after having a little *altercation* with Mr. Williams," that fuck face Muñoz says before strolling away. I walk over to Izzy, still fuming from finding her in the hallway with our fucking *rival*. I can't touch him while he's here, so right now I'm focusing on getting the answers from my wife.

"What were you doing with him, Iz? And happened to your dress?" I say while taking the snapped strap and beginning to tie it together for her.

"I came out of the bathroom and some asshole thought he could leer at me," she sighs. "He started rambling about how I'm too pretty for a mobster like you, then tried grabbing me, I stopped him from going any further with a kick to his balls, since I don't have any knives on me," she says and gives me a pointed *I'd have stabbed him even though we're at a gala for the mayor* look.

I finish with the strap and clasp her chin between my thumb and finger, raising her head so she's peering into my eyes.

"Are you okay, baby? Muñoz said something about Williams, was it him?"

"I'm fine," she says with a reassuring smile. "And that's what he said, he came around the corner just after he the man dropped to his knees clutching his dick. As soon as he saw Muñoz, he scurried off. I was trying to tell Muñoz I was fine as you arrived."

Huh, for once, it's not Muñoz I'm pissed at, grateful he turned up when he did and then gave me fuckers name before he left. I'll be having a little date with *Mr. Williams.*

"Are you mad? I know I shouldn't have kneed him but—" I cut her off by pressing my mouth to hers in a slow and gentle kiss, trying to reassure her.

"I'm pissed, baby. But not at you, never at you. You did good, if it was me instead of that asshole who walked over when he did, he'd be leaving in a body bag," I growl before pulling her into my chest and pressing a kiss on the top of her head.

"Come on, let's get out of here."

O nce we get inside our building, I guide Izzy into the elevator and as soon as the doors close, I pounce. I hold her against the full-length mirror, hand wrapped around her throat and bring my mouth to her ear.

"Wh-what are you doing?" she stutters.

"You don't get gentle tonight, baby. You haven't been a good girl for me, so you don't deserve my nice side. No, tonight you've been my little slut, and little sluts get *fucked*, hard. But not until you've been punished," I growl and the elevator door opens, I pull back and pull her into the apartment.

"I thought you weren't mad at me?" she asks with a fake-ass pout and a look of innocence.

"I'd never punish you for defending yourself, Izzy. But what I will punish you for is making me walk around all night with a cock that's hard as steel and the knowledge that you're walking around bare under that dress. So be a good little girl for once in your life and *take your fucking dress off*."

CHAPTER TWENTY-FOUR

Izzy

*S*o *be a good little girl for once in your life and take your fucking dress off.*

Oh. Fuck. *This man.*

He has the ability to turn my insides to mush. It's like he's altering my DNA to fit with his. I've never been the obedient type before, but one order from him and I'm ready to submit. I'd gladly render my inhibitions, follow his orders, do anything he asks of me as long as he gives me those sweet kisses, fucks me like his life depends on it then takes care of me after.

I slide the straps of my dress over my shoulders, letting the gown slip from my body and pool around my feet before carefully stepping out of it, leaving me stood in the foyer in nothing but my six-inch heels.

I start to bend to undo the clasp on my heel when Luca's arm darts out to stop my movement.

"I only told you to take off the dress, little demon. Leave the heels on."

He advances on me, the look on his face is pure, feral lust. He's the predator, and I'm his prey.

"You have no idea how hard I've been all night, imagining slipping my hand up the slit in your dress and playing with your tight pussy, I bet you would have let me, wouldn't you?

"Yes," I breathe, feeling dizzy from his closeness, he bends down and brings his mouth to my ear. "I knew it, you're my dirty little slut, aren't you? My problem, wife, is that I'm the only man who will ever get to touch your sweet cunt, no other man is allowed to see, touch or smell you ever again." He pauses and wraps his mouth around the shell of my ear, lightly biting down on it. "So, for you to be walking around a room full of men, who were hell-bent on eye fucking you—because you looked like a wet dream—with no panties? Without my permission? I'm not okay with that, baby. So, for your punishment? Well... you better run *mia regina,* because if I catch you? All bets are off," he whispers darkly before pulling back, the heat in those dark eyes of his has my legs shaking and my whole body lighting up.

I've never allowed a man to control me the way he does. If it were anyone else, I'd tell them to get fucked. But Luca, him telling me what to do, how to do it? It's so hot, I want to hand over all my control, drop to my knees and submit to him, worship him, I want to be anything he wants me to be. I want to be everything he needs me to be.

And with that realization, I spin on my heel and bolt through the apartment, I can hear him chuckling from where he's striding after me.

Not the best footwear to be running in.

I run through the kitchen and dart through the living room with him hot on my heels, maybe if I could loop back around, I could make it to the—

"Too slow," Luca says triumphantly in my ear as he spins my body to face him, he bends down and wraps his arm around my thighs, picking me up and flinging me over his shoulder before I can even blink. I try to wiggle free from his grasp but it's no use and he stalks to the bedroom, his arms a band of steel around my thighs.

We reach the bedroom and he all but throws me on the bed, the predatory gleam in his eye should scare me, terrify me, even. But all it does is make me want to sink to my knees and ask him to use me.

"Get on your hands and knees," he orders, and I immediately comply, excitement shooting through me. "Crawl up the bed and hold onto the headboard."

I do as he says, turning my head to sneak a glance at him, his eyes are locked on me as he shrugs out of his tux.

"What's your safe word, little demon?"

I think for a second before making my decision.

"Vanilla." I smirk, and he raises an eyebrow but doesn't comment.

He runs his hands up the back of my thighs, reaching my ass, he spreads both of my cheeks, exposing me.

"You look so good like this baby, ass in the air, your wet cunt begging for my cock," he murmurs. "You don't get my dick yet though, I'm gonna turn your pretty little ass red first, and you're gonna count each slap for me."

I don't even have the chance to process his words before his hand rains down on me, causing a sharp sting and a bolt of pleasure to run through me that makes me let out a loud moan as he massages the spot his hand is connected to.

"Count for me, little demon," he rasps.

"O-one," I manage to say as I try to catch my breath.

"Good girl," he coos before bringing his hand down again.

"Two."

He brings his hand down again, raining three more slaps in quick succession.

"Th-three... four, f-ive," I stutter. The pain is intense, but not as intense as the pleasure that comes along with it, it's freeing, giving him control over me. All of my senses are heightened, and my brain turns to mush as he spanks me another four times.

"You're doing so well, baby, I'm so fucking hard seeing my marks on your perfect skin, knowing that I'm marking you as mine, think you can take one more for me?"

"Yes, please."

"Fuck, I love it when you beg," he groans, landing a final slap to my ass. He bends down and kisses my tender skin before pulling back.

I turn my head to look at him, his eyes almost black, the intense, unadulterated lust in his eyes weakens my knees. His hand goes to his length, and he gives himself a quick tug before lining up with my entrance and slamming inside me.

"Fuuuck," he groans. "You took your punishment so well, Iz. Such a good girl for me," he says before slowly pulling out and slamming back inside me, my walls clench around him but it's not enough.

"More, please. I need more, Luca," I say, and he grunts in acknowledgement before wrapping an arm around my chest and pulling me up, so my back is pressed against his chest, the change in position makes his thrusts deeper and I struggle to remain upright, I have to twist my arms backwards and wrap them around his neck, so I don't collapse from pure bliss as my orgasm builds.

He reaches out and grabs my chin, turning my head so my face is inches away from his, the look in his eyes is downright feral as he slams his lips to mine, kissing me and fucking me in tandem. He fucks me like he's exercising his demons, opening himself up and showing me everything, he's letting me in to see the deepest parts of himself.

He pulls back and bites down on my neck, causing a sharp pain to flow through me, only intensifying the pleasure of him fucking me with abandon.

"I can't get enough of you, baby; it'll never be enough. Each day you consume another part of me," he rasps in my ear, his words pushing me closer to the edge. "Let go for me, Iz, just let go," he groans and brings his mouth back to mine, resuming the passionate kiss from before.

Luca swallows my cries as my orgasm builds and builds until I'm pulled under, like I'm caught in a wave, fighting for breath yet begging it to take me under all at once. His movements become erratic, he jerks inside me and lets out a groan before he finally stills, his mouth still fused to mine. Gone is the feral kiss, his lips are no longer attacking mine but are now caressing me softly, as if he's savoring my taste.

Luca lets me go gently, he removes my heels and lies down beside me before wrapping an arm around me and dragging me towards him, tucking me into his side while we both catch our breath.

"That was..." I begin to say but unable to find the words to describe the experience. It wasn't just fucking, it was intimate, primal, like nothing I've ever experienced before.

"Everything," Luca finishes for me.

He's right, it was everything. He is *everything*.

CHAPTER TWENTY-FIVE

Luca

I'm not a good man, in any sense of the term. My only redeeming qualities are that I refuse to hurt women and children. I don't show kindness to people unless they're from my close circle, which includes my brothers, my father, Alec, and now Izzy. I don't really have anyone else; I have an aunt from my mother's side and a couple of cousins, but they're not part of the Mafia life, my aunt left this life behind before her kids were born and never looked back. We speak on occasion but keep our distance for the sake of their safety.

I didn't lie earlier when I told Izzy that tonight I wouldn't be gentle. That was the truth. The lie was that I was only fucking her. As I lie here, catching my breath after the most intense sexual experience of my life, I realize something.

That was not—in any way—me *just fucking* my wife. That was me consuming her, showing her a part of herself that she didn't know existed. That was me letting her inside me, showing her the deepest, darkest side of myself. That was me letting her in completely, and it was me—in my twisted, depraved, messed up way—making love to her for the first time.

"Hey, Iz?"

"Yeah?" she mumbles sleepily in reply.

"Why did you go through with the marriage? You don't seem to particularly like your father—so it wasn't for his approval, and you can take care of yourself just fine, you could have ran at any point, so why didn't you? Why did you marry me?" I ask, it's something I've been wondering about since she came to the gym to tell me about her phone call with Antonio. It's clear she is in no way his biggest fan, she can physically take care of herself and she's always working, so it's not like she needs money.

Izzy tenses in my arms before she swallows and peers up at me.

"My mama always believed in arranged marriages, I can't understand why, but she did. Her and my father's marriage was arranged, but they loved each other fiercely, unlike anything I've ever seen. A part of my father died the day my mother did, he wasn't always this bad, he could be, but it wasn't his constant personality like it is now. Mama always used to tell me tales about how one day, they would arrange a marriage for me, to someone who would be fierce and strong, someone who could protect me, always. I guess I married you because I thought that it would make her happy, even though she's not here anymore. I felt like I would be disappointing her—letting her down—if I didn't go through with it," she says with misty eyes, but she blinks before any tears can fall. My strong girl, my fierce little queen.

"I may not be the man you dreamed about when you were a child, but I'll always take care of you. I'll always protect you and give you choices, I don't want to dull your light or your fight, Izzy. You're a queen, *mia regina*. I'll help you fight any demons you have, baby, but you don't have to be strong all the time, it's okay to fall apart too. I'll be here to help you put yourself back together," I say, and she snuggles closer into my side, her body shakes, and her silent tears soak my skin. I hold my wife in my arms as she sobs silently, she doesn't let me see her fall apart, but she lets me hold her through it, drawing strength from me as she breaks my heart in two.

It's been five days since the gala, and I've spent the last few days catching up with work on our legal side of business, spending time with Izzy and tracking the movements of Elias Williams.

Turns out, the asshole who dared to lay his hands on my wife isn't just some dumb fuck nobody. No, he turned out to be a prominent businessman, and the mayor's cousin. And while under normal circumstances, I'd happily bring him to one of our warehouses and torture the stupid fuck before putting him out of his misery, unfortunately, that would be a danger to me and my family.

Needless to say, I am in no way letting him get away with touching what's mine, I just can't make it a public display to warn others of what happens if they decide to do the same, much to my dismay. So, I'm having to settle for killing him quickly, with a less personal touch than I would like but I'd rather that than let the slimy little fucker live.

I've spent some time following him, learning his patterns, his routine, his schedule. Which is how I'm currently sat in an armchair in the corner of his bedroom, knowing he'll be arriving home in approximately seven and a half minutes.

I take in my surroundings, cringing at the over-the-top, pretentious bedding, to the watch collection he has on display as though it's a piece of artwork. Elias Williams likes to fancy himself as a god, it seems. He's egotistical, has no concerns in taking what he wants, like his attempt on taking my wife for himself—very poor judgement on his part—and seems to enjoy gambling, spending his money in strip clubs, owned by *my* fucking family and tends to act like he's the center of the universe.

That ends tonight.

I hear the car engine rev as it pulls up to the house and into the driveway before cutting off.

Elias likes to give the impression that he's vastly wealthy, but if that was the case he'd have better security, or security at all for that matter. It was embarrassingly easy for me to break into his home, I'd expected more of a challenge if I'm honest.

I hear his footsteps coming up the stairs and approaching the room I'm currently waiting for him in. I feel like I'm in one of those movies where someone's waiting in a dark corner, who turns on a lamp to announce their presence. The asshole opens the door and removes his watch, placing it in his glass cabinet with the others. *Figures.*

I clear my throat to grab his attention and he startles, jumping back like a scared little kitten and—best of all—crashes into the dresser, sending the cabinet of watches crashing to the floor before it shatters at his feet, making me chuckle.

"You made a mistake Elias; do you have any idea of what that might be?" I sneer. Moonlight bathes the room enough for him to make out my face, so I can see the instant he realizes who's in his home, a mixture of recognition and fear passing his features.

"Mr. Rom-mano, I've just come from one of your clubs, the girls are great. W-what are you doing here?" he stutters like the little bitch that he is.

"I could give two fucks about any of that, you piece of shit. I'm here because you dared to lay your filthy hands on my wife," I growl, and all color leaves his face as he blanches. *That's right motherfucker, be scared.*

"It was... it was rumored to be an a-arranged marriage. I did...didn't think you'd care if I helped myself," he whispers and backs himself into the corner of the room, the *opposite* side of the room to the exit I might add. Idiot.

I take a deep breath to try and keep my rage from taking over. The asshole *didn't think I would care* that he touched my wife? My Izzy? *Mia regina?*

Fuck, *breathe Luca.*

Images of what could've happened if my girl hadn't managed to fight back infiltrate my mind and the edge of my vision turns black, my control snaps and I let the rage take over.

I'm barely conscious when I approach him and beat the living shit out of him, or when I finally see the light go out in his eyes, the rage inside me is unlike anything I've ever known, so strong and so fierce that I'm numb as I set his house up to look like a break-in and it isn't until I'm making the drive back to the city that I start to feel like I'm coming back to myself again.

Fuck, that was bad. I've had bouts of rage before. Usually when someone in my family gets injured or attacked, but I have *never* blacked out before like I did tonight.

Christ, this love thing really messes with your head.

My ringtone fills the car as Izzy's contact pops up on the dash, which is unusual as she normally prefers to keep our communication to texts. Immediately on high alert, I accept the call.

"Izzy? Are you okay?"

"I'm fine, just wondering where you keep your first aid kit," she says casually, as if she didn't just send my panic from five to fifty with a few words. I can hear her moving around the room in the background, what the fuck is happening?

"Why? What's wrong? Why do you need a first aid kit? Should I send a doctor? I'm on my way home but it'll take me thirty minutes to get there. Should I send Marco over? I'll call Marco now, he can—"

"Jesus, Luca! Calm the fuck down. I'm fine, I just needed some aspirin, I couldn't find any and remembered there were some in the first aid kit you used to clean up my arm," she says before mumbling something that sounds a lot like *overprotective* and *psycho* under her breath.

"Why do you need aspirin? Are you okay?" I say, still worried.

"I'm fine, I got my period and I've got cramps, okay? You can stop your worrying, if you're like this every month it happens, you'll have a heart attack, Luca," she says in a sexy as fuck assertive tone and I begin to breathe again. Jesus, I've never been so protective over a woman before. Then again, I've never known a woman like my wife before, she's in a league of her own.

I let out a sigh of relief before telling her where she can find the first aid kit and I can hear her rummaging around in what I assume is the cupboard under the sink in the main bathroom.

"I've got it, thank you."

"Do you need me to get you anything else? I can make a stop on my way home," I say. I want to help her, but I have no idea how, this is so far out of my comfort zone. I've never had to deal with a woman on her period before, why would I?

"I'm good, Luca, but thank you. I'm just gonna chill on the couch and watch some tv. I'll see you soon," she says and ends the call, leaving me apprehensive as fuck. Don't women cry and get all moody when they're on their period?

My wife is slightly psychotic and stabby on a normal day, so who the fuck knows what she's like when she's hormonal. She can be crazy sometimes, but she wouldn't be herself if she wasn't.

I ended up stopping at a store on my way home and stocking up on snacks, chocolate and ice cream for Izzy, as well as a whole selection of sanitary towels and tampons. According to a quick google search, these are must-have's for when a woman is on her period. The poor old woman in the store picked up on what I was doing after hearing me curse to myself for the third time and took pity on me, helping me gather a selection of items that will "make her feel better."

According to Google, orgasms help too. Though I'm not sure whether to test that theory, the last thing I want is for Izzy to think I only want her for her body. Yes, her body is amazing and sex with her is like nothing I've ever felt before, but I want more than that, I want more of her, I want fucking everything she'll give me.

I'm making it my mission to capture her mind, body, heart and soul, just like she has captured mine.

I enter the apartment and find Izzy fast asleep on the couch, bundled beneath a blanket. My sleeping angel doesn't even stir as I slide my arms beneath her and pick her up. I carry her into the bedroom and place her on the bed, pressing a quick kiss to her hair. I quickly put the bag of groceries away and get undressed before sliding into bed and gathering Izzy back into my arms.

She nuzzles her head into the crook of my shoulder, and I finally feel like I can breathe again. Nothing feels right anymore unless I have her in my arms.

"I love you, Izzy," I whisper into the darkness, knowing that there's no way in hell I can tell her when she's conscious, she's not ready for that. She's not there yet, but that's okay. She will be, I'll make sure of it. I'll make my wife love me, even if it's the last thing I do.

CHAPTER TWENTY-SIX

Izzy

The past few weeks have been nothing short of bliss. Ever since the gala—and the amazing sex me and Luca had—we've been closer than ever before.

Around a week after the mayor's event, I was watching the news and a story about the man who attacked me that night, Elias Williams, had been victim to a break in which resulted in his death. I had no doubts in my mind that my husband was behind it and when I asked him what happened he just shrugged and said, "That's what happens when someone touches what's mine."

Turns out Luca is extremely possessive, it wasn't enough for him that I bruised the assholes balls and his ego, Luca needed his blood for himself.

And I'm pretty sure I shouldn't find that wildly romantic.

As well as being possessive, it seems my husband also has a softer side. Luca is attentive, he cares about my day, and he takes care of me. It was strange at first, I'm not used to having someone care so deeply for me and it put me on high alert, looking for a lie but after a while I realized that's just him, he's the kind of man who will take care of those close to him, and he hates when I'm in pain or hurting.

I stand in the bathroom mirror and smile to myself as I remember Luca's need to take care of me while I was on my period.

Fuck, these cramps are killing me.

Every month I end up out of commission for a couple of days. I've always had bad cramps, according to the doctor I'm just one of those women who get them really bad.

It's two in the afternoon and I ended up having to come and lie down in bed, figuring I wasn't going to get much work done today anyways.

I'm flicking through Netflix, trying to find something to watch when the bedroom door flies open, and Luca walks in with a frantic look in his eye.

"Iz? What's wrong? You never spend time in here during the day,"
he says and makes his way over to me.

Last night he must have found me asleep on the couch because I woke up this morning snuggled into his side.

"Stop your stressing, I'm fine. I've just got cramps and needed to lie down for a while."

"Is this normal? Should I call a doctor? Have you taken medicine? What do you need from me, baby?" he asks, his tone desperate.

"What I need is for you to calm the hell down, it's completely normal so don't you go calling any doctors," I say sternly. "And why are you here anyway? You're not normally home during the afternoon."

"I just wanted to check on you." He removes his suit jacket and I'm about to ask what he's doing but he leaves the room before I have chance.

He comes back a couple of minutes later, arms full of snacks and he piles them on the bed before climbing in next to me. He grabs a heat pack from the pile and lifts the blanket so he can place it on my stomach.

"What are you doing? You need to work," I say to him, completely confused as to why he's still here.

"My wife is in pain, you're staying in bed for the rest of the day, and I'm not going back to work. We're gonna spend the day watching shit on tv while eating snacks, don't bother arguing because it's fucking happening," he says before he kisses my forehead, gets himself comfortable and pulls me closer to him.

"I've told you before, I'll always be here to take care of you."

We ended up spending the rest of the day in bed, snuggling up under a blanket while watching the latest Marvel movie.

I've never been this happy before, and I feel like this is the calm before the storm.

I apply the last of my lipstick and check myself in the mirror one last time. I'm wearing simple black skinny jeans, a pale blue blouse and classic black Louboutin heels with my hair curled and light makeup covering my face.

We're going to his father's estate for a family dinner. To say I'm nervous would be an understatement. I'm fine when it's just me and Luca alone, I feel like I can just be myself, but around others? I've been acting a certain way for so long it's hard to get myself out of that cycle. Luca says I should just be me, but he doesn't understand what it's like to suppress yourself for so long around others.

You'll be fine, Izzy, stop your worrying.

I take a deep breath and walk through the apartment to meet Luca at the elevator. He's stood waiting for me, wearing one of his usual suits. It's rare I see him wearing anything else, when he's in the apartment he'll wear sweats or shorts, but he never leaves the apartment unless he's in a suit.

"Ready?" he asks.

"Ready," I say with a nod.

"You look beautiful, *mia regina*. They already love you. You'll be fine."

He presses a quick kiss to my lips before taking my hand and leading me into the elevator.

Once we're in the car, Luca places his hand on my thigh as he drives us to his childhood home.

"Have things calmed down since you took out Novikov?" I ask, he doesn't mention his work much, which I don't mind—I just don't like the idea of him being in additional danger.

"Yeah, Muñoz has gone underground to regroup for now, he knows it would be suicide to hit us right now, why? You worried about me?" he says with a raised eyebrow.

"Of course, I am. Who'd give me so many insane orgasms if you were gone?" I tease.

"If another man touches you, I'll come back from the dead and rearrange his organs. No one, and I mean fucking no one, touches what's mine, Izzy."

"Relax, no one could replace you. But use that as an incentive to not get yourself killed."

"No one could replace me, huh?" he says as though he's joking but I can sense a hint of vulnerability. Is he really worried about that? Surely, he knows no one could mean anything to me like he does.

"I promise you, no one but you, Luca," I say, and he gives me a blinding smile that showcases his dimples and gives me butterflies. He takes my hand and presses kisses to my knuckles before he rests our interlocked hands on his lap.

We pull up to his father's estate and I stare up at the structure, I didn't take much in the last time I was here, considering it was my wedding day, I was a tad preoccupied. It looks like what I always imagined the Pemberley estate from *Pride and Prejudice* would be like.

Luca gets out of the car, and I open my door and do the same before he can come and open my door for me. He gives me a stern glare but lets it slide, he should know by now that I don't need him to protect me, but there's no telling him that.

Luca takes my hand, and we walk up the steps to the entrance. A small woman—who must be in her fifty's—opens the door giving Luca a warm smile before doing the same to me.

"Beatrice, this is my wife, Izzy. Izzy, this is Beatrice, my father's housekeeper."

"It's nice to meet you," I say with a smile, and she returns the sentiment before guiding us to a sitting room accompanied by Salvatore and Marco.

Salvatore stands and walks towards us. "Son," he says to Luca and gives him a nod.

"Thank you for joining us, Izzy," he says to me and squeezes my shoulder. "Dinner should be ready in a moment. Enzo stepped out to make a phone call, he can meet us in the dining room."

We sit and wait at the dining room table for Enzo to join us. Salvatore is at the head of the table with Luca on his right and Marco on his left while I sit next to Luca. Enzo strolls in without a care in the world and takes a seat next to me, I furrow my brows, why would he sit next to me instead of Marco?

Just as I think it, Luca tenses.

"What the fuck are you doing, Enzo?"

"What? I have business to discuss with my favorite sister," he says, nonchalant.

"You've never had a sister you idiot."

Enzo shrugs but mumbles something that sounds like "I nearly did" under his breath. I know Luca has never had a girlfriend before, does that mean Marco did? I'm sure Luca mentioned Marco has never been in a committed relationship before.

The evening turns out to be surprisingly comfortable, not at all like the family dinners me and my father would have. We eat dinner and Salvatore and Luca talk about business, Enzo switches between adding in to their conversation and trying to rile Marco up while he sits there like a man made of stone, a cool expression marring his features.

"Hey Bella, about that business we need to discuss," Enzo says to me with a boyish grin that makes him seem even younger.

"It's Izzy, asshole, not Bella," Luca says from beside me making Enzo roll his eyes.

"What business?" I add before Luca can say anything else.

"What do you like to do in your free time? Do you go shopping? Save puppies? Or do you... read?" he says with a look of innocence. What the fuck is he up to?

"I hate shopping. No, I don't save puppies and yes, I like to read. What's your endgame, Enzo?" I sigh.

"No endgame, just wanted to get to know my new sis," he says, acting innocent but I see a calculating look flash across his face before he masks it.

I swear he gets weirder each time I talk to him.

After dinner, Salvatore announces he needs to speak to Luca in his office so the rest of us move to the living room to wait for them.

"I need to make a phone call," Enzo says with a furrowed brow before stalking from the room and leaving me with Marco.

He stares at me from where he sits opposite me. There's no malice in his gaze but his stare threatens to send a shiver down my spine, nonetheless.

"Is there a reason you dislike me?" I say, breaking the silence.

He cocks his head, and he appears contemplative. "I don't dislike you, Izzy, you make Luca happy so I could never not like you. I'm not much of a talker, I observe."

"I'm the same, but the stare you usually give me is anything but welcoming, you don't like being around me, why is that?" I ask and cock my head the way he did.

"It's not you, you just remind me of a different time in my life," he says in what's almost a whisper, there's pain in his eyes and I'm brought back to what Enzo said earlier. I'm starting to think Luca was wrong about his brother, I think he has been in a relationship, and there's a reason he hid it or hasn't been in one since. But it's not my place to pry, no matter how curious I am.

I give him a nod of understanding and his shoulders drop in what I think is relief just as Luca emerges from the office and comes and stands behind me where I'm sitting in the armchair. He bends down and presses a kiss to my temple before straightening.

"You ready to go?"

CHAPTER TWENTY-SEVEN

Luca

We say our goodbyes to my family and head back to our apartment. The evening went well, Marco was his usual stoic self, but he seems more on edge around Izzy and I'm not sure what that is all about. Enzo was surprisingly well-behaved, and our father seems to be really taken by Izzy.

I was apprehensive as fuck when Dad pulled me into his office to talk business because I didn't like leaving Izzy alone with my brothers. I know neither of them would ever try anything with her, I just don't like leaving her alone. Fuck, I'd have her with me twenty-four-seven if I could.

All my life, I've been adamant I'd never settle down, I'd never become attached to a woman and now look at me, I'm pussy whipped by the woman sat beside me and I wouldn't have it any other way.

Dad wanted to speak to me to see if I'd heard anything about the Colombians—which I haven't. They're suspiciously quiet and I don't like it. Either they're licking their wounds or they're planning something big, but it'd be idiotic on their part for them to try it. We have the Russians backing us now as well as a truce with the Chicago outfit. We're also on friendly terms with the Irish, so

Muñoz would be better off proposing a truce rather than planning another attack, but he's never been right in the head, so who the fuck knows what'll happen. We'll have to keep our guard up for now until he resurfaces.

Once we get home, Izzy gives me a tender kiss on the cheek and excuses herself to shower. Does she really think I won't be joining her? Jesus fucking Christ, I've had to share her for half of the day, I'm not letting her out of my sight for the rest of the night.

Fuck being attached, that's the understatement of the century.

I make quick work of undressing before I make my way into the bathroom and I'm greeted by the sight of my wife in the shower, she has her back to me and hasn't sensed my presence yet while she tilts her head back to soak her hair. Fuck, she's a goddamn vision.

"Are you just going to stare, or are you going to join me?"

So much for her not sensing me.

I walk towards her and step into the shower before shifting her so we're both under the cascading spray of the shower and press my lips to hers. She tastes like strawberries and honey, like sunshine and home. She's my fucking home.

I deepen the kiss and lightly bite down on her bottom lip which rewards me with a moan. Fuck, that sound alone could make me come like a fucking teenager. I push her backwards so her backs against the wall without breaking the kiss, my hands caress her breasts before I lower my right hand down her stomach and to her wet cunt.

"Fuck, baby, you're drenched. Is this all for me?" I pull back from the kiss to look into her hooded eyes.

"Always," she moans as I stroke my thumb across her clit and slowly slip two fingers inside her.

I finger fuck her while I kiss up and down her neck, occasionally biting down and giving her the pain that I know she loves. It doesn't take long until the bathroom is filled with her moans and whimpers as she shatters on my fingers.

"Oh god, Luca," she moans. Her walls pulse around my fingers and fuck, I need inside her right the fuck now.

I pull my hand back and lift her up; she wraps her legs around me as I line my cock up at her entrance and slam into her, making us both groan in unison. I don't think I'll ever get used to the feeling of being inside of her. No other woman would ever compare to my girl.

"Fuck, baby, you always feel so fucking good." I bring my lips to hers, and she hums in agreement as I continue thrusting into her.

"You're fucking mine, Izzy, say it," I order. I pull back and latch my lips onto the shell of her ear as she winds her arms around my neck.

"I'm yours, Luca. Always yours," she whimpers and tugs on my hair to lift my head and we stare into each other's eyes while I keep up my pace. I can tell she's close, I can feel her pussy tighten around my cock and it drags a moan from me. My eyes travel from her face down to where our bodies are joined, and it takes all of my control to hold on and not come before she does.

"Shit, baby, you look so beautiful taking my cock like this. You're so wet for me. You're a fucking dream, Iz," I grunt as the water from the shower continues to soak us both.

It's an erotic sight, seeing my wife cry out in ecstasy with water dripping down her tits. Her nipples are so hard they look fucking painful from how turned on she is.

"Come for me, baby," I rasp and pick up my pace. "I need you to come, *mia regina*."

Her walls tighten further, and she lets out a scream as she comes all over my cock, and it's impossible to hold on any longer. I slam my hips another three times, and I'm spilling my cum inside her and groaning her name.

I hold her close as we both come down from our orgasms and whisper in her ear, "You're amazing, Iz. Beautiful, stunning, breathtaking... You're everything I didn't know I needed, and I do need you, *mia regina*."

I pull her into one last kiss, pouring everything I feel for her—all the gratitude, gratefulness and love, so much fucking love—since I can't say the words aloud just yet. She'll be ready one day, but today is not that day. I set her back down on her feet but keep her pulled to my chest, savoring the feel of her body pressed against mine. Skin to skin, heart to heart.

After we clean ourselves up, I wash Izzy's hair and dry her before I pick her up and carry her to bed where we both lie naked under the blanket, her snuggled into my side with one of her legs flung over mine. We sleep like this every night now, gone are the days of her having a guest room to herself—fuck that, wherever she is, I am. If she wants to sleep in the guest room then I'll fucking sleep in there with her, I really don't think I'd be able to sleep without her beside me.

This is the favorite part of my days, lying in bed with my wife by my side. I stroke her hair as her eyes flutter, and I can tell she's fighting sleep.

"Sleep, little queen," I whisper as I continue staring down at her in awe. She's fucking amazing and I'm one lucky bastard that she's mine. I'll never take this woman for granted.

I rub my finger against her wedding ring, and it makes me feel like shit as I realize she doesn't even have an engagement ring. I know she said she grew up knowing what she would have to do for her family, but she still deserves everything this life has to offer and the least I could have done was meet her before the wedding and give her a goddamn engagement ring.

She had to move to a different state, leaving the only life she's ever known behind. She had to move to a place where she didn't know a single soul to live with a man who she didn't know. Thinking about it makes me realize just how strong my wife is, she never once cowered or appeared worried. She took my life by storm; she came into my life and flipped it upside down in the best possible ways.

She's the light I didn't know I needed to brighten up my day, she guides me through the darkness. She's the fucking sun, and I'm just one of many planets who can't help but gravitate towards her.

I need to show her that I'm in this, that she's not just a temporary fixture in my life. Pretty words mean nothing without the actions to back it up. She deserves the world and I'll use all the fucking power I have over this city to give her it if that's what she wants.

A smile tugs at my lips as I think about tomorrow, I have a stop to make on my way to work, both Izzy and this city need to know that she's mine for good, that includes putting a rock on her finger.

CHAPTER TWENTY-EIGHT

Izzy

For the second time since I moved into this apartment, I wake up feeling eyes on me, except this time I can sense it's not my husband.

I gently reach under the pillow for my gun while I pretend to still be sleeping. Luca doesn't like the fact that I sleep with a gun under my pillow, he says that I don't need a gun to protect myself when I have him, yet I still don't feel safe without it. Call it old habits, I guess.

I slowly turn off the safety before quickly sitting it and pointing it at the asshole sat at the end of the bed.

"What the fuck are you doing in here, Enzo?"

He looks at me with wide eyes, clearly, he didn't expect me to be armed, never mind point the gun at him. I knew it was him as soon as I sensed him, but the little fucker needs to be taught a lesson about watching women sleep.

He lifts his finger in a *just a moment* gesture and pulls out his phone and brings it to his ear.

"Uh, bro, your wife currently has a gun aimed at me, please call her off," he says into the receiver before putting the call on speaker and placing it down on the bed.

"What do you mean Izzy has a gun aimed at you?" he speaks slowly as if he doesn't quite believe he heard what Enzo just said.

"Well, I was watching her sleep and then suddenly—" He's cut off by Luca bellowing into the phone.

"What the *fuck* do you mean you were watching her sleep? Izzy, shoot him. I give you my blessing," he says seriously, which makes me laugh.

"Again, what are you doing here, Enzo?" I ask with a sigh, it's too early in the morning for this shit.

"You like books, you said that two nights ago at dinner, so I want to take you book shopping," he says with an eager nod and suddenly everything clicks into place. When I gave him the information about the girl he saw in the club, I found that she owns a bookstore a few blocks away, he's using me as a stalking tactic.

"Of course! I can't wait to meet Robyn," I say with a grin. "Now get the fuck off my bed and make me a coffee while I get ready."

"He's on our bed? Enzo, what the fuck is your problem? Get off my bed and away from my wife, I swear I'll castrate you," I hear Luca growl as Enzo grabs the phone and makes his way out of the room.

Huh, I forgot about him being on the phone.

I take a quick shower and get dressed before meeting Enzo in the kitchen where he's waiting with a fresh cup of coffee for me in a to-go cup.

"I asked Luca how you liked your coffee, now let's go."

"Why are we going there, Enzo?"

He bites his lip in a contemplative gesture as though he's trying to find the right words.

"I've been watching over her, keeping her safe. I don't want to get her involved in my life, but I can't stay away either. The only thing I could think of to be close to her just once was if I'm a customer in her store, but I know nothing about books. Which is why you're dragging your reluctant brother-in-law with you." He nods, and he reminds me of a little lost puppy.

He's clearly conflicted about this girl, and if he's determined to keep her safe? Well, at least that's one good thing about this while fucked up situation.

We leave the apartment and Enzo leads me to a sedan parked near the entrance to our building. I expected some flashy sports car considering his age, not a fucking sedan. Then again, this ties in better with his *watching girls from the shadow's* aesthetic.

Enzo drives for a couple of blocks before pulling up outside a building which I'm guessing is about a block away from the bookstore. And gets out of the car.

"What are you doing?" I ask when he opens my door.

"We can't just park outside of her store, what if she sees my car? Nope, we're walking the next block."

Jesus fucking Christ, he's thought of everything.

I shake my head at him, at a loss for words and we walk side by side towards our destination. Enzo tells me how Robyn bought the store with the inheritance she got from her parents' deaths, as if I didn't already know from the search that he had me do for her. I let him keep talking, he seems like a different person when he's talking about her, his face brightens, his eyes light up and he gets all animated. It's adorable.

We enter the store and a bell chime's, alerting any staff to our presence. Robyn rounds the corner, she's short like me, but with dark brown hair and green eyes. She's pretty, I can see why Enzo has taken a liking to her. She's dressed in ripped jeans and a cream sweater, nothing like the women from our world would dress—other than me.

She gives us a big smile, welcoming us to her store and asks if there's anything in particular we need. Enzo seems to be stuck staring at the poor girl.

"Hey, I'm Izzy. This is my brother in-law Enzo, I recently moved to the city to move in with my husband and left a lot of my books back home in Chicago. Can you give me any recommendations?" I say with a smile to break the weird silence that seemed like it would never end, and I elbow Enzo in his stomach to bring him out of his daze.

"Nice to meet you," he says cooly with a nod, and I give him a *what the fuck* look. He needs to get his shit together before he scares her.

Thankfully, he takes the hint and starts asking her questions about the types of books she sells. He makes a big production about how he wants to build me a library as a wedding gift, and I internally roll my eyes as I follow them both through the shelves while Robyn points out different genres that she thinks I might like.

I actually really like her, she's the same age as me and we'd probably make good friends if I wasn't helping the idiot in front of me stalk her.

I pull out my phone while Enzo and Robyn are deep in conversation about some new thriller that's just been released.

> You should see the state of your brother. He clammed up like nothing I've ever seen before when we came into the store. He just stood and stared at her like he couldn't believe she was real.

Luca

> I still don't understand why you had to spend the day with my idiot brother.

> Why? Jealous?

Luca

> When it comes to you? Always. You're mine, I don't like other men near you, especially when the fucker invited himself into our bedroom. If he wasn't my baby brother, I'd fucking kill him.

> I'm helping him stalk another girl, jealousy should be the last thing you're feeling.

Luca

> Just hurry the fuck up, I've got a meeting in Queens soon then I'm coming home. You better be there when I get back, I miss you.

I miss you.

I smile to myself feeling like a giddy teenager, how the hell he elicits these feelings from me I have no idea.

I miss you too x

I tuck my phone away and focus on what Robyn is saying to Enzo, he'd been picking up books as we walked around the store. We make our way to the register so Enzo can pay for the stack of books he's been carrying for my "new library" before we thank Robyn for all of her help and make our way back to the car.

"Feel better now that you've spoken to her?" I ask after we've walked for a couple of minutes in silence.

"Yes. No... I don't know. I just want to keep her away from the world. She's too fucking light to be tainted by my darkness, but she's also like a fragile little bird that needs caring for," he says on a sigh and squeezes his eyes closed.

He's so conflicted about this and it makes me think about what my life would have been like if I grew up away from the Mafia. Don't get me wrong, it can be a dark life to live, but the Romano's are also pure, they're good men who put others above themselves and they genuinely care about their Cosa Nostra family. I could have had it so much worse.

I used to dream about growing up in a different life, away from the danger, violence and death. But when I think about that life now? I think about how I wouldn't have Luca—and that's just not worth it.

"I know you didn't ask for my advice, but you're getting it anyway. I grew up in this world, like so many other women. But I got lucky to be a part of your family. You may see our way of life as darkness, but there's light within it, Enzo. Think of how much safer Robyn would be at your side, you wouldn't have to keep her safe from the shadows anymore, her being known as yours would offer her a layer of protection as it is, but if the whole *famiglia* was behind her? She'd be untouchable."

"She shouldn't have to change her entire life for me though, and there's still the dangers that comes with being mine. What if someone wanted to use her to hurt me? She's my weakness," he says, not understanding my point.

"How much would really change? She'd still be able to work at her store, she'd still be able to do everything she usually does, she'd just have bodyguards to protect her. Is that really a bad thing? You're so hell bent on doing things your way. Have you ever thought about what she would think? I saw the connection between the two of you just now, maybe you should try and date her, tell her who you are from the beginning and let her have a choice." We reach the car and I turn to face him.

"Take it from someone who's had decisions made for her for her whole life, you need to let her decide."

Enzo gives me a nod, lost in thought about what I've said and goes to open the passenger side door for me, but before I can step forward Enzo grabs me and throws me to the floor, covering me with his body as there's a loud explosion.

Someone blew up the car. Who? Were they wanting to kill Enzo? Or was it me as Luca's wife? And why the fuck am I thinking about this shit when we clearly need to *fucking move.*

We don't get the chance to move, the force from the explosion jolts my body backwards and my head cracks against the pavement. I can feel the heat from the fire, and it prickles at my skin. The hit makes me dizzy; I can hear Enzo shouting to me, but I can't make out the words that he's saying. My vision blurs and white spots begin to take over, I try to blink to clear it but it's no use. Enzo's panicked eyes are the last thing I see before everything fades to nothingness and my world turns to black.

CHAPTER TWENTY-NINE

Luca

Marco and I are just walking into a meeting with the Irish to discuss a new deal when my phone rings and Enzo's caller ID appears on my screen.

Why the fuck is he calling me while he's out shopping with Izzy and making her help him in whatever cocked up plan he has to stalk his girl? Me and her will be having words when I get home, she should just leave him to it before he thinks he can drag her into whatever the fuck he's up to and think she'll be at his beck and call whenever he needs her.

He probably just wants to try and piss me off. Knowing him, it wouldn't surprise me. The little shit loves getting on my nerves and Izzy is the easiest way to do that. He knows I'm beyond territorial when it comes to my wife.

I swipe the screen to decline the call and sit down opposite Finn O'Brien, ready to discuss business. But before I can even get a word out, Marco's phone rings. He glances at the screen and rolls his eyes before answering. Whatever he hears on the other end of the call has his face paling and he swallows before his wide eyes meet mine and I just know that somethings wrong.

"We need to go. Now."

I know he doesn't want to reveal whatever the fuck has happened in front of the head of the Irish so we give him our apologies before we turn and leave the restaurant, before I can ask Marco what the fuck is happening, he's running towards the car and jumping inside. I follow and get in the passenger seat, and he pulls out into the traffic as soon as my door closes.

"You better tell me what the hell is going on, Marco," I say. I can hear the desperation in my own ears. Whatever it is, it's fucking bad if it has my brother spooked.

"Someone rigged Enzo's car to blow when the passenger door opened," he says and he swallows before continuing, "He managed to shove Izzy out of the way, but the blast knocked her backwards and she hit her head, he knew we'd usually use our own doc, but he didn't have a choice. An ambulance turned up at the scene and he put a gun to the EMT's head and told them to fucking fix her. They're on the way to the hospital now, she still hasn't woken up," he says and looks at me with haunted eyes.

No. Fuck no. There's no way.

I can't breathe; my heart feels like it's about to fly out of my fucking chest and I have to force myself not to picture the scene or I'll lose my goddamn mind.

She's fine, I tell myself. She fucking has to be. I can't lose her when I've only just found her. *She'll be okay. You'll be okay, baby.*

I lean my head against the headrest and close my eyes, trying to fight the nausea crawling up my throat.

"Get me there. Take me to her, Marco," I whisper, pain evident in my voice.

Marco breaks every speed limit there is on the way to the hospital, getting us there in under fifteen minutes. He doesn't speak, there's nothing he could say to me right now that will make me feel any better. As soon as the car slows down in front of the entrance, I'm jumping out the door and leaving Marco to deal with parking.

I enter through the ER and glance around but I don't see Enzo or any of my men he called in as security so I make my way to the desk, as soon as I tell the girl my name her eyes widen, and she points me to where I can find Izzy. At least Enzo had some sense and got my girl a private room.

I walk down the corridor and spot two of our men stood outside Izzy's door, I enter the room and the sight that greets me nearly brings me to my knees. Izzy is laid in bed, looking so fucking fragile with a bandage wrapped around her head, I can see dried blood matted into her blonde hair. She seems so small and the thought that I could have lost her guts me.

Enzo's sat in the chair next to her and he looks as bad as she does. In fact, is that a piece of metal sticking out of his back? Jesus Christ.

"What did the doctor say? Is she okay? When will she wake up? Why haven't you been seen yet?" I fire at him as I make my way to her bedside and take her hand in mine, brushing my thumb over her wedding ring. It was only this morning I went to the jeweler to get her an engagement ring and now she's laid in the hospital, unconscious.

"They did a scan, and everything looks fine, the doc said she should wake up soon and he suspects a mild concussion, but he'll have to check her over thoroughly once she's awake. I haven't been

VOW TO ME 177

seen because I'm not leaving her side until she's awake. I can't, it's my fault. I should have protected her better, I should have noticed something was wrong, I'm so fucking sorry, brother." He closes his eyes and tips his head back before swallowing and turning to me. The regret in his eyes is clear as day.

"It's not your fault, little bro, and once I find whoever did this, they'll wish they were never fucking born. Hell, I might set Izzy on them, she can be fucking terrifying when she wants to be."

I stand and walk to the door, telling my men to get a doc in here to check Enzo over.

It feels like an eternity waiting for Izzy to wake up. It's been an hour. Enzo got checked over, the doc had to remove a chunk of metal from his shoulder and stitch him up from where he sat next to her bed because he refused to move. Marco arrived and called our dad, they're both waiting in the waiting room, wanting to give us some space. I'd kick Enzo out and tell him to wait with them, but he's so broken up over this I don't have the heart to do it.

I keep whispering to her, telling her I need her to wake up but it's no use. I feel helpless, there's nothing I can do but wait. Trust me, I asked the doctor.

I stand up and pace around the room, muttering to myself as I hear her voice.

"My head is fucking killing me." My head snaps towards her, and the relief I feel to see her staring back at me is like nothing I've ever known.

"Iz? Are you okay? How do you feel?" I rush towards her, and of course, the stubborn as fuck woman that she is tries to sit up. "Lay back down, woman. You're not going anywhere."

"Fuck, sis, you cared the shit outta me," Enzo says and presses the call button to alert the doctor she's awake.

I take Izzy's hand and bring it to my lips, pressing a tender kiss to her knuckles while they both recall what they remember from the attack. Honestly, I'd rather not hear the details—because I hate the fact that she got hurt—but I need them if I'm going to find the asshole that dared to hurt my wife and brother.

Enzo leaves to update Marco and our dad, finally giving me some alone time with my wife.

"Fuck, Izzy, I've never been as fucking scared as I was when we got that phone call, you're not leaving my sight for the foreseeable future." I lean down and press a kiss to her forehead and her lashes flutter. Even banged up and bruised, she's still the most beautiful woman I've ever seen.

"I'm fine, Luca. I'm right here, and I'm not going anywhere."

"Damn fucking right you're not, I'm gonna speak to my father at some point later today, I want to take you way for a couple of weeks. Give you a honeymoon and give us both a break from all the chaos. What do you think?" I ask, and I'm suddenly nervous.

Will she want to go away? Does she even still want to stay married after what happened? My life put her in danger so it wouldn't be a surprise if she didn't.

"You should know by now that I'd follow you anywhere," she says with a sweet smile, and I give her one in return before I press

my lips to hers in a light kiss, I pull back after a couple of seconds.
I don't want to hurt her further.

T hree days. Three fucking days we've been stuck here in this
hospital. The doctor checked Izzy over and declared she did,
in fact, have a concussion and insisted on her staying here under
observation. Izzy argued that it was unnecessary, but I put my foot
down. I wasn't risking anything happening to her if she left the
hospital before advised.

I spoke to my father-in-law and told him what had happened,
he thanked me for letting him know and hung up on me without
even asking if his daughter was okay, asshole.

Marco has been busy tracking down the fucker who set up
the explosive, he asked Alec for help hacking the security cameras
around the area and they found footage of a man fucking with the
car while Izzy and Enzo were in the bookstore. Enzo and Marco
managed to find him and currently have him waiting on ice for me
in one of our warehouses.

I also spoke to Dad about getting Izzy away from the city for
a while once she's recovered. While it may not be the best timing
given the circumstances, he agreed that I should take her away and
even offered us the island he bought for my mother before she
passed. He and Marco will take over my responsibilities while I'm

gone and keep me updated on everything that's happening back home.

I haven't left the hospital once while Izzy's been admitted, like fuck am I leaving her side. I had Tomasso bring me some clothes to change into and everything Izzy needed from the apartment rather than me having to leave.

We're currently getting ready to go home. The doctor finally gave Izzy the all clear and gave me instructions to keep a close eye on her.

Close eye on her? Not a problem. I'm not letting her out of my sight.

"I'm going to change in the bathroom, don't fucking follow me, Luca. It's time I start doing shit for myself without you hovering." I go to tell her that I'll help her anyways, but she carries on talking before I can. "You heard the doc, I'm fine," she huffs before standing and gathering her clothes.

Fucking stubborn woman.

"For fuck's sake, fine. But I'll be right outside the door if you need me," I say and plead with her with my eyes not to argue, she sighs but nods in agreement.

"Can I use your phone? I need to arrange a team to follow us home and mine is dead," I ask.

She unlocks her phone and hands it to me before retreating into the bathroom. I call Tomasso and arrange for three cars to escort us home, I'm not taking any chances of an ambush on the way home. We still don't know the reason behind the attack, the man we have in the warehouse was hired by someone, and we won't know who hired him until I go over there and torture it out of him.

I hang up the phone just as a text comes in. My brow furrows when I see it's an unknown number and I click on it to see the message.

Unknown

I miss you, little one.

Who the fuck is this asshole and why the fuck is he telling my wife that he misses her? I trust Izzy with my life, I know she would never go behind my back. It's probably someone from her old life in Chicago. Rage bubbles up inside me at the thought of one of her past lovers telling her he misses her. Fuck that, she's mine. I swipe and delete the text from her inbox before locking the phone and leaving it on the bed for her and gathering the rest of our things.

I'm ready to get the fuck out of here and get my girl home where she belongs.

CHAPTER THIRTY

Izzy

One week. Seven days. One-hundred and sixty-eight hours. That's how long it's been since I was let out of the hospital. That's how long it has been since Luca decided he wasn't going to let me out of his sight. I can't even go to the bathroom without him attempting to hover over me.

The man is driving me *insane*.

I thought it was cute at first, but now it's just getting ridiculous. If he doesn't stop soon, I'm going to end up fucking stabbing him in the arm and sending him to the hospital just to get some peace.

I'm sat on the sofa, watching him pace around the room and muttering to himself about who the fuck knows what.

"What the hell is wrong with you?" I eventually give in and ask.

"I need to deal with the cocksucker who was hired to rig the explosive on Enzo's car, it's been over a week since the incident, and we can't wait much longer. I also don't want to leave you here alone, so I don't know what the fuck to do."

Hmm, maybe I shouldn't complain about him not letting me out of his sight.

"Easy, take me with you," I say with a shit eating grin. I want to get my hands on the asshole who tried to blow me and my little brother-in-law to pieces.

He stops his pacing and turns to me, he runs his eyes over me as if assessing for injury, I'm completely healed so it's not like he's going to find anything. I've been fine for days and he won't even touch me, the most action I've got from him is a quick kiss and him holding me at night.

He really needs to stop treating me as though I'm made of glass that will shatter at any moment. I won't break, I'm a hell of a lot stronger than that and that's just something he's going to have to realize.

"Fine. But if you get dizzy, feel nauseous or feel even the slightest headache then we're getting the fuck out of there and coming straight home. I won't let you mess around with your health," he says with a pointed look, and I roll my eyes before jumping up and pressing a kiss to his cheek and making my way to the bedroom to get ready.

I dress in black leather pants that could've been painted on to my skin, a cropped black sweater that hugs my breasts and I pair them with a pair of heeled, red ankle boots—and of course I add a red lip to match.

I eagerly walk back into the lounge to meet Luca, thankful that I'm getting to leave the apartment for the first time in a week. His eyes widen as he runs his gaze over me, his brows tugging down in a frown.

"What the fuck are you wearing?" he growls.

"What do you mean? What's wrong with it?" I say in the most innocent tone I can muster and bite my lip to hide my smirk.

"Like fuck are you leaving the apartment looking like that, Izzy. I'll end up shooting every man we come into contact with, is that really what you want?"

"Tone down the caveman act, there's nothing wrong with what I'm wearing and I'm not changing. Now, let's go," I say in a no-nonsense tone and walk towards the elevator. Luckily, Luca realizes this is *not* the hill he wants to die on and joins me with a sigh but doesn't make a retort.

He stays silent the whole drive to the warehouse and he's starting to make me nervous. Does he not want me involved with this? Does he not trust me?

"You're freaking me out Luca, why are you being so quiet?"

"I'm regretting letting you come, what if you see the other side of me and hate me afterwards?" he says quietly and turns to me, the vulnerability in his eyes would floor me if I wasn't already sat down.

"Are you being serious? You do remember giving me a tongue in a jar with a bow made from flesh, right?" I say with a chuckle and take his hand in mine. "Nothing would make me hate you. Besides, I want a go at the asshole who tried to blow me up, are you going to hate me after that?"

"Of course not, I already know you're a stabby psycho when you want to be," he says, his tone is full of pride, and it makes my breath hitch knowing that I can completely be myself with him and not have to worry about what he'll think of me.

I lean over and press a kiss to his jaw as we pull up outside the warehouse. Luca turns off the ignition and shifts so he's facing me.

"If you want to leave at any time, just say the word and we'll leave with no questions asked, if you start to feel sick at all just say the word and we leave. Don't worry about anything else Izzy, okay? You come first, always." He's out of the door and rounding the car before I can reply.

We walk into the building side by side with Luca's hand on the small of my back. The guards around the warehouse give Luca an inquisitive look before masking it and nodding to us, they're clearly not used to seeing a woman involved in business.

We enter the main room and I see a man tied to a chair in the middle of the room, he must be in his early thirties, has shaggy blonde hair and brown eyes. There's nothing recognizable about him, nothing at all that would make him stand out in a crowd. I see Marco stood in the corner with his usual mask of indifference in place while Enzo is standing behind the asshole strapped to the chair, he's bent down and whispering in his ear with a manic look on his face.

Over the past week, Enzo has visited me nearly every day, he apologized profusely about what happened the day of the incident. He feels guilty that I got hurt, I ended up telling him that if he apologized one more time it would be him that had a concussion and he soon stopped. Yet, he still came to sit with me, and gave me a break away from my overbearing husband. Enzo glances up and spots us as we enter.

"Izzy! Oh, fuck dude, you thought having to wait for Luca to deal with you was bad? It's even worse now that my favorite sister is here with him," he sing-songs to the fucker and I give him a grin.

I go to stand next to Marco in the corner to let Luca do his thing and get any information out of him. There's three of their men stood around the room who remain stoic, they ignore our presence until Luca orders one of them to bring me a chair—I internally roll my eyes because he's such a fucking mother hen.

I sit and watch the show as Luca uses various torture methods to try and get information out of him. He clearly lives for this shit; he's loving it. The sadistic look in his eyes as he removes parts of his anatomy is a thing of beauty.

Huh, a thing of beauty? I guess I'm just as sadistic as he is.

It's clear the asshole doesn't know much, he says he was hired through an online forum which I'm familiar with, the thing about that forum is that it's virtually impossible to trace the hit back to whoever placed it, but that won't stop me from at least trying. Apparently, he was paid twenty grand to set up the explosives and the attack wasn't aimed at me or Enzo in particular, the ad was placed for any member of the Romano family. The guy thought it would be easier to go for Enzo's car since he uses less security than the rest of the family.

Once it's clear our new friend—Elliot Barnham—doesn't know anything more that's of use, Luca turns to me and raises his brow. An unspoken agreement passes between us, he knows I'm pissed about the attack and that I want to inflict some pain on him myself. I won't kill him—I'll leave that part to Enzo who's been jumping around the room wanting to get on to the killing part of the process.

I stand and make my way over to them. There's a hint of relief in his eyes, thinking that I can't be anywhere near as brutal as my husband, and I inwardly smirk at his misogynistic views.

"I spent three days in the hospital because of your little attack," I say, feigning hurt. "It wasn't very nice what you did to us."

"I'm s-sorry, Mrs. Romano... please... please ask him to let me go," he pleads, and I tip my head back in a laugh.

"Let you go? Sorry sweetie, that's not how this is gonna go." I grin at him before pulling a switch blade for my boot, I fucking love these boots. There's a hidden strap inside to keep my knives in place—plus, they're pretty. Luca sighs when he sees me retrieve the blade, for some reason he doesn't like me carrying them. I shrug at him and casually walk towards my new friend before bending down and cutting the ropes that tie his legs to the chair.

"Stand," I order as I nod to Luca and Marco, gesturing for them to hold him in place. They both comply, letting me run my little show while Enzo giggles, yes fucking *giggles*, from where he's stood. Psychotic idiot.

This whole time Elliot has been sat in nothing but boxer briefs that are now covered in blood from Luca's antic's, I walk around him and stand behind him before I crouch and bring my blade to the back of his knees and slashing along the tendons in the back of both knees.

He drops to the floor and is now in a kneeling position while I walk back around him so I'm standing in front of him, him kneeling at my feet.

"I do love bringing men to their knees," I say with a sweet smile while Luca growls at the insinuation. I ignore him and bring my attention back to the little fucker who thought he could hurt me and Enzo.

"Beg me," I say, and he starts pleading at me to let him go. I stare into his eyes and the dryness of his face makes me frown.

He's not very good at begging for his life. *There should be tears.*

I bring my knife down to his face and make a slice at both of his eye lids, so it looks like he's crying tears of blood.

Hmm, that's better.

Marco makes a sound in the back of his throat, I'm not sure whether it's from approval or not, but that's what I'm going to class it as.

"You should have cried for me, I didn't want to do that, but you weren't begging hard enough," I say with a mock pout before nodding at Enzo, I'll let him have his fun since it doesn't seem like Elliot is going to last much longer after everything me and Luca have done to him.

I glance around the room and the men the guys have in the room are staring at me in shock, they're not used to a woman having bigger balls than most men it seems. I clean up in the attached bathroom once Luca is finished and walk back out into the main room where Luca holds his hand out for me. "*Mia regina,*" he says clearly enough for the others to hear when I place my hand in his before bringing my palm to his lips and placing a sweet kiss.

CHAPTER THIRTY-ONE

Luca

I lead Izzy out of the warehouse and back to the car, I sent a message to Tomasso while Iz was busy cutting up Elliot to tell him to pack us some things. Now that she's well enough to torture someone, I'm pretty sure she's well enough to travel.

I've never felt more pride than I did watching Izzy cut up that asshole, and the fact that she left him for Enzo instead of finishing him herself shows me just how much she understands him. Not many people understand that crazy bastard.

They've grown close in the past week, spending time together every day. I'd be a raging lunatic consumed by jealousy if he wasn't my little brother, but I know it's a purely platonic friendship. I think it's good for them. It's good for Izzy to have a friend in a new city and it's good for Enzo because that kid has always had problems getting close to people, I don't know if it's his quirky personality or if he just eventually scares them away, but he's always had issues making friends.

"Are you sure you're feeling okay?" I ask once we get in the car. She's probably sick of me asking, but I never want to see her laid up in a hospital bed again, there was a point when I really thought I was going to lose her. That pain has stayed with me ever since, it didn't go away when she woke up. No, it just kept building and building, leaving me an overbearing, annoying as fuck husband who can't let his wife out of his sight for longer than thirty minutes unless I want to start imagining ten different scenarios in which she's hurt or sick or injured.

I hate feeling this way, like if I don't hold on tight enough, she's just going to float away.

"I promise, I'm fine. I would tell you if I wasn't," she says softly, trying to reassure me. And it does, her voice alone does weird things to me. It's like she's put some sort of spell on me—all I can ever see is her.

I put the car in drive and make the drive to the airport, after around fifteen minutes, Izzy realizes were going in the opposite direction to home.

"Uh, Luca? Where are we going?"

"I told you I wanted to take you on a honeymoon."

"What? Luca! Where the hell are we going? I haven't packed my things! We can't just up and go away somewhere!" she bursts, clearly not on board with the last-minute plans.

"It's a surprise, I had Tommaso pack us some things and he's meeting us at the airport. I want to get you away for a couple of weeks, give you the honeymoon I should have given you after the wedding. You deserve the world, Izzy, let me give it to you," I say as I take my hand in hers and give it a squeeze.

We arrive at the private hangar at the airport and Izzy looks out at the jet while mumbling something that sounds a lot like "Of course the asshole has a jet" before she jumps out of the car and waits for me to do the same.

"Where are we going? I've never left the country before," Izzy says casually, and it makes me pause. What does she mean she's never left the country? She grew up the same way as I did, it's not as though her father ever struggled for money. Christ, I bet he has billions sat doing nothing but gaining interest.

"Why haven't you left the country?" I ask, my voice gruff. I'm pissed she's never had the experiences she should have. Hell, she should have at least visited Italy before, she's fucking Italian and I'm sure she has cousins that live there.

"Sheltered princess, remember?" Sarcasm is evident in her tone. "My father left me at home with Alessi whenever he traveled, he always said that there was no need for me to leave Chicago."

It takes everything in me to control my anger and not plan a stop by the Windy City so I can strangle Bianchi, the asshole.

We board the jet and take our seats; Izzy rolls her eyes as the embroidered seats with our family emblem on. I've learned my wife isn't one for over the top, pretentious things most women in her position would be.

By the time we take off, she's asleep with her head resting on my shoulder. As soon as the flight attendant informs me that we can remove our belts, I unfasten her belt and lift her before walking to the back of the jet and placing her on the king size bed. I grab my laptop that Tomasso had left in the jet along with our things and sit next to where Izzy lies asleep to get some work done, I've never been able to sleep while flying.

Izzy sleeps for six hours before I finally give in and wake her up for dinner. I at least had the foresight to have a coffee ready for her because Izzy when she's just woken up? Not an Izzy I like engaging with.

Okay, that's a lie, I'll take her any way I can get her.

We eat dinner and Izzy peppers me with questions about where we're going, she really fucking hates surprises.

I sigh, she's not going to stop unless I tell her. "We're going to an island just off the coast of Italy. My father bought the island for my mother as a wedding gift, we visited every year until she died. None of us have been since but we have staff who live on the premises to maintain everything," I say, and she gapes at me with wide eyes.

"We don't have to go if you're not comfortable Luca, it's clear it was a very special place for you to visit with your mom. I don't want to take away from that," she says and bites her lip like she does if she's nervous.

I lift her and sit her on my lap so she's straddling me. "I want to go there with you, I think it'll make me feel closer to her. And she would have wanted me to take you there. She would have loved you." *Just like I do.*

It's getting harder and harder to not blurt the words I mean with every piece of my soul every time I look at her.

Finally, after the longest eight hours of my life, the pilot announces over the speaker that we're getting ready to land. I lift Izzy off me and strap her into the seat next to me while she huffs and complains that she's fully capable of doing it herself.

After we land at Naples International Airport, we jump in the helicopter and make the short flight to the island just off the coast of Capri.

Once we reach the island, I help Izzy jump down from the helicopter and walk her up to the mansion that sits in the middle of the island. It's a huge villa that was built around the time I was born with another two houses sitting at the back of the property for staff.

Rosita, the housekeeper who lives on the island comes out to greet us and envelopes me in a hug. Even though it's been nearly twenty-three years since I visited, I still remember the small woman who would dote on me and Marco when we visited.

"*È così bello vederla, signore,*" she whispers in my ear. I return the sentiment before ushering both women inside the house.

"Welcome to our home for the next two weeks, *mia regina,*" I say and wrap my arms around Izzy from behind and press a kiss to her temple.

CHAPTER THIRTY-TWO

Izzy

The island that the Romano's own is truly beautiful. I've never seen sand so white, water so clear, or skies so blue. I was apprehensive about coming here once Luca told me the story of his mother. This place is clearly a very special place for his family so I felt like I would be intruding on their sanctum or something.

I'm sitting on the kitchen counter nursing a coffee while looking out of the patio doors at the view of the ocean as the sun rises. For the first time ever, I'm awake before Luca and it's weird, but I think it may have a little something to do with the six-hour nap I took yesterday on the jet.

Once we arrived, Luca gave me a tour of the villa—if that's what you can call it, it's huge—before Rosita cooked us supper and he took me to bed and cuddled me to sleep. He still hasn't touched me, and the man is driving me insane.

Before I met him, I would go months without sex and it wouldn't never bother me, now I'm reduced to a pile of crazy lustful hormones which he won't satisfy for whatever ridiculous reason he's cooked up in that head of his.

I'm so lost in thought that I don't even notice Luca stood in the doorway staring at me. Considering I usually pride myself on being able to sense people, I'm a little pissed that I didn't hear him come in.

"I woke up and you were gone," he states casually, but there's an emotional storm behind his eyes, yet I can't pinpoint what emotion it is.

"I've slept more in the past week than I normally would in a month," I say with a shrug, and he stalks towards me, reaching me within three strides. He steps in between my legs, wraps his arms around my waist and presses a kiss to my lips. "I didn't like waking up without you beside me, you should wake me next time."

"You deserve rest too. Besides, I kinda liked being the first one up for once," I say with a grin and take a sip of my coffee.

He reaches his hand up and tucks a piece of hair behind my ear. "Mmm, you missed out on waking up in bed with me though, is that really a good thing?" he says and takes my coffee from me, bringing the mug to his mouth and taking a sip.

"Depends. Are you over whatever ridiculous notions you have about touching me yet?"

"You want me to touch you, wife?" he says and runs his hands up and down my thighs. "Have you missed me kissing you here?" He rubs his thumb over my clit above my panties.

"Have you missed tasting me, Iz? Have you missed me fucking that tight little cunt until your walls pulse and you're milking me dry?" He leans forwards and swipes his tongue up my neck. "Have you missed me making you scream my name while you fall apart underneath me?"

Luca brings his lips to mine and devours my mouth like he's been starved and I'm his only source of nutrition. He tastes like my coffee and sin, I wrap my arms around his neck to pull him into a deeper kiss while moaning into his mouth.

"Do you need me, baby? Do you need me to take care of the ache that's been building all week while I haven't touched you? Tell me, Izzy, did you touch yourself to thoughts of me fucking you? Spanking you? Teasing your clit with my tongue while finger fucking you?"

"Yes... all of it. I need you, Luca... please," I moan and plead with him, desperate for him to touch me, fuck me, use me, just do *something.*

"Lie back, baby... I want my breakfast," he whispers as he lowers me down so that I'm laid across the kitchen counter, ass to the edge while he removes my panties and presses kisses up my thighs before he reaches my sex and pressing an open-mouthed kiss to my clit, making me arch my back and moan his name.

"Fuck, Izzy. You're soaked," he rasps against me before circling his tongue around the bundle of nerves and inserting two fingers inside me. "You need me to take care of you, huh?" he says between licks. "Say it."

I groan and whimper while he continues working me with both his fingers and tongue. "Fucking say it, Izzy," he murmurs against me.

"Yes... fuck. I need you," I groan, and he increases his pace until I'm writhing beneath him, I need more, I need something, fuck. As if sensing I'm on the edge, he nips my clit with his teeth and the sharp pain coupled with his fingers hitting my G-spot has me spiraling into an orgasm while bucking against him, coating his face with my juices as I cry out.

Once I come down from my high, Luca releases his grip on my thighs and helps me sit up. Before I can reach for him, he's already turning his back on me pulling ingredients out of the fridge.

What the fuck is happening?

Like, seriously. What. The. Hell.

"What are you doing?"

"Making breakfast," he says as if it's obvious, but the smirk he throws at me from over his shoulder tells me he's teasing.

"What if I wanted something of a different variety for breakfast?" I ask and flash my brows which makes him chuckle.

"Trust me, I'd love nothing more than have you drop to your knees and fuck your mouth with my cock until I'm coming down your pretty throat or flip you over and fuck you in the middle of this kitchen. But we have plans today, and you need to eat," he says and tips his head towards the bedroom in a *get a move on gesture*. I sigh before hopping off the counter, I press a kiss to his cheek as I pass him before leaving him in the kitchen to get ready for the day.

I must still be in my post-orgasm high because I didn't even bother to ask what these plans we have are.

S hopping

Fucking shopping.

Does he not know me at all? Or is he just trying to torture me?

After we ate breakfast and Luca took a quick shower, he drove us from the island to Capri on a speedboat, where I'm now standing in the middle of Louis Vuitton, wondering whether the locals would mind if I strangled my husband for bringing me here.

This is my worst nightmare, we've already been to three different stores where I followed Luca around as he picked up different dresses, shoes, bikini's and what-the-fuck-ever else caught his eye that I apparently need.

"Tomasso couldn't pack you much because you didn't have much to begin with. We're here to remedy that." He'd said as if I gave a shit about the size of my closet or which brands of clothes I own.

I grew up with more than enough money, wearing clothes that I hated because my father wanted me to dress like the other girls my age in our circle did.

I'd be perfectly content wearing an oversized tee and a pair of shorts from Target, but no. Of course, that isn't good enough.

"Is this the part where you start trying to change me? Dress me up like a doll, use me as your plaything? What's next, you start telling me what I can and cannot say when we're in public, telling me how to act? This is how it starts you know," I say with a raised eyebrow.

He tips his head back and stares at the ceiling as if he's praying to the lord to give him strength. It goes on for so long I'm about to ask him what the hell is so interesting about it but his dark gaze pins me in places and keeps my mouth quiet before I can.

"The last thing I want to do it change you, you're perfect just the way you are. You don't like anything in these stores? That's fine, I'll take you somewhere else. You want to order online? Also fine. What's not fine is having six or seven outfits because you left the rest of your things back in Chicago. What's not fine is you thinking I'm doing this for any reason other than to spoil you. I've done nothing but accept every single thing about you, Izzy. I love how you're nothing like the spoilt little princesses you grew up with, I love that you have a backbone and don't take any shit, from anyone, including me. I love that you challenge me and aren't afraid to speak your mind."

He steps in front of me grasps my chin with his thumb and forefinger to tip my head up so my eyes clash with his and the sincerity in his gaze makes me heart ache. His words hit me right in the chest and it has my throat closing and my eyes stinging. I blink away the sensation before tears can start to fall.

How did I find a man that knows me so perfectly and accepts all of me? From an *arranged marriage*, no less.

A tidal wave of emotions hit me, and I realize that the one thing I never thought would happen, happened. It came out of nowhere and the realization threatens to bring me to my knees.

Holy shit.

How?

I made a promise to myself years ago that I wouldn't allow myself to fall in love. After seeing the change in my father after he lost

Mama, I vowed to never fall for a man, to let a man change me, for better or worse. I stare into Luca's eyes, he's looking at me so intently, the kindness in his gaze showing that every word he just said to me is the truth.

Oh fuck.

What does this mean?

Do I tell him? What if he doesn't feel the same? We were forced into his union after all, what if he thinks it's fucking ridiculous that I could love him after such a short amount of time? What if he—

He must sense the change in my demeanor and sense me panicking because his voice cuts through my thoughts, bringing them to a screeching halt before I can spiral even further.

"What just happened? Where did you go?" he asks, and I stare at him with wide eyes and no answers to his questions. I swallow the lump in my throat but can't bring myself to answer him, I can't. I just fucking *can't*.

What would I even say? *Oh. don't worry, I just realized I'm in love with you, thanks for buying me all the dresses and shoes and shit.* I think the fuck not.

I shake my head and pray he doesn't push it further. Luckily, he takes the hint that I can't voice my thoughts right now and instead changes the subject, guiding me out of the store and towards the little café we planned on going to for lunch.

CHAPTER THIRTY-THREE

Luca

W e've been on my family's island for a week, and things haven't been the same between us since that first day when I took Izzy shopping. She's pulling away, closing herself off and I hate it. I have no idea what went wrong, but something happened.

We've still been sleeping wrapped up in each other on a night, we've been having sex as we usually would now that I'm certain she's fully recovered. We've been doing everything we usually would, but it's as if she's closed herself off emotionally to me. We used to lay in bed at night and talk about shit; we would be open with each other and talk about the past and the future and everything in between. We'd talk about the big things, the little things, the things that make us both who we are and those little details that we'd have in common that have no real meaning but came together and fused us as one.

But now? Now she's a closed book and I have no idea what started it... or how to fix it.

I stand in the doorway of the dining room, watching her where she sits at the table working on her laptop. She's in her element, oblivious to me standing here watching her for the last five minutes. Whatever she's working on has her brows furrowed and irritation coiling through her if the straightness of her spine and her tense shoulders are any indication.

I walk over and close the lid of her laptop; her head snaps up and she stares at me with angry eyes.

"What do you think you're doing?" she snaps.

"We need to talk." I shrug nonchalantly, acting as though her attitude towards me lately hasn't bothered me in the slightest when really, it's been tearing me up inside wondering where we went wrong.

"What about?" she sighs.

"What the fuck is going on, Iz? We were fine before we came here, now we're on our honeymoon and you're acting as if it's an inconvenience being near me unless we're intimate. What happened?"

She swallows and her eyes dart around us as if she's looking for an escape.

Not happening. You don't get to run and hide from me, baby.

"Just talk to me, would you?" I say when I've had enough of waiting.

"What is your problem Luca? What do you want me to say? Everything is fine, you always need to fucking fix everything."

If it's a fight you want, it's a fight you'll get, little demon.

"You're full of shit Izzy, you're running and hiding. But why? What happened that day when we left the island? You were fine one minute and the next you're acting like a completely different woman. You're hiding from me, or from something, so what is it?

Because we can't go on like this," I sigh and shake my head, not knowing whether to keep fighting to break through to her or save it for another day.

I expect her to argue, to push her point further, to walk away, curse me. What I didn't expect was for a gut-wrenching sob to fall from her lips before she breaks down, tears streaming down her face as she shudders uncontrollably.

I'm at her side in a second, picking her up from the chair before sitting down and holding her on my lap. My arms band around her waist as I hold on to her. I don't ask questions, I don't pry like I want to, I just let her get out whatever it is that's she's feeling, murmuring encouraging words in her ear so she knows she's not alone.

"I've got you, baby," I whisper to her.

"It's all your fault," she says on a sob and my brows wrinkle in confusion before she continues, "I promised... I promised myself I wouldn't ever let this happen. T-then you happened... and now I'm going to end up like him." She buries her head in the crook of my neck and lets out a shaky exhale.

She's not crying anymore, just sniffling every now and then while tears continue to mar her face.

"What did I do? And who are you going to end up like?" I ask softly, not wanting to trigger her into another panic attack.

"You were you. You were everything. Just like Mama was to him. You're the heir, Luca, a man who faces death every single day. What will I become if you die? What will happen to me then?" she whispers.

"You're worried about what would happen if I died? My family would take care of you, Iz."

She jumps off my lap and glares at me.

"That's not my point, Luca!" she yells and clenches her fists in anger.

"Then what is your point? Explain it to me."

"My point is that my father loved Mama more than life itself and when she died, he became the man he is now. He's a tyrant that would use his own daughter to make a deal, he's a man that would belittle me and use me for whatever means necessary. He doesn't give a fuck about me or anyone else anymore. He's cold. He's distant. I promised myself I would never become like him! I promised myself I would never, *ever* fall in love because that would risk me becoming *him*. But you had to be so... so *you*. You cared for me in a way no one else ever did, you accepted me for everything that I am, you saw the real me and didn't shy away, you made me fucking love you and it's ridiculous because I've known you less than two months." She stops her rant and takes a deep breath, her chest heaving and a wild look in her eyes. She's beautiful, perfect, she's everything and she's fucking mine, and she loves *me*.

Fuck, she's in love with me.

All of my worries from the past few weeks fade away as I stare at the woman who owns every single part of me, I stand and step in-front of her. She goes to step back, but I clutch her shoulders and pin her in place.

"No more running, Izzy. You want to know what would happen if I died? I won't tell you, because it's not going to happen. I'll always come home to you, I'll always be here, driving you crazy, taking care of you, being the one you can cry to and laugh with and watching those shit tv shows you force me to sit through. I'll be here *with* you, I'll be here *for* you, I'll be here loving you every single day, Izzy. You don't get to hide from me anymore, okay? Because I love every single fucking part of you, the good, the bad, the insane. You came into my life and flipped it upside down, you've changed everything. You've changed me and I wouldn't want it any other way because I can't imagine my life without you in it. You think I'm going to leave? Fuck that, I'm not giving you the chance to move on to another man, Izzy. I'll cheat death to make sure you'll always be mine."

I don't give her a chance to say anything else as I slam my lips to hers and pour all my emotion into the kiss. Her lip's part on a gasp and I use the opportunity to slip my tongue inside her mouth, leisurely swiping my tongue against hers before nibbling on her bottom lip.

I pull back to look down at her. Even with her eyes puffy and red from crying, her hair a mess on the top of her head, her face free of makeup, she's still the most goddamn beautiful sight I've ever seen.

"You love me," she whispers so quietly I barely hear her.

"Of course I do, baby. How could I not?" I give her a lopsided smile, and she rewards me with a wide smile that pulls the air from my lungs.

"I'm sorry I'm so crazy and freaked out," she says with a frown, making me chuckle.

"You wouldn't be you otherwise. I told you I never want you to change. Never apologize for being everything that you are." I press my lips to hers in a quick, tender kiss before lifting her up bridal style and carrying her towards the bedroom.

"Are you gonna fuck me now, Luca?" she asks sweetly, and I shake my head while making a tsking sound.

"You've shut me out this past week, you've been a brat, gave me attitude and made me second guess myself and us, you're not getting fucked, Izzy. You're getting punished," I say and throw her on the bed where she lands with a squeal.

I pull her t-shirt over her head and slide her shorts down her legs, leaving her naked on the bed and staring up at me with hooded eyes.

"I'm all yours, Luca. Punish me, use me, fuck me, love me. I'm yours to do what you want with, always."

Fuck me.

CHAPTER THIRTY-FOUR

Izzy

The hungry look in his eyes, the outline of his hard cock straining against his shorts that's begging me to reach out and touch it, the heaving of his chest, the ragged breath that leaves him as I say the words that I mean with every part of me. He craves me just as much as I need him.

He loves me, he's been loving me for a while, I was just too blind to see it. Too scared, too worried about the *what ifs* to open myself up to the possibility of loving a man who's in danger more often than not and being loved by him in return.

"Fuck, I love you," Luca says before he strolls over to the dresser and pulls out a tie. He comes back to me and motions for me to give him my hands and I do so willingly.

"Remember your safe word?" he asks before wrapping the tie around my wrists and adjusting me so he can tie my wrists to the headboard. I nod my head and tug on my arms to see how much wiggle room I have. The short answer? *Not a lot.*

"Just say the word and I'll untie you," he says softly and presses a kiss to my forehead before he strips out of his shirt and shorts leaving him naked for me to stare at him unabashedly.

His abs ripple as he climbs on the bed and crawls up towards me.

"Do you know what this past week has been like for me, Izzy? Having to watch you pull away from me has gutted me, baby," he whispers and positions himself between my legs, the stubble on his cheek grazes the side of my thigh and I shuffle on the bed needing friction.

"I'm sorry," I whisper sincerely.

"I know you are, but I'm still gonna teach you a lesson so you know not to do it again," he whispers against me before he dips his head and swipes his tongue across my clit. I'm so fucking turned on that I whimper at the slightest contact.

Needing more, I tilt my hips up, but he pulls back. "You need to stay still. You move and I stop, got that?" I nod in agreement.

He lowers his lips down and his tongue licks at my opening before sliding up my seam and he wraps his lips around my clit and sucks. I fight every instinct I have and keep still, not wanting him to stop.

He slowly sneaks two fingers inside me and continues licking and sucking at a tortuous pace. The ache inside me builds and builds. But he doesn't up his pace. He continues at a slow pace and I'm beginning to see why he would call this a punishment. It's *torture.*

"*Please,*" I beg, it comes out as a hoarse whisper and he *finally* picks up his pace, my walls tighten and I'm right fucking *there* but the asshole pulls back at the last second with a chuckle and it takes all my self-control to not wrap my legs around his neck and strangle him.

"What sort of punishment would this be if I let you come straight away?" He raises his brow and I glare at him in defiance while inwardly cursing him.

"I'm sorry, please... *please*, let me come," I whimper, and he gives me a sadistic smirk in return as he lowers his head back down to my center. This time he picks up his pace, fucking me with his fingers and mouth in tandem. But, *of course*, once I get to the edge, ready to fall headfirst into a blissful orgasm, the asshole pulls back and chuckles.

Once again, he dips back down and continues the process, bringing me to the edge before pulling back right as I'm about to orgasm. I'm seriously debating removing my hands from this tie and just getting myself off.

"Have you had enough yet?" His voice is a deep rasp and I nod my head enthusiastically while begging him with my eyes to let this be over.

"Okay, baby," he says and leans back, grabs hold of my legs and flips me so I'm lying on my front. He maneuvers me so I'm on my knees. My hands are now crossed over each other but still tied to the headboard so I grab hold of the bar that runs across it to keep my balance and to stop myself from falling face first.

He lands a sharp slap to my ass which makes me wince before pleasure shoots through me and I wiggle, trying to get closer to him, trying to feel something, *anything*. Tears stream down my face as I beg and plead with him while he continues to spank me.

I'm so fucking desperate to come that at this point I'll do just about anything.

"Do you think you've been punished enough?" he says and lines his cock at my entrance. "Do you think you've learned your lesson, *mia regina?*"

My head bobs up and down in a nod. "*Please,*" I whisper so quietly I'm not even sure if he hears me before he slowly thrusts inside me.

"You can come, baby." He picks up his pace and my insides tighten in anticipation before pleasure rolls through me and I'm screaming his name while my pussy strangles his dick through my orgasm.

"Fuck, fuck, *fuck, Izzy,*" he chokes out. As the wave of my orgasm subsides, he leans over and loosens the tie around my wrists, freeing me from the headboard while continuing his pace. He slams into me another few times before pulling out and flipping me back onto my back and lining himself back up and shoving back inside me again.

"You feel so fucking good." *Thrust.* "So fucking tight." *Thrust.* "So fucking wet." *Thrust.* "So fucking mine."

"You look beautiful laid beneath me, completely at my mercy," he groans as he brings his lips to mine in a heated kiss.

He pulls away and sits back on his heels before he grabs my hips and adjusts the angle so he's lifting my ass in the air and he's hitting that spot that has me seeing stars. "Come for me, baby, let me feel your pretty little pussy flutter around me, let me feel you tighten around my cock once more before I fill you up with my cum."

His words are all it takes to push me over the edge and then I'm freefalling into another orgasm. His movements become erratic, and he groans my name as he spills inside me.

I'm so exhausted I can't even keep my eyes open, I vaguely feel him cleaning me up with a warm cloth and whispering that he loves me as he pulls a blanket over me before the darkness pulls me under.

It's our last day on the island. We've spent the last week wrapped up in each other, happily living in our little bubble. We've explored the island, cooked dinner together before Luca sat me on his lap and we ate from the same plate. We've gone back to Capri for dinner when we wanted a change of scenery. He tells me he loves me every chance he gets and makes love to me—or our version of making love—every morning, every night and in between too.

The time away from New York has been perfect. We leave to go home tomorrow morning and I can't help but wonder if we'll continue the way we have been once we get home or if we're just too wrapped up in our bubble that once we leave, things will be different.

It doesn't help that Luca's been acting weird all day. He fucked me against the kitchen wall this morning, but he's distanced himself from me since, he's acting skittish and he's definitely hiding something.

My phone rings and I sit up from where I've been lying on the couch to reach it, I pick it up and see Enzo's contact on the screen.

"Hey," I say when I answer.

"Hey, sis."

I roll my eyes at the nickname. "What's up? Why are you calling me and not Luca?"

"I just wanted to tell you that since the books I bought you got destroyed I went back and got you some more, I just dropped them at your apartment," he throws out casually, and I inwardly groan that he's keeping up this idiotic ruse with his girl.

"Enzo, for fuck's sake. Just talk to the girl, take her to dinner, coffee, a drink, I don't fucking know. Just stop lurking in dark alleyways to watch her, coming up with excuses to visit her store and just *talk* to her. And STOP letting yourself into our apartment while we're not home, you're a pain in the ass."

"But you love me." He chuckles, and I huff out a breath. "When have I ever told you that I love you? I barely tolera—" I'm cut off as Luca snatches the phone out of my hands and looks at the screen before bringing it to his ear.

"I suggest you delete my wife's number before I catch the next flight home and fucking strangle you, Enzo," he growls and hangs up before swinging his gaze to me.

"Well, hello to you too, husband. How nice of you to grace me with your presence. Now tell me, is there a reason you're avoiding me?" I ask and bat my eyes at him.

His mouth opens and closes but no sound comes out and he spins on his heel and stalks out of the room.

What just happened?

I take a deep breath before standing and following after him, he walks through the kitchen and out of the double doors. As soon as I get outside my breath catches in my throat and my steps falter.

The sun is just setting so the sky is a deep blue. There are candles set up as a walkway across the sand to where Luca stands in the middle of the beach, my eyes meet his and his gaze is so full of love that all I want to do is run and fly into his arms.

CHAPTER THIRTY-FIVE

Luca

I'm not sure why I'm so nervous, but I feel like I've been walking on eggshells all day waiting for this moment. I've barely spoke to Izzy all day out of fear that she'd see right through me and realize what I was up to.

I've never made a romantic gesture before, considering I've never had a girlfriend before, so this is a big step for me.

When I walked into the sitting room to grab Izzy and overheard her on the phone to someone saying something about loving them, I saw red at the thought of her telling another man that she loved them. Then I realized it was my annoying little brother and I calmed the hell down before she decided to ask what was going on with me. I got the fuck out of there and made it out to where I had everything set up rather than reply to her, figured it was easier because I knew she wouldn't let me get away with saying nothing, I knew she'd follow me. Stubborn pain in the ass that she is.

Izzy storms out of the patio doors and halts as she takes in the scene surrounding her. Her eyes meet mine and they widen before she takes measured steps towards me, never breaking eye contact.

"What's going on?" she asks as she reaches me, and I swallow as I take her in. She's dressed in a pale blue summer dress with her feet bare. She's not wearing any makeup and her hair is piled on top of her head as usual. She's fucking breathtaking.

I clear my throat and do the one thing I thought I would never do—drop down on one knee.

Izzy's mouth pops open and she stares wide-eyed at me and whispers my name. I pull the small box from my pocket and flip the lid, making her breath catch. She doesn't even bother looking at the ring, she just stares into my eyes and waits to hear what I have to say.

"Izzy, you deserve the world. You deserve sunshine and roses and rainbows and fucking unicorns. You deserve everything little girls dream of, and everything grown women read in those ridiculous romance novels and wish they had. You deserve to wake up each morning knowing your husband will come home to you and only you. You deserve to be treated like the queen you are." I take a deep breath and take hold of her hand.

"I don't deserve you, baby. You should have had a real proposal, a real wedding which you got to plan yourself, you should have been able to choose your own husband instead of being stuck with me." She shakes her head at me, but I continue. "You deserve everything, and I'll give you it if you let me, this is me letting you choose, I want you to choose me, baby. I want to re-do our wedding, I want to have a real marriage, I want to spend my life with you. I want to stand up in front of a room full of family and friends—not business associates there for appearances—and vow to love you forever. I want you to vow to me that you'll spend the rest of your life loving me, vow to me that you'll never leave, no matter what hard times we go through or arguments and fights we have. Vow to be mine, baby. I love you so fucking much. Marry me, Iz, properly this time." I finish my speech and hold my breath as she stares at me with tears pooling in those gorgeous eyes of hers that I get lost in every single day.

Her legs buckle and she drops to the ground in front of me, she wraps her arms around my neck before bringing her mouth to mine in a passionate kiss. I freeze for a second before responding and my tongue tangles with hers, it takes all of my self-control to pull back and not take the kiss further, but somehow, I find the strength to lean back and look into her eyes.

"That's not an answer, *mia regina*."

"I love you, Luca. So fucking much. Did you doubt my answer would be anything other than yes?" She smiles and it's my favorite type. The type of smile that lights up her whole face, making her eyes shine and making my chest constrict. "I can't wait to spend the rest of my life loving every single part of you. I see you, Luca. Thank you so much for seeing me too. You've been everything I never thought I could have. I came into this marriage expecting to have to fight tooth and nail every day for my place in this world, but you've shown me that not all men are the same, you've shown me what love feels like, what safety feels like, what compassion feels like. Of course, I'll marry you, *amore mio*."

My breath catches at the nickname. I never thought I'd be one to engage in fucking pet names. But here I am, sat with the love of my life. She's my little demon, *mia regina*, my *everything*.

"Thank fuck," I say before slamming my mouth back to hers and pulling her to me so she's straddling my lap before realizing I'm still holding the ring box in my hand. I break the kiss and rest my forehead against hers for a beat then sit back so I can pull the ring from the box and place it on her finger.

Izzy stares at the ring, it's a three-carat diamond ring on a white gold band. But the thing that makes it *her?* There are tiny diamonds nestled around the large one in the middle, made to look like a crown.

She is my queen, after all.

"It's perfect," she whispers, and I smile, relieved that she likes it since I had no fucking clue what I was doing that day as I explained my vision to the jeweler, only hoping that he could make my vision come to life.

"You're perfect, baby." That word doesn't even begin to describe her, but it's the best I can voice. It's like she was made for me, she fits my jagged edges perfectly and brings light into my previously gray life.

Izzy brings her lips back to mine and shifts so that she can undo the zip on my shorts, I lift us both up as I help her pull them down and my cock springs free. I've been hard since the moment I pulled her onto my lap, but I wasn't going to ruin the moment by trying to fuck her. Seems like she has other ideas. I run my hand up her leg and find her pussy bare and already ready for me.

Fuck, she hasn't been wearing anything under this dress all day.

She probably removed them while I was avoiding her as an act of rebellion. *My little demon.*

I shift and slowly sink inside her. I start to thrust up into her, but she puts her hands on my shoulders to stop me and takes control. She rides me slowly while we continue kissing under the night sky, shrouded in candlelight. It's passionate, it's loving, it's intimate, it's everything.

It's the complete opposite of how we usually have sex, we both like our sex rough and hard but this just feels so fucking right in this moment.

Her walls clamp down and I can tell she's on the edge, I bring my thumb to her clit and rub small circles around the bundle of nerves. She lets out a long, throaty moan as she finds her release and it's the most beautiful sound that I've ever heard. Her movements stutter because she's so lost in her pleasure and I grab onto her hips so I can help her keep her balance while I thrust up into her, it only takes a couple of seconds until I'm groaning into her mouth as I fill her with my cum.

"*Ti amo*," I whisper into her hair as I hold her to my chest. I don't want to ever let her go, I want to freeze us in this moment forever, sat under the stars with my girl in my arms seems pretty much like peace to me. Only I can't freeze this moment, we have reality waiting for us once we land back in New York tomorrow.

"*Ti amo tanto.*"

We've been home for four days, and all I want to do is kidnap Izzy and drag her back to the island, away from other people and away from our responsibilities. I've hardly seen her these past few days; I've been too busy catching up on everything I missed while we were away. The only time I've had with her is on a night where I've fucked her into a slumber then held her in my arms as we both slept.

Luckily, I didn't miss much while we were on the island, just the usual shipments and day-to-day business. Marco met with the Irish without me since we rushed out the last time we met with him. The only interesting thing that happened was Muñoz finally came out of the woodwork and contacted my dad for a meeting. We're on our way there now to meet him at a restaurant in neutral territory.

We're taking five SUV's full of men with us because while it's likely the bastard won't try anything; we'd rather be on the safe side in case he does. We pull up in front of the restaurant and me, Dad and Marco file out of the car. We opted to not bring Enzo on the off chance he flipped and shot the place up at the sight of Muñoz.

"Bet you wished you'd stayed in bed with your wife, huh?" Marco says with a raised brow, and it takes me by surprise seeing the emotion in his eyes, there's something that looks a lot like regret flash across his face before he masks it and I give him a nod but don't verbally respond, too confused by the exchange to voice it.

We walk into the building, and I scan the inside for threats. The asshole we've been at war with for the better part of the last year is sat at a table in the corner casually sipping from a glass of whiskey, he has two men stood behind him and I spot another four dotted around the room that are trying—and failing—to blend in.

The three of us walk over and take a seat at the table, our men know to surround the perimeter in case something goes down.

He swallows a gulp of his drink and clears his throat.

"Thank you for meeting with me," he says in his thick Spanish accent and looks between the three of us before settling his gaze on our father.

"Why are we here, Alejandro?" Dad says, and his brow raises at the insult of him calling him by his first name, but he doesn't offer a retort. *Smart man.*

"This war has gone on long enough, don't you think? I think it's about time we called a truce and called it a day with all the attacks on each other."

I hold in a snort and refrain from pointing out that he and Novikov were the ones who started this war to begin with. He only has himself to blame for the lives and business his organization has lost.

"And what do we get out of this truce?" I ask instead.

His gaze flies to me and I notice the subtle way his eyes dart around. He's nervous. He should be.

"I want to reinstate our old deal, so we keep our territories and form an alliance on other factions threatening our shipments coming in at the docks." he says with a nod as if we give a fuck about what he's saying.

"What's stopping us from doing with you what we did with Novikov? You did see the message Luca here left, didn't you?" our father asks, and Muñoz audibly gulps, this time I can't hold in my snicker and Dad jabs me with his elbow, subtly telling me to behave.

"Nothing is, but this has gone on long enough, if I lose any more men the balance of organizations will tip, and we all know that that's bad for business not only for me, but for everyone else. Just take the deal, shake on a truce and let's finish this."

Dad looks to me and I give him a sharp nod, I might fuck around with him, but we all know we're better off just taking the truce, we don't want to lose any more of our men either.

Our father holds out his hand and Muñoz shakes it before standing and taking a few steps towards the exit but before he leaves, he turns back to face us.

"In light of our truce, there's something you should know. Someone close to a member of your family is the one behind your recent attack, they won't stop until they get what they want," he says before strolling out of the restaurant and leaving us all to wonder the same thing.

What the fuck was that?

And who the fuck was he referring to?

Someone close to a member of your family.

None of us are really that close to anyone. I'm close with Alec, but he's out of the question. Dad keeps to himself and the higher capos, Marco barely tolerates our presence, never mind anyone else's. Izzy doesn't know anyone in the city. The only one left is Enzo, but he's as reclusive as you come unless you count the girl he's stalking, but she doesn't even know he exists so she's out of the question.

So, *who the fuck* could it be?

We leave the restaurant in silence and pile back into the car, I'm in the passenger seat while Dad drives and Marco is in the back.

"Any ideas?" Dad asks once all of the doors are closed, and I shake my head.

"What about someone close to Izzy?" Marco asks from the backseat, and I shake my head again.

"She doesn't know anyone in the city, the only people she has regular contact with is me and *fucking Enzo*. Besides, she could rival you for her inability to tolerate other people."

"Well, we need to figure out who tried to kill my son and daughter-in-law. And when we do? I'll display their head in Times Square as a warning of what happens if some *idiota* tries to harm my children."

CHAPTER THIRTY-SIX

Izzy

"Do you really have to go out? Can't you just ask Enzo to pick it up for you? I'm sure he'll do it happily," Luca sighs into the phone and I roll my eyes.

It's been just over three weeks since we got back from our honeymoon, and I haven't left the apartment once. I got so bored that I ended up reading some of the books Enzo dropped off while we were away. What he didn't realize was one of the books was part of a duet and now I *need* to read the second one.

I called Luca and asked him to send Tomasso over so I could head out to the bookstore, but the asshole would rather keep me under lock and key.

"I've been cooped up for three fucking weeks, I'm going out, so either send Tomasso or I'm going alone."

"Fuck, *fine*. But if you sense even the smallest hint of danger, you call me, okay? Or maybe I should skip my meeting and come with you? I could talk to Dad and see if—"

"For fuck's sake, Luca!" I yell into the phone. "I'll be fine! You're not skipping anything, you're going to go to that meeting and do whatever it is that you have to do while I go to the bookstore to buy a book like a fucking normal person, normal people don't need their husbands trailing after them all of the time."

"I'm sorry," he sighs, and I feel bad for yelling at him. "I just want you to be safe, baby. I can't stand the thought of something happening to you."

I swallow the knot in my throat and promise him that I'll be fine before hanging up and heading to the elevator.

Luca

I love you, be safe.

I love you too x

I persuaded Tomasso to walk to the bookstore rather than drive. It's only a few blocks away and I've really been slacking on my training since moving here. I need to get back to my routine.

He grumbled something under his breath but didn't argue with my reasoning that it would be just as easy to walk than it would to drive.

We walk into the store and come face to face with Robyn who gives me a big smile.

"Hey, Robyn, right?" I ask as though I don't know so much more about her—or her entire life—and she nods.

"That's right and you're... Isla? Izzy?"

"Izzy."

"Right, sorry. Your brother-in-law came back in again after that first time," she says with a tight smile and something flashes in her eyes.

For fuck's sake, what did he do?

"Yep, I've just got back from my honeymoon and came for the second book in a duet he bought me," I say.

She shows me the book I need before taking it to the counter and ringing up the purchase.

"I know this is really unprofessional, but can I ask what the deal is with your brother-in -law?" she asks, and I bite back a laugh.

Oh sweetheart, you really don't want to know.

"He's single, if that's what you're asking," I say with a grin and she smiles shyly as she shakes her head.

"No... that wasn't what I meant, but—you know what? Never mind, just forget I said anything."

My brows furrow at her obvious discomfort.

"Is everything okay?"

"Of course," she says and gives me a forced smile. "Thank you so much for coming back."

I can't blame the girl for not wanting to talk to me, I just hope she has *someone* she can confide in.

I make a mental note to call Enzo later to tell him to sort his shit out, this has gone on long enough and clearly, something is going on with her.

I grab the bag she hands out to me and thank her before making my way out of the store with my shadow following me. Me and Tomasso stroll through the streets of New York back towards the apartment, he doesn't speak much, which I'm grateful for because my mind is scattered thinking about the mark on Robyn's arm I spotted as she handed me the bag.

I know that Enzo would never hurt her, so who the fuck did? I would have asked her about it, but I know she wouldn't tell me, she doesn't know me, so why should she?

We're just walking past a group of people, and I go to grab my phone from my pocket to call Enzo when I notice Tomasso's no longer beside me. I turn around to see if I can spot where he's disappeared to, but it's like he's vanished into thin air. I spin back around, confused as fuck about where he could have gone and I choke on my breath at the sight in front of me,

Stood next to a parked car on the side of the pavement is a man I never thought I would see again. His face is a welcome familiarity and I stand slack jawed staring at him. I blink a few times, worried that my mind has conjured him up, but my view stays the same. The man who meant everything to me, the man who I never thought I would see again is standing right in front of me.

He's really here.

I take off in a run towards him and fling myself at him. I wrap my arms around him, and he does the same, pulling me into tight hug and tears stream down my face. People around us give us funny looks but I don't give a fuck, they can think what they want. He's fucking here, my arms are wrapped around him.

He's here.

He's fucking here.

I can't believe he's really fucking here.

"What... what the—"

"Shhh, not here, *piccolina*," he says and tilts his head towards the car we're stood next to.

He lets me go and opens the door for me, I slide inside, and he rounds the car and gets in the driver's side.

"I missed you so fucking much," I say with a watery smile as I stare at him, taking in every inch of his face.

CHAPTER THIRTY-SEVEN

Luca

I step out of the meeting being held for one of our legal business dealings to answer my father's phone call, knowing he wouldn't be calling me during a meeting if it wasn't important.

"What's wrong?" I ask.

"Get to the estate, there's something you need to see. Make it quick," he says before hanging up.

I instruct my assistant to tell the others in the conference room that I've been called away in an emergency before leaving the building and driving to my father's estate. I drove like a bat out of hell to make it here in just under twenty minutes.

I walk into the office and my steps falter when I see Marco and Enzo glaring daggers at each other. "What's going on? Why do you two look like you want to kill each other?" I ask before closing the door and taking a seat in front of Dad.

"Because he won't give her the—" Enzo starts but is cut off by Marco.

"E-fucking-nough Enzo!" he bellows. "It's as clear as fucking day," he growls and gestures towards a small brown package on the desk. I can't remember the last time I saw Marco lose his temper the way he is right now.

I stare at the envelope as if it'll give me the answers to whatever the hell is going on.

Dad clears his throat and slides the package towards me before he swallows. There's pity in his eyes and I fucking hate the sight.

What the goddamn hell is going on?

I take the package and study each of them with a raised brow before opening it and pulling out a note and thumb drive.

Did you ever wonder how we always
knew how to find your pretty little
wife, Romano? You should keep a closer eye on your toys.

My breath stalls and I choke down the denial crawling up my throat before inserting the thumb drive into the laptop in front of me. I click on the file with Izzy's name on and I furrow my brow while examining the picture I'm presented with.

There's a photo of Izzy in a store at the mall and she's stood next to a tall, black-haired woman. It looks like they're talking as Izzy passes her something.

I click to the next image and it's the same woman again, only this time it's an image of her handing something to Muñoz.

Rage, like nothing ever before bubbles up inside me but I push it down and click to the next image.

The image that greets me makes me sick to my stomach and black dots line my vision. It's Izzy, my fucking wife, sat on Muñoz's lap in a club. She's wearing a wig, but I'd know my wife anywhere.

What the fuck were you doing, Iz?

The time stamp on the image is from a few days before the wedding, so she could have just been getting the information she needed about the Amate's.

I click the screen again and this time, it's a video. I press play and force myself to watch as my wife grinds her ass up against Muñoz in the middle of the club. They're wearing the same clothes as the image before in the video. I feel sick.

I'm going to kill him. I'll rip out his insides while I make her watch.

I'll string him up by his balls while I carve into his fucking chest, I'll—

"There's one more you need to see, son," my father whispers, and I take a deep breath before clicking the screen again. It's another video, only this time, it's dated with today's date.

I press play and my head swims. It's Izzy on the sidewalk about a block away from our apartment. There's a man stood next to a black car and once she sees him she stands and stares as him for a beat before running into his arms, they stand and hug each other for what feels like minutes, she's crying, and I have to sit and watch the woman I love more than anything in this world get into a car with another man. It's like a scene out of a goddamn romance movie. I can feel the emotion wafting off her through the screen and if I weren't already seated it would have brought me to my knees. *Christ*, I feel my heart shatter inside my chest as my soul fucking crumbles to pieces at my feet.

My chest aches and I can't breathe. My eyes sting and I blink to try and clear my vision.

The pain.

The lies.

The fucking *betrayal*.

I take out my phone to call Izzy, but the line cuts off without ringing.

I press Tomasso's contact but it just rings and rings before going to voicemail.

"It might not be what it looks like, we could have it all—" once again, Enzo is cut off. Only this time it's by a knock at the door. Dad yells for whoever it is to come in and one of our foot soldiers comes in, his face pale.

"Sorry to interrupt, but Tomasso Greco was found dead in an alley with this hanging out of his neck," he says before handing a plastic bag to Marco and leaving the room.

Marco glances at me before taking the object out of the bag and I see fucking red.

It's a five-inch blade with a gold embossed handle.

It's one of Izzy's knives.

I'd know it anywhere considering she treats them like her fucking children.

She refuses to leave the house without at least one strapped to her.

She killed him then ran off with another fucking man.

She left her knife, so we'd know it was her who killed him.

I'm going to fucking find her, then I'll make her fucking pay.

What a goddamn joke, I gave her everything. I gave her all of me, and she stabbed me in the heart the same way she did Tomasso in his neck.

Tomasso.

Fuck, a man I've known nearly all my life is dead, and it was my *wife* that killed him.

"There's nothing else to it, Enzo. I think the picture painted is pretty clear. My wife is a lying, traitorous bitch. We need to find her. We don't tolerate treachery, even if I am married to her," I growl and throw the laptop at the wall where the screen shatters. Just like my mind. I don't know if I'm going to be sick or go on a murderous rampage, the emotions swirling around inside me make my head ache and I have to close my eyes while trying to focus on my breathing.

Fuck this.

Fuck *her*.

Fuck it all.

Fuck *everything*.

Run and hide, little demon. I'll stop at nothing to destroy you, just like you've destroyed me.

She was my queen, my love, my life. And now she's my prey.

F ive days and nothing. There's no sign of her. She left everything in the apartment. She didn't take a single thing; I came home five days ago, and fucking destroyed the place in a fit of rage. She even left her laptop, but I refrained from setting it on fire on the off chance it can help us locate her.

I keep thinking back to that text she got while we were in the hospital. Clearly, I'm an idiot for believing I could trust her and thinking it was just some random from her past.

I'm up on the roof of our building, staring out at the city below me. For some reason, we never came up here together, which I'm glad for because it's now the only place in the building that isn't haunted with memories of her.

Every time I'm in the apartment I see her lying on the sofa, rolling her eyes at me while I talk shit about whatever she's watching. I see her sat at the kitchen island working on her laptop as she scrunches her brow in that adorable way at what she's reading. I can't even sleep in my own bed because it smells like her.

I miss her. And that's ridiculous, I'm supposed to hate her, yet I feel like I'm missing a piece of myself.

The pain hasn't left since I watched her jump into another man's arms. I just wish I could forget about her, forget about the good times we had spent laughing, forget about that fucking night on the beach.

Jesus. None of it was real. It was all a lie.

We've turned the city inside out looking for her, but she left no trace of herself anywhere. We tried following the car they left in on the city's cameras, but it was no good. They've vanished into thin air. I debated calling her father, but he doesn't give a shit about her so it would be pointless. We also need to find out who the fuck sent us the thumb drive, because they're the ones who tried to blow up my brother.

Did you ever wonder how we always knew how to find your pretty little wife, Romano?

Fuck, does that mean that she planned it? She knew what would happen. My brother could have died. *She could have fucking died.*

I take a large gulp from the bottle of whiskey I'm holding to swallow the bile that claws up my throat at the thought.

I hear the door to the roof click open and a quiet curse from behind me. Great, just what I need.

Marco and Alec take a seat on either side of me, and I inwardly groan. *This better not be a fucking intervention.*

"Fuck, Marco, I knew it had to be bad when it was you who called me, but I didn't fucking expect this," Alec says.

"I told you, asshole. We need him to get his head on straight."

"We need to take him out to get him laid, or burn all the bitch's clothes, that will help, right? Or we could get him a voodoo doll that looks like her for him to stick pins in."

"Why the fuck did I call you?" Marco groans.

"Have you found her yet? Have you killed her yet? That's the punishment for treachery in your world, right?"

"No one's laying a hand on her," I bark as I finally join the conversation that they've been having as though I'm not sat right fucking between them.

"Luc—"

"No, Marco. I don't give a fuck what you say, you won't fucking hurt her, you won't lay a hand on her, you'll let me deal with her."

"We need to fucking find her first."

"Right," I say with a nod and turn towards Alec. "Can you help? Can you try and find her? And find out who the fuck sent us the thumb drive? Our resident computer geek is useless, we need your help, man."

"Sure, man. But only if you sober the fuck up and sort your shit out. Drinking yourself stupid isn't helping matters," he says and squeezes my shoulder.

"Thanks," I say and settle my gaze on Marco. "Where's Enzo? I'm surprised he didn't join in on this little outing of yours."

He quietly curses before peering up at the sky. "He still doesn't believe it, he won't speak to me or Dad because he thinks she's innocent," he says with a swallow, and I shake my head with a sigh.

It wasn't only me she fucked over, Enzo let her in, he let her get close and now he'll refuse to believe the evidence that's clear as fucking day because of her Oscar worthy acting skills and the fact that it seemed like she understood him when no one other than us ever has.

"He'll see the truth for himself once we find her. It'll hurt him the same way it's hurting me, but at least he'll see the truth." I give him a confident nod and hand him the bottle I'm holding. We may as well get fucked up tonight, because starting tomorrow I'm putting all my effort and resources into finding my little liar of a wife.

CHAPTER THIRTY-EIGHT

Izzy

FIVE DAYS AGO.

I wake up with a groan.

Why the fuck is my head pounding? Why are my muscles aching? And why the hell am I sleeping on what feels like the floor? I search my memory for the last thing I remember.

The bookstore.

The bruise around Robyn's wrist.

Tomasso disappearing into thin air.

The ghost of my past having his arms around me.

Getting into the car.

A sharp pain in my neck.

Feeling like I was going to pass out before everything faded away.

Holy shit. Alessi is alive.

And he fucking drugged me.

I'll kill him.

My eyes fly open, and I drag my body into a sitting position. I'm on the floor of what looks like a basement, my left wrist is cuffed and chained to the wall, and I do a quick check of my body. I'm still wearing all my clothes, and I'm not injured anywhere other than my pride, but any weapons I had on me have been removed.

Of course, they have. He's the one who taught you everything you know.

I pull on the cuff around my wrist but it's too tight for me to wiggle out of. I grab the chain and try prying it from the wall but it's too secure. There's no way I'm getting free from it.

Why the fuck would the man I considered my best friend, the man who was like a brother to me, my family, fake his death and then over a year later kidnap and me and lock me in a fucking basement? What does he have to gain?

T HREE DAYS AGO.

I have no clue how long I've been here. There are no windows for me to be able to see the time of day. I haven't slept, not wanting to leave myself in a vulnerable position.

I've had no food, no water, no fucking bathroom to use since I've been here. It could be hours, it could be days, it could be a week. I don't fucking know. What I do know is that Luca will be searching for me, surely, he's close to figuring out where I am? He wouldn't stop until I was back with him.

I keep that thought on repeat, because if I don't? I'll lose my goddamn mind.

The deadbolt on the door on the opposite side of the room clanks and I shift my gaze towards it as Alessi steps inside the room,

I glare at him but stay silent. If he wants me to beg him to release me, he'll be waiting for a fucking lifetime. The only man I'll ever beg is my husband.

He looks the same as he did before he "died" except for the fact the has more scruff surrounding his jaw. He's tall, standing at 6'4, with a wide build and broad shoulders. If I was at my full strength and wasn't chained to a fucking wall, I might have been able to get the jump on him. But I'm weak, I have no chance in hell of getting free without a weapon.

"I missed you, *piccolina*."

The nickname he's called me since I was a teen makes my gut churn. How dare he call me the pet name I always used to associate with safety? How dare he speak to me so casually, as though were catching up over coffee? How fucking *dare* he?

"What the fuck am I doing here, Alessi?"

"You're going to tell me everything you know about the Romano family and their empire, their business dealings, their alliances, everything."

"Like fuck I am," I growl as I glare defiantly at him.

He chuckles and raises his brow. "You've been here for two days, little one, and your husband thinks you've run off with your lover—that's the way me and your father made it seem when we sent him a thumb drive with some pretty damning evidence." He grins.

Your father.

My father helped him kidnap me. Of course, he did. Dear old Daddy strikes again. I want to ask what evidence, but I know that's what he's waiting for, he wants me to question him.

Once he realizes I'm not going to voice the questions swimming around inside my head, he sighs before taking a seat on the bench in front of me.

"There's you dancing with Muñoz at the club and you sitting on his lap. We even set up a little run in you had with a woman. Remember the woman who asked for your opinion on which hard drive she needed? We paid her and took a picture as you handed her the hard drive best suited for her, then we took a picture of her flirting with Muñoz and set it up like she was passing him something... see where this is going?" He gives me a manic grin and I shake my head. There's no fucking way Luca would believe this shit, right? *Right?*

"But the best part was your reaction when you saw me on the street. The way you greeted me? How you ran and wrapped your arms around me? That's fucking Hallmark shit, *piccolina*."

Fuck. I know exactly how it appears, and now I know that Luca will be looking for me for the wrong reasons. He'll want me dead.

"So, save yourself some trouble and tell me everything you know. Your husband won't be coming to save you, the only one fighting for you is *you*."

"Go fuck yourself," I say with a smirk. Luca may think I'm capable of betraying him, but I fucking won't. He may have believed the worst of me, and that cuts deep. But I'm not going to do shit for the asshole in front of me, he can try however he likes, but I'm no traitor.

TWO DAYS AGO.

Alessi left me some water and a piece of bread yesterday after realizing he couldn't get me to talk, so at least I've had something to keep me going.

The deadbolt moves again, only this time instead of being greeted by the face of my dead best friend, I'm greeted by the view of my father.

Oh, joy.

"Hey, Papa. Good to see you," I say sarcastically with a nod.

"Enough, Isabella. You'll tell us everything you know about the Romano's, you'll help us take them all down." His voice is gruff and commanding, and I don't bother to hide my eye roll. Gone are the days where I'll play pretend and hide behind the mask of perfect princess.

"Ah good, you're not hiding anymore. Did you know it was my idea for Alessi to train you? Did you know that we worked together in faking his death?" he asks with a smirk. "We've had everything planned for years. We'd use you to take down the New York outfit, and you will marry him once the Romano boy is dead, and he will be the one to take over as my heir. I've always seen something in him, something promising. Over the past year we've been slowly moving into different... business ventures. You exceeded our expectations with your ability to use computers, you'll make a great addition to our team that finds our *buyers.*"

Buyers. He's talking about sex trafficking. I've been keeping my eye on suspicious disappearances in and around Chicago, but I never once thought it was my father. I even flagged it and sent it to Alec for him to investigate it.

This *motherfucker* has started selling girls. Jesus fucking Christ. I need to find a way to contact Alec so he can locate the girls. Fuck everything else, those girls need rescuing.

I keep quiet, still not telling him anything about my husband or his family, and he pulls out his phone to send a text.

A few minutes later, Alessi strolls in and gives me a wicked grin.

"You won't talk the easy way, *piccolina*? That's fine, we'll see if you can survive the hard way," he says and nods towards the table in the corner of the room. It looks like something that belongs to a mental institution, used to strap patients down.

Oh fuck, this is gonna hurt like a bitch.

ONE DAY AGO.

My body aches. I'm covered in bandages from where Alessi let loose, he cut up my skin, burned my skin, broke my fingers and dislocated my shoulder.

The only thing that's keeping me going is knowing I survived without telling him a thing. Most of the injuries are superficial because he "wanted to keep me pretty for when I'm his wife" the sick fuck.

I'm lying on the floor, staring up at the ceiling and wondering what's going through Luca's head right now. It hurts that he really thinks I would do that to him. He's shown me more love in the last two months than I've seen for most of my life, and for him to believe I could really do that to him? Well clearly, it can't have been that real or he would have known better, he would have seen through the lies, he would have had faith in me.

That's the part that hurts the most. Not Alessi's betrayal, not my father's antics, not being tortured while tied to a table. No, the most painful part of this whole thing was knowing Luca didn't fight for us, that he didn't trust me, that I would blindly follow him anywhere, in anything. But he couldn't extend the same courtesy to me.

The door opens and I brace myself to see the two men who were supposed to love me like family but instead used me for their own gain. Only it's not either of them, it's a foot soldier who approaches me and releases the cuff on my wrist, I pull my arm back to go to hit him, but he slaps me across the face so quickly I didn't see it coming. I slump back down but he grabs my forearm and drags me

S. WILSON

from the room. It's only as we're ascending the stairs that I realize I've been in my childhood home this entire time.

He shoves me into a room that's filled with computers, and I glance around for a way to escape as he backs out of the door.

Before I can make a move to follow him, my father steps into the room.

"You're going to repay me for all of the years I had to put up with you living under my roof, the spitting image of your mother and reminding me of everything I've lost. It should have been you that died, not her."

The mention of my mother sends a pang of hurt through my heart. *If only you could see the man that you once loved now, Mama.*

He explains how he wants me to build a database of all of the girls he has for sale, giving me a folder filled with pictures of girls who've clearly been through hell. It makes me fucking sick that this is happening in this day in age, it's even worse that it's my own flesh and blood who's doing it.

He sits in the corner of the room, observing me as I work. I know there's no point in trying to fight him, I'm too weak and fragile, not to mention he'd just shoot me before I could even make a move.

I play my part and develop a database while swallowing down bile as I do so. My father doesn't understand computers, which is the only thing I have going for me right now.

The computer I'm working on only allows me to go through a certain systems mainframe. But luckily for me, I set my laptop up on the same one when I bought it two years ago. The laptop that's currently sitting in New York. And if I know my husband like I think I do, he'll give it to the one person he knows with the ability to hack into it.

The one person who can put a stop to this shit and help those girls.

After I've sent a message to Alec, and my father deems me to have done enough work for the day, he orders a guard to deliver me back to the basement.

The guard isn't as tall as the others or well built. If anything, he's a scrawny little thing and I use the opportunity of being alone with him to my advantage. I wait until we're stood in the basement, where no one will be able to hear the commotion before I jump him, I grab his gun from its holster and shoot him between his eyes before he can even blink. The poor fuck didn't even see it coming.

Once Alec unravels the codes that I've sent to him on my laptop and he sees my message, Luca will be here within hours. Too bad for him I won't be here when he arrives.

CHAPTER THIRTY-NINE

Alec

I stare out at the city below from where I sit behind my desk. The view from my office is the only reason I bought this building. It's the only place I find peace—and yet, right now I'm plagued by the thoughts running rampant around my head as I flick my gaze to the laptop and thumb drive Luca gave me last night, something about the whole situation feels off.

I've spent the last three hours going over the images and videos on the thumb drive while simultaneously hacking the cameras of the locations the images were taken. The first image of Izzy at a store talking to a black-haired woman are just that—from the store's security cameras, it seems like she's just helping the woman pick a flash drive. In the image sent to Luca it looks as though she's passing her something—and she is, what the image doesn't show is that she's passing her a hard drive that she took from the shelf. And while I'm unable to place where the image of the woman and that Columbian fucker takes place, I'm willing to bet my billion-dollar empire that it's a set up to perceive Izzy as a villain.

The security cameras in the club are a different story, and while she did flirt and dance with him, after she sat with a group of his friends, he appears loose lipped, and she appears calculative before slipping out of the back entrance of the club.

When I met my best friend's wife at the mayor's gala, she didn't come across the type to do what everyone currently suspects of her. I'm usually good at reading people, and even though I could tell she had demons behind those chocolate brown eyes of hers, I really don't fucking think she would do this to Luca. Which is why I'm conflicted about the whole thing. Luca is adamant that she's a traitorous bitch, whereas I'm more inclined to agree with Enzo.

Not that I'd ever voice my opinion. If I ever muttered the words "Enzo is right" in the presence of Luca, Marco or my brothers, they'd all lock me up and bleed me dry of the insanity swimming in my veins without a second thought. What they don't realize, is that while yes, he's a fucking lunatic, he's also a fucking genius and anyone who disagrees is just too blind to see it.

I sigh and run my hand through my hair before flicking my attention to her laptop, I flip open the lid and furrow my brow. While at first glance, it may seem like a regular laptop, anyone in my line of work would be able to tell it's been modified to some degree.

I power on the device and go to hack my way in but I'm immediately hit with firewalls.

And not just any firewalls.

Firewalls I fucking recognize.

Holy shit.

I take my phone from my pocket and dial Luca before bringing the phone to my ear, he answers on the first ring.

"Did you find anything?"

"Not sure yet, I just wanted to ask... what does Izzy do for work?"

"Something to do with consulting, I'm not really sure..." he continues talking but I tune it out.

I know exactly what she does for work, she's my fucking partner in the side business I run alongside the public one.

When I needed help two years ago in setting up the systems for FreeThem, I found *The Scorpion* online and hired them to help. They were so fucking good that I asked them to help me full time, and they did. I spent months trying to figure out their identity, but I'm no fucking match for them.

They were a ghost, and I respected that.

While I may not have been able to figure them out, there's no way in hell they didn't figure me out. I'm fucking good at what I do, but even I wouldn't be able to hide my identity away from them. Her. *Izzy Romano.*

I think back to the night I met her, when Luca introduced us, there was a flicker of surprise and recognition in her gaze. At the time I just figured she recognized me from the magazines that hound my ass, now I know different. She knew exactly who I was.

Jesus fucking Christ. This just got so much more complicated.

This whole thing could be because of her online persona and not the Mafia. Or her supposed lover that I'm becoming more convinced by the second isn't true.

I can't exactly reveal any of this to my best friend. She didn't tell him for a reason. Just like I haven't told him about it for a reason.

Luca thinks I run things completely on the up and up apart from the odd times I help him out. He has no idea that my security company is basically just a front for a group of mercenaries who save sex trafficking victims and kill off the scum who buy and sell them.

Fuck.

"Alec? You there?" *Fuck, I forgot about him.*

I clear my throat. "Here, I'll call you if I find anything." I hang up the phone before he could question me further.

I focus back on the laptop, determined to breach the firewalls and figure out what the fuck is going on.

Hours go by and I slowly make progress, if this was Izzy hacking into my security she would have been in within an hour. I've been at it for four and I'm not even halfway there.

I'm just about to get up to stretch my legs and an alert pops up on the screen. It's written in the code we usually use to communicate locations of victims she's uncovered.

I set up my laptop so I can unravel the code while still trying to breach her systems. After an hour or so I finally gain access to her laptop and at the same time the decoding finishes so I can ready her message.

Alec, if my husband is even half as smart as I think he is, he will have given you my laptop. Alessi Donetti is alive and helped my father kidnap me. AB is involved in ST, send a team BHB Docks. And tell my husband to go fuck himself for ever doubting me.

Well, *fuck*.

There's no way in hell I'll ever be able to explain any of this to Luca without telling him about mine and Izzy's partnership.

And to do that I'll have to explain what I've been up to for the last two years.

And then I'm going to have to tell him about my reasoning behind it all.

Goddammit to hell.

I spend another hour going through Izzy's files to try and understand the video of her little lover's reunion. Or what appeared like a lover's reunion.

Turns out the man in the video is this "Alessi" she mentioned. Her childhood friend and guard who has recently risen from the dead from what I've gathered from the information on her laptop.

I brace myself and pick up my phone, not only do I have to tell my best friend that while he's been setting fires all over the city for the past six days searching for his wife thinking she ran off with another man when she was actually kidnapped and subjected to who the hell knows what, I'm also having to reveal my biggest secret and my only regret. I press the phone to my ear to give the man who saved mine and my brothers'—along with my mother's—lives twenty years ago a courtesy call first.

"Uncle Sal, it's time."

CHAPTER FORTY

Izzy

I exit the gates of my childhood home, determined to never set foot on the grounds again. I was limping from the brutality that I've been subjected to for the last five days as well as the fight I've just endured, so I decided to borrow a car from my dear old dad.

My father had nine guards on the property, and I've just killed them all.

I did leave my husband a gift for when he arrives though. I liked the poetry of leaving him a gift. It's what I did at the beginning of our union. It's only fair I do it at the end too.

That asshole can go to hell for all I care, he'd rather believe anonymous sources over me, leaving me to be tortured and held against my will.

And while I may be done with the man that I once considered the love of my life and the Romano family, I can't stop thinking about my visit to the bookstore before I was taken.

Once considered? Liar.

I shake my head and internally reprimand myself. I want nothing to do with him. *Nothing*, I remind myself as I reach for my phone that I took back from Alessi, he already made sure to turn off any tracking services so at least he's done one right thing, this way my darling husband won't be able to find me.

I press on Enzo's name and bring the phone to my ear since my phone isn't connected to the car.

"Hello? Izzy is that you?"

"It's me."

"Jesus fucking Christ, Izzy, I've been worried as hell. No one in the family is speaking to me because I told them you wouldn't do it. I know you wouldn't, Bella, so what the fuck is going on."

"Not the time, Enzo. I visited the bookstore the day I was taken, Robyn had bruises around her wrists. You need to protect her," I say.

"What the fuck do you mean she had bruises?" he growls in a deathly tone, and I can feel the danger emanating through his voice.

"Just keep an eye on her, En... oh, fuck!" I cry as a sharp pain ricochet though my shoulder as I sit back in my seat.

"Izzy... are you okay?" he asks, worry clear in his voice.

"I'm fine, but if you tell Luca I contacted you I'll slice your neck from ear to ear in your sleep," I threaten, but it's weak since I'm in too much pain to put any real effort into it.

"Come back to the city. I have an apartment you can lie low in until you figure things out, and my brother can go fuck himself in my opinion, the *stronzo* should have had more faith in you, sis," he says before giving me the address and telling me to head to the nearest airport. Apparently, a friend of his has a jet I can borrow so

I don't have to drive, and since I don't have any identification on me, it's not as though I can just catch a commercial flight.

"Thank you, for everything," I whisper before hanging up.

Looks like I'm going back to New York, let's just hope it takes my husband a while to find me, since I don't think he'll appreciate the message I left for him.

CHAPTER FORTY-ONE

Luca

For the second time this week, I've been summoned to my father's office.

I knock on the door before opening it and walking inside. When he called me and asked me to come over, I figured it had something to do with regular business. Which is why I'm shocked as shit to see both of my brothers and my best friend waiting for me.

Alec has never even been to the estate before—other than the one time for my wedding. So, I'm confused as hell as to why he's here now, unless this shit with Izzy is even worse than we first thought.

Fuck, what else could she have possibly been up to?

"Sit down, Luca," Dad orders and I comply, taking a seat so I'm sat facing both him and Alec. The latter glances to my father, who gives him a nod.

"There's some shit I need to tell you, and you need to keep quiet and listen," Alec says with a pointed look.

Get the hell on with it, I want to say, but I refrain and give him a nod instead.

"When I built my company eight years ago, I did it with one goal in mind, building it up to the point it could be used as a front for my real plans. Two years ago, I put those plans into motion. Now, you know I'm good with tech, but I still needed help, which was why I reached out to one of the web's best-known hackers, *The Scorpion*. They liked the idea of what I was doing and agreed to a partnership of sorts, and we've been working alongside each other ever since," he says and swallows before darting his gaze around the room—seeming to focus on anything other than me.

"We created FreeThem, a platform in which we can track sex traffickers and trace their buyers. My company—while also doing what the public perceives it to do—is essentially a mercenary group focused on wiping the assholes who run the flesh trade from the face of the earth and helping the victims get back to their normal lives or giving them new lives altogether." He sighs and runs a hand through his hair before taking a gulp from the glass of whiskey that my dad passes him.

"What made you do all of this?" I ask since he's never once mentioned any of this to me. In fact, now that I think about it, I know fuck all about his childhood. I know his brothers and his mom, but none of them talk about the years that happened before I met him.

"That part is irrelevant for now, what has this got to do with anything, Alec?" my father interjects before a pained Alec can answer and he lets out a breath of relief. There's a haunted look in his eyes and it makes me wonder just how well I actually know my best friend.

What the hell happened to him for him to go to such lengths?

"Right... remember how I called you yesterday and asked you what Izzy does for work?" he asks, and I nod—still not understanding where this is going.

"It was because I noticed the signature used in the security systems on her laptop."

What the fuck does that mean?

"Are you telling me that Izzy, my wife, is involved in the flesh trade?" I snap.

Jesus fucking Christ, it's one fucking thing after another. She deserves some sort of fucking award because she really had me fooled.

"No, Luca, your wife has been my partner in bringing them down for the last two years," he states and even though I'm confused as hell, I let out a breath of relief, it's bad enough what she's done to me, but if she was trafficking women and children? I'd have no choice but to put a bullet between her eyes.

"There's more..." I bring my gaze back to his face and he looks pained at what he's about to say. "I hacked into security systems and cross checked the images that were sent and the video footage..." he goes on to explain how it seems as though it was all set up to incriminate Izzy and I feel fucking sick.

I've spent the last six days cursing her out when it may not even be true, but that still doesn't explain her little boyfriend that I'm going to stab in the dick for touching what's mine. I may not own her heart like I thought I did, but she's still my fucking wife. She bears *my* name, and it was *my* cock that was buried deep inside of her every single night throughout our joke of a marriage.

"So, she's innocent of betraying the *famiglia*, that doesn't mean she didn't run off with her lover," Marco quips, speaking up for the first time and voices what I was thinking while Enzo has been surprisingly quiet throughout this whole thing.

Alec rubs his eyes, he looks exhausted, and I feel like shit because this has clearly been a lot for him, I really don't know what the fuck I would do without him to be honest.

"The man in the video was her childhood friend, Alessi Donetti."

"Impossible, he's dead," I say with conviction, but the doubts start to trickle in. *Did she lie about his death to throw me off?* The pain in her voice and eyes as she told me about him flash through my mind and I internally shake my head. *She's just an expert liar and manipulator.*

"Luca... Izzy knew you'd give me her laptop. She sent me a message asking me to send a team to Chicago to stop a ring that's happening over there and that..." he trails off again and leans forward resting his forearms on his thighs and clasping his hands together.

"And what?" I ask impatiently.

"From what I can gather, Alessi and Antonio Bianchi faked Alessi's death to isolate Izzy so that when he had the chance to propose an arrangement between your families, she'd feel more alone and go through with it without a fight. Bianchi has moved into the skin trade and I'm guessing he needed your deal so he could send shipments in and out of the state without being questioned."

"So, Izzy was in on it the whole time? That's why she left?" I ask, trying to ignore the pain in my chest that's been present since the second she left.

"For fuck's sake, she didn't leave, man. She was taken." He gives me a sympathetic look and the world blurs around me.

She was taken.

She was fucking taken. Kidnapped. She didn't leave. And while I've been drowning myself in whiskey, thinking about all the ways I've planned on punishing her. She's been going through who the fuck knows what. Jesus fucking *Christ.*

Where did they keep her? What did they do to her? Did they fucking torture her? Thoughts of Izzy hurt and beaten swim around in my mind and my gut tightens.

I dart up from the chair and hunch over the trash can just in time to empty my stomach into it. This time, instead of pushing the pain of Izzy being gone away, I let it consume me. I let all the emotion hit me at once. It's the fucking least I deserve for turning my back on her when she needed me the most. For not trusting her when all she ever did was open herself up to me. All she ever did was love me, and I left her to the wolves.

"Fuck!" I roar, I swing towards my father and brothers. My dad and Marco are both pale, probably thinking the same thing as me. While Enzo glares at me from the corner. He doesn't need to voice his thoughts. He's been the one saying she was innocent all along and I've been too much of a dick, letting my hurt pride and ego get the best of me instead of listening to him.

"You lot can go to Chicago and deal with everything while I stay here and keep an eye on things," he says with no emotion in his tone before walking out of the room without a backwards glance at the rest of us.

"She's been held at her father's estate for the last six days," Alec says, and me, Dad and Marco immediately spring into action, preparing a team and planning the best way to approach the situation.

Alec gets ready to head out but clears his throat, so we all stop what we're doing and turn to him.

"There's something else, she wanted to give you a message..." he says while keeping eye contact with me. "She wanted me to tell you to... to go fuck yourself for ever doubting her." He squeezes my shoulder in a show of comfort while I take a deep breath and close my eyes.

I'm so fucking sorry, baby.

Though I know, in the very depths of my soul that sorry will never be enough. In fact, I think I may have lost her for good, and it'd be exactly what I deserve. I failed her. I failed *us*.

We make it to Chicago within three hours, which still isn't quick enough in my opinion. I'm fidgety as fuck as we pull up to the Bianchi home. I couldn't sit still the whole flight here, I ended up pacing back and forth down the aisle the whole two hours we were in the air, unable to think of anything other than the horrendous ordeal Izzy must have endured these last six days.

I'm opening the car door and climbing out before Marco even has the chance to stop the car. We brought forty men with us in three separate jets since we're not sure of the security my asshole father-in-law has around his home.

"Everyone remember the plan?" I ask and there's a breakout of murmurs around me.

We decided to have twenty men surrounding the property to keep an eye on things and to be on standby in case we need them while me, Marco, and our father lead another twenty men inside.

My father, brother and I lead the men up the steps towards the entrance, the former steps ahead of Marco and me and uses a battering ram to breach the front door. My dad may not be as young as he once was, but he never turns down the opportunity to jump in and get his hands dirty, especially when it comes to his family.

We enter the home and are immediately hit with the sight of three dead guards laid out in the hall, all lying in a pool of their own blood. My brow furrows and I look towards Marco.

What the hell is going on?

Panic hits me at the realization that someone could have attacked the compound and taken Izzy. If what Alec said was true and Antonio is, in fact, involved in the flesh trade then this could be a revenge hit, and who the fuck knows what someone would do with the daughter of a slimy fuck like Bianchi.

"Luca," my dad says and my head snaps towards him to see him holding out a note that contains one word. *Basement.*

I rush forward and make my way towards the basement; we studied the blueprints of the house when we were setting up the plan, so I know exactly where to go. I swing open the door at the end of the hall and run down the steps with my gun raised and a heavy feeling of dread settling in my gut. At the bottom of the stairs there's a large metal door that's been left cracked open.

I inch forward and slowly open the door while attempting to prepare myself for whatever the fuck I'm about to find inside.

I step inside the room and my gaze focuses on the two figures who occupy the space. I was preparing myself to find my wife injured, beaten, or fucking *dead.*

What I did not expect to see was my father-in-law tied to a chair or that little bitch Alessi strapped to a table whimpering. I let out a breath of relief before the realization that I have no fucking clue where my wife is hits me.

I walk over to Antonio and slap him, so he wakes up. His eyes pop open as soon as I make contact and he lets out an aggravated groan.

"Where the fuck is Izzy?" I bark.

"How the fuck should I know where my bitch of a daughter is? She's the one who fucking killed half of my men, mirrored the marks on that sack of shit that he gave her..." He gestures towards where Alessi is tied to the table. "And then tied me to a fucking chair like a pig. The little cunt is fucking crazy, muttering to herself about how she wanted to leave you a divorce gift," he says shaking his head and staring at me expectantly, clearly waiting for me to untie him and let him go. By now, Marco and our father have joined us in the room, but they stand back, letting me take the lead.

I have to force myself not to think about what he said about Izzy mirroring the marks Alessi gave her. The thought of her being hurt makes me want to burn this entire godforsaken city to the ground. And divorce? *Over my dead, mutilated fucking body will that ever happen.*

"Don't look at me for help, you piece of shit. You kidnapped my fucking wife, and what? Fucking beat her... I'm gonna do so much worse to you. Hell, you deserve to lose a limb or two for daring to call the most fucking precious woman to walk the earth a bitch and a cunt."

Not like you didn't call her that and more over the last few days.

You're just as bad as them.

You don't deserve to avenge her.

Her life would be better off if you weren't in it.

No. Nope. Fuck that. I only have one reason for living, and that's *her*. I'll carve my own goddamn heart out before I ever let anything happen to her again.

My gaze flicks over to the asshole who stabbed Izzy in the back after letting her believe he was a man she could depend on for most of her life and this time, I let the rage take control.

I stroll towards him and take in the bruises and wounds that mar his body. I swallow down the nausea that threatens to make an appearance for the second time today at the sight of him. Not because I give a fuck about him, but because I know that Izzy also has the same marks covering her body.

A body that should remain encased in glass, which should be fucking worshipped and not scarred.

"You did that to her?" I ask while gesturing to his body and he looks up at me with wide eyes. Now that I'm closer and able to see his injuries properly, I can see how his shoulder is dislocated, he has a black eye and blood dripping from his forehead. His arms and legs are covered in tiny slices. His shirt has been ripped open and he has bruises covering his ribs and torso.

My breath catches in my throat, thinking about how alone Izzy must have felt while locked up down here. There's a chain attached to the wall and blood on the floor in the corner of the room and I know, *I just fucking know*, that it's hers, that this was where she was kept.

I'm also stuck by a bolt of pride that she was able to single handedly take down her father's men and free herself. It really shouldn't surprise me, she's the strongest person I know.

"Please... I was just following the Dons plan," Alessi whispers and he's either a stupid fucker or he's got balls of steel since he's blaming Bianchi while he's also in the room, but then I realize I don't really give a fuck which he is, he's going to die either way.

I've thought about killing the man laid out in front of me a thousand times over the last few days, I pictured torturing him, dragging his death out for days and doing every sadistic, twisted, fucked up thing imaginable to him. But now that he's in front of me? I realize it's not worth it, I just want to end this and get the hell out of here so I can find my wife and beg her for forgiveness.

I reach down to my ankle and grab one of Izzy's knives from the sheath. I brought a couple of them along so I could have a piece of her with me, and I think it's fitting to kill this asshole with something that belongs to her, she did do all the hard work of getting him in this state, after all.

I bring the blade to his neck and slice, watching as the life fades from his eyes, as he fades from existence.

I turn around to face my dad and brother, silently communicating with them that we need to hurry this up so I can get out of here. They both give me a slight nod and I look at my father, tilting my head towards Bianchi in a silent question.

In normal circumstances, we'd just kill him. But he's the Don of Chicago, and I can't just kill him without thinking about the effect it will have on us. Technically, if he's dead, Izzy is next in line—not that anyone would accept her because they're all sexist, misogynistic assholes, so the role would go to me. And like fuck am I moving to another state.

My dad shrugs before pointing his gun at Bianchi. "You had the nerve to fuck with, kidnap, and hurt my daughter," he hisses, and warmth spreads through me at my father addressing Izzy as his daughter. "You're lucky I care more about her than dragging out my revenge." Before I can even blink, he pulls the trigger and lands a shot between his eyes.

"We'll figure out the Chicago situation later, let's go find your girl," Marco says and pats my back before we make our way up the stairs and towards the exit. Just as I'm about to pass through the door that leads outside, I see an envelope lying on the table with something resting on top of it.

The pit returns to my stomach as I slowly approach it, and I blink rapidly as I realize it's Izzy's wedding and engagement rings resting on top of a letter that's addressed to me.

CHAPTER FORTY-TWO

Luca,

I wish I could say I'm surprised at the turn of events that have happened since we returned from the island, but I'm not.

We were so happy, weren't we? I knew something would happen; I knew I could never be happy for too long. People like you and me will never deserve that type of happiness. We're too dark to be granted the gift of light.

I grew up around the most powerful men in the state, I knew the types of lives they led, I knew their hearts were made from stone and that their souls were black, like a dark abyss that would swallow you whole if you got too close. I don't know why I ever thought you would be different.

Don't feel bad, Luca. All you've done is what any other man in your position would do. I don't care what you do with Alessi and my father, I just want to be left out of it.

I walked into his marriage knowing the man I married would probably break me physically. But I never thought it would be possible for you to break me mentally, but you did. And now I'm left feeling shattered, not knowing how to put myself back together.

I feel like I've lost a part of myself these past few days, not because of the betrayal from Alessi, not the ruthlessness of my father, and not from the torture they put me through when I was locked up in that basement and cut into because I refused to give them any information on your family—but from knowing that you could honestly think I could betray you like you did. That you really thought I would ever be with another man, that I would ever give anyone information on you and your family. That's what fucking broke me, Luca. You broke me, but don't worry, I'll find a way to fix myself.

I'll do it, because I'm not the type of woman who will let a man bring her down and keep her there.

I'll be having an attorney draw up divorce papers, I know that's probably not what you want, but I also know you're not the type of man who will force me into a marriage I want no part of. So please, just accept it, Luca, if any of the love you ever felt for me was real, just sign the papers and let me move on with my life because I don't want to live with this pain for any longer than I have to.

Thank you for giving me a glimpse of the sun before I was dragged back down into the darkness.

Isabella

CHAPTER FORTY-THREE

Izzy

The apartment Enzo has that he told me to lie low in? It turns out the apartment is the one he's currently occupying because it happens to overlook a certain bookstore. I honest to God don't know what the fuck to do with him anymore.

I've been here for two days and haven't heard a single thing from Luca, though he did find out that Enzo helped me back into the city, he has no idea I'm currently staying with him—he'd have a fucking coronary if he found that little tid-bit of information out.

I had Enzo sneak my laptop from his father's office for me so I can at least work while I'm here. I've been focused on helping the women and girls that were in my father's custody. Alec managed to send a team to intercept a shipment, saving thirty women. But it still doesn't feel like enough, it never will.

No matter how hard I try to distract myself, all my thoughts keep coming back to Luca. I don't even know who I am anymore. This isn't me; I've never been the type of woman so sit around and mope over a man. My heart aches when I think about what we could have had, but I know deep in my bones that if it wasn't for what happened with my father, something else would have torn us apart in the end. It was inevitable, we're both too stubborn, too hot headed, and far too alike for us to ever have a balanced relationship.

The ringing of my phone pulls me from my thoughts, and I frown as I see an unknown number calling me.

Could it be him? But why wouldn't he try calling me from his own phone first?

I tentatively reach out and accept the call, bringing my cell to my ear. "Hello?"

"Izzy?" a familiar voice asks, and it takes me a minute to recognize the man on the other end of the call.

"Why are you calling me?" I sigh.

"Can we meet? I want to talk to you," he asks, and I inwardly groan.

"Fine." Resigned but curious as to why he wants to meet me, I agree to meet him at a coffee shop downtown.

I end the call, call an Uber and grab my coat before walking out the door. The drive to the coffee shop doesn't take long. I walk inside, and I'm hit by the strong smell of coffee and cinnamon before seeing the reason for me being here sitting at a table in the middle of a shop with a coffee waiting for me.

"What am I doing here, Alec?" I slide into the seat opposite him and shrug out of my coat.

"I wanted to see how you were doing, check up on you." He gestures towards my face. I look like shit, I know I do. There's no amount of makeup that can hide the bruises covering my face and body.

Enzo had a doctor meet me at the apartment as soon as I landed in New York, he popped my shoulder back in place and stitched the deeper cuts that cover my body.

"I'm fine," I answer briskly, and he gives me a resigned nod.

"It's not your fault, you know," he says to which I give him a confused look before he continues. "I've seen everything you've been doing. What your father did was not your fault, you shouldn't blame yourself for something you were unaware of and powerless to fight."

Right, *that*.

"Cut to it, Alec. Did Luca send you here?"

"Fuck no. And he has no idea I'm here, he'd probably threaten to kill me if he did, you know he's sorry right?"

I peer out of the window and murmur, "It's too late for that, he may have been there for me eventually, but he wasn't there when I needed him the most."

"You're right, but I want you to know that I'm grateful for everything you've done in the last two years. I don't want yours and Luca's relationship to come between our partnership. If you want to completely ignore my identity and carry on as Hurricane and Scorpion, I completely respect that. But I would like us to get to know one another better. You're my biggest asset, Izzy." He slides a thumb drive across the table and stands. "That's a copy of everything that Luca was sent, I thought if you saw that, then maybe you could try and see things from his point of view." And with that little parting gift, he strolls out of the coffee shop, leaving me to wonder what the hell just happened.

I'm in a daze as I take a cab back to the apartment, Alec's words repeat in my mind over and over until I'm on the verge of a breakdown. I take the elevator up to Enzo's floor and walk down the narrow hall but my steps falter once I see the man that I'm helplessly in love with sitting on the floor in front of the apartment door.

Luca must sense my arrival as his head snaps up and his eyes widen when he blinks as though he doesn't think I'm really here.

"Izzy," he whispers and the pain in his voice makes me want to wrap him in my arms and tell him everything will be okay. But I don't, because it won't, I really don't think we can ever come back from what's happened.

"Why are you here, Luca?" I murmur.

He climbs to his feet, and I take in his appearance. His usually pristine suit appears disheveled, his hair seems ruffled, and he has dark circles under his eyes, as if he hasn't been sleeping.

I guess that makes the two of us.

"I had to see you with my own eyes, baby. Can we talk? Please."

I sigh before unlocking the door to Enzo's apartment and waving my arm to gesture for him to come inside before closing the door behind me.

I take a seat on the armchair—not wanting to sit on the sofa and give him the opportunity to sit too close to me. But rather than sitting on the sofa, he sits down on the coffee table in front of me. His hand twitches and he clasps his hands together and leans his arms on his knees as if he's trying to stop himself from reaching out to me.

"I'm so fucking sorry, Iz, I know that won't mean anything to you, but I just needed to say the words. You're my life, baby. My everything. Please tell me there's some way we can fix this." There's desperation in his tone and it breaks my heart to see him so fucked up over this, but I can't risk my own heart breaking again.

"I know you are." I give him a sad smile while willing myself not to cry. "There's nothing to fix, Luca. This was always going to end one way or another." I stand and walk to the window to look down at the street. "I'm grateful for everything we shared, but I can't do it anymore. I always thought I was strong, I thought I could handle anything. But I'm not, you broke me, Luca." My voice cracks on the last word and I turn to face him. I didn't even hear him approach me, but as I turn, I realize he must have gotten up while I was speaking, because he's standing right in front of me, unshed tears in his eyes that threaten to weaken my resolve.

Luca drops to his knees right in front of me, his chest heaving as though he's struggling to catch his breath.

"I can't do any of this without you, Izzy. I can't fucking breathe without you. Every second I'm away from you I feel like I'm struggling to take a breath, I'm drowning and you're the only hope of my survival. I'm begging you, Izzy, please just give me a chance to prove just how much I fucking love you. You know I'm not the type of man to ever beg for anything, but I'll happily stay on my knees for the rest of my life if that's what it takes. I'll do anything, Iz. You want space for a while? I'll do that. You want dates and flowers? Done. You want me to burn the city to ashes for you, baby? Just say the word and I'll light the match while kneeling at your feet. Just give me a chance to love you with everything I have."

He heaves in a breath and hangs his head, but I can still see the tears running down his face.

"I'm sorry. I love you, Luca, but I can't be with you." My lips tremble as I force myself to say the words, and he nods silently before standing. He approaches me carefully, as if he's worried that I'll bolt the second he comes close and wipes the tears from my face before pressing a light kiss to my forehead which only makes me cry harder.

"I'll always love you, Izzy," he whispers into my hair before he pulls back. He gives me one last look, full of shame, remorse and heartbreak before he turns and walks out the door with his head tilted down.

As soon as the door closes behind him, I fall to my knees, my legs unable to keep me standing any longer. The remnants of my shattered heart scatter to the floor around me while the other half of my soul just walked out of the door.

CHAPTER FORTY-FOUR

Luca

The door closes behind me and I lean my back against it. The sounds of Izzy's cries are faint as she breaks down on the other side and the sound guts me. All I want to do is walk back in there, take her in my arms and comfort her. But she's not mine to comfort, not anymore.

My eyes sting, the result of leaving myself bare in front of the only woman I'll ever love. I use the sleeve of my jacket to wipe my face, trying to regain my composure and tilt my head back, attempting to take a deep breath.

I hear footsteps coming down the hall and I know who it is before I even open my eyes. The asshole always has the worst possible timing.

"How the fuck did you find—" He cuts off as I turn to him, his eyes widening as he takes in my appearance. Yeah, I probably look like shit, yet I really can't bring myself to give a fuck.

"Fuck," he mutters before closing the distance between us and wrapping his arms around me.

The gesture brings me a sense of comfort as I mirror him and sob into his shoulder. I can't even remember the last time I hugged one of my brothers. Hell, the last time I cried was when my mother died twenty-two years ago.

"Come on, let's get you home where we can drink all of our problems away." He pulls back and nods before walking towards the elevator.

I follow him with my head bowed. "I can't go back to my apartment, Enzo. I can't fucking do it."

He nods in understanding. "Then we'll go to Marco's and drink a bottle of his expensive whiskey, he can't refuse to share like he usually would, you're hurting brother. What kind of brother would he be if he didn't let us drown out our issues," he says with a smirk, and I roll my eyes at him. Marco likes to collect the expensive shit, and Enzo's always harping at him to share, yet he never does.

Enzo drives us across the city to our brother's apartment. I'm not one to normally turn up at my brother's apartment unannounced, but apparently, I'm just letting Enzo take the reins for once.

"You knew, didn't you? That's why you didn't come to Chicago, because you knew she wouldn't be there," I say.

"Yeah, I did. I'm not sorry, Luca. She needed me, and I was there, I won't apologize for that."

"I know," I murmur. "Thank you for being there for her, for believing in her when I wouldn't, and taking care of her when she needed it."

"I didn't do it for you, bro. She's like a sister to me and I'll always be there if she needs me, just like I am to you. I don't know what will happen between the two of you, but if you can't work it out, don't expect me to choose sides. I won't do it, Luca."

"I wouldn't expect you to. I'm glad she has you, man. She needs someone in her corner—even if that someone isn't me," I whisper the last sentence, not trusting my voice not to crack and he gives me a solemn nod, the emotion that flashes behind his eyes tells me he knows exactly how close I am to having a fucking breakdown and I slump back in my seat, closing my eyes for the rest of the drive.

"We're here, man, come on." Enzo parks the car on the pavement in front of the apartment complex and we make our way up to the penthouse that Marco occupies. My father bought us a penthouse apartment on each of our eighteenth birthdays and we all still live in them to this day—other than Enzo's new apartment that's conveniently located opposite a certain bookstore.

The elevator opens into the living room, where we find Marco casually leaning back in the chair, whiskey in hand while frowning at his phone. He glances up as we approach, and he shares a look with Enzo before getting up and going to the kitchen. He comes back a moment later with two empty glasses in hand before sitting back in his seat and pouring us both a glass of the whiskey that was left on his coffee table.

"Are we going to talk about it? Or are we going to mope?" Marco asks and it takes me by surprise. The last thing I expected Marco to do was initiate a conversation, especially about *feelings*.

"I lost her," I murmur, the words sending a pain through my heart, and I wish I could just fucking rip the fucking organ out of my chest and be done with the everlasting pain that's coursing through me.

"Do you love her?"

"What sort of question is that, Marco? Of course, I do. With everything that I am." I glare at him from across the room, but he remains unaffected as always. Always so fucking stoic, my brother.

"Then don't give up. I know that if you could go back in time and change the course of events, you would. *I know.* She's hurt right now, she's pissed, and she needs time to process everything that's happened. You'll regret giving up if you do..." He stares off into space, his mind taking someplace else. "You'll regret it for the rest of your life," he says and swallows the rest of the drink in his glass before closing his eyes and shaking his head. Why does it sound like he's speaking from experience? I've never known my brother to have a girlfriend, or even a regular fuckbuddy, so why does it sound like he understands my pain? I'm about to ask him just that when Enzo subtly shakes his head from where he's standing near the window, so I lean my head back on the sofa and stare up to the ceiling, wondering how and why the hell my brothers have kept it from me.

"Well, this is fucking depressing," a voice sounds from behind me and my head snaps towards it. How the hell did I not hear the elevator?

"What the fuck are you doing here? I ask.

Alec smirks at my attitude and slumps down into the armchair next to mine. "Marco texted me as you arrived, inviting me to the pity party. You look like shit. Then again, your wife's appearance wasn't much better," he says with a laugh, and it takes everything in me not to lunge myself at him and strangle the little fuck.

"What the *fuck* do you mean by that? When did you see Izzy?" I say through gritted teeth.

"Today. We had coffee together, we're besties now," he says with a wink and my control snaps. I jump to my feet and go to reach for the gun in my waistband but my brothers grab me before I can grab it. *Assholes.*

"You can't shoot your best friend," Marco says in my ear while I struggle to get out of their hold.

"Jesus, you've lost it, man. I've worked with Izzy for two years. Granted, I didn't know who she was, but she's been killing herself lately trying to fix the wrongs of her father and I asked her to meet me so I could check up on her and try and talk her into taking a break. I like the girl, and I don't want her working herself to the bone because of misplaced guilt. I also might have given her something that could help your case. So, chill the fuck out and sit the fuck back down," Alec barks and I stop fighting against my brothers' hold and give him a reluctant nod before they let me go and I sit back down.

"What did you give her?"

"A replica of the thumb drive that was sent to you," he says, and I don't know whether her having that is a good thing or not. I'm not sure anything could help me at this point. I'm pretty sure I've lost her for good, and I've lost a part of myself in the process.

I stare at the headstone in front of me, the headstone that I haven't visited in years because I've been too busy. Or more like I couldn't face the pain of coming back here.

Maria Romano
Loving wife and Mother
"Fight for those you love. Whether that's beside them, for them or with them."

Marco's words from yesterday reminded me of the words our mother always used to say, she used to say that love is the most powerful thing in the world, and it can also cause the most devastation. I'm going to have to agree with her on that one, because of the pain that I'm feeling? Yeah... it's fucking devastation alright.

"Hey, Ma," I whisper into the cold morning air. "I met her. My reason for living, I mean. But I fucked up and now I've lost her, and I have no idea what to do... How am I meant to live without the other half of my soul? You'd have loved her, Ma. You'd probably kick my ass for what I did to her, and I'd deserve it. I miss you and I wish you were here so you could help me through this, I'm sorry for not visiting more often, it just fucking hurts." I close my eyes and breathe in the bitter cold air, allowing the cold to pierce my chest. "I love you."

CHAPTER FORTY-FIVE

Izzy

Once I finally managed to pick myself up off the floor, I showered and sat on the bed in the guest room Enzo assigned as mine before allowing myself to study the images Luca had been sent the day I was taken. I examined the images for hours, trying to understand what was going through Luca's mind when he saw them.

I must admit, it does look bad. If I received something similar, would I really think any different?

I hardly slept last night, my thoughts running rampant, wondering whether me and Luca could ever really work. I'm sitting and working at the dining table when Enzo walks in the door. He didn't come home last night, and I have no idea whether that's normal for him or not.

"Hey, are you okay?" I ask, he appears hungover and like he could use a good shower before a six-hour nap.

"Been better," he grunts as he opens the refrigerator and grabs a bottle of water before sitting down next to me and fiddling with the label on the bottle.

"You stink, Enzo, what the hell happened to you?"

"Marco's whiskey happened, sis. You should try it sometime." He smirks but it falls flat. "How are you doing, Iz? I know Luca was here yesterday, I found him in the hallway as I was coming home last night, and I ended up dragging him to Marco's."

"I can't do it, Enzo. I can't give myself to him, when I can't trust him to give me himself in return," I whisper, my voice cracking and I will myself not to cry again. I'm so fucking sick of crying.

"I know it's fucked up how he didn't have faith in you, Izzy, but can you imagine how he felt when he saw those images? The videos? I know Alec gave you the copies. And then the thing with Tomasso too. It was all too much," he says, giving me a sympathetic smile but my brows wrinkle in confusion. "What does Tomasso have to do with anything?"

Enzo pales. "Fuck, Izzy, didn't they tell you? Tomasso was found dead in an alley, with one of your knives embedded in him. Luca was always close to him, he was one of our most trusted men, that's why he had him guard you."

Tomasso's dead? Fuck, why the hell didn't I know this?

"I... it wasn't me Enzo, I'd never..." I stutter, and he grabs my hand, giving me a gentle squeeze.

"They know that now, Izzy, but at the time? At the time, it was a lot of information. A lot of *incriminating* information." He gives my hand one last squeeze before getting up and heading to his bedroom. Leaving me to think about how Luca lost someone so close to him, and how he thought I had killed him. He must have hated me for everything he thought I had done. Even though it wasn't true, can someone really come back from that hate? I don't think I could.

I stand and stare up at the building in front of me, not knowing if I really want to be here or not. So much has happened, so much has changed, everything is broken, and this is the only thing I can think of to fix it.

I take a deep breath and walk into the building. It's busy, people scattered around the lobby as I walk up to the reception desk.

"I need to see Alaric Dean," I tell the receptionist and she abandons whatever she's doing on her computer to glare up at me. "Do you have an appointment?"

"Nope. If you could just point me in the direction of his office, that would be great."

Her sharp gaze narrows on me, as if she can't quite believe I have the gall to say something like that. *Oh, honey, you have no idea what you're getting yourself into if you keep looking at me like that.* Luckily for her, her mask of professionalism slips back into place before I lose my temper.

"I'm sorry, ma'am, unless you have an appointment, you can't see him," she says, and I roll my eyes at her and walk away. I'm not fucking around waiting for an appointment, I'll find his office myself. I take the elevator up to the executive's floor and glance around until I spot a door with his name engraved on the front.

I walk up to the door and knock before I walk in, he sits behind his desk and looks up at me with his brows furrowed when he sees me. His assistant, who was sitting outside at her desk scurries inside after me, clearly flustered with my unexpected arrival. "I'm so sorry sir, she just walked in, I couldn't stop her," she says, and he waves her away without even glancing her way, she side-eyes me before rushing back out of the door, closing it behind her.

"Who are you and what the hell are you doing just walking in here?"

"I'm here because I need to divorce my husband."

"And you couldn't have made an appointment?" he asks and arches one of his brows. I walk over to the floor length windows and gaze out at the city below. "No, I couldn't. I need the papers drawn up today, I don't want any assets, I just want the marriage ended."

I've thought a lot about this over the last few days and I've realized that this is the only way to fix this shit.

"I see. Is there a reason you're in such a rush Mrs..."

"Romano," I finish for him and turn my head to see his eyes widening in recognition before he masks his reaction.

"Alright... assuming your husband doesn't shoot me for representing you, is there a reason this needs to be done today?" he asks, and I bite back a laugh. If only he knew I was more likely to end up shooting him than my husband.

"I love him, that's why it needs to be done today and he won't shoot you if I ask him not to, don't worry."

CHAPTER FORTY-SIX

Luca

After I left the cemetery, I came to the warehouse used by Alec's organization. Last night, after he told me about how hard Izzy is being on herself, I wanted to do something to help them, so I asked Alec if there was anything I could do. Which is why I'm standing here, covered in another man's blood after I've just beaten the shit out of him to get him to spill his secrets.

Alec knows I have a knack for gathering intel—just not in the same way he does. The guy in front of me was one of Bianchi's most trusted men and I've been asked to find out everything he knows about my now dead father-in-law's dealings within the skin trade.

We left the Chicago outfit in the hands of our family friends, the Rossi brothers. They weren't actually part of the Mafia; they just have the same values and thirst for violence as us. They'll clean up the city and keep things on track. We've done business with them numerous times and we know they can handle it. The four brothers will be an unstoppable force in Chicago.

"P-please... just stop," he whimpers, and it sends a thrill through me. This is the first time that losing Izzy hasn't been at the front of my mind, and I'll gladly take the distraction.

"Who else was Bianchi working with?"

"I d-don't know much... just that he... h-he was trying to make a d-deal with O'Brien, but he refused... the boss didn't tell me much, I s-swear," he cries, and I roll my eyes at his dramatics. So, Bianchi was trying to make a deal with the head of the New York mob, everyone knows that none of the leaders of New York tolerate sex trafficking.

"Who else in New York was he in talks with?" I ask and kick him in the stomach as an incentive to hurry the fuck up and start answering my questions with good enough answers.

"There were whispers about a low-level gang... Blue Vipers, I swear that's all I know."

Blue Vipers? What sort of fucking gang name is that? Ridiculous.

"Are you sure that's all you know?" I grunt as I bring my knife to his arm and carve my initials. His screams fill the room as he sobs and begs me to stop.

"I-I don't know anything!" he yells, and I believe him. You always get to a certain point and know that there's nothing else to know. I bring the knife up and stab him in the side of his neck, letting blood spurt across my bare arms as I revel in his screams, thankful for the momentary distraction of the shit show that is now my life. It doesn't last long, life without Izzy is unbearable and I'm not sure how much longer I can survive like this.

I head to the bathroom and clean off his blood before I shrug my suit jacket back on and pull out my phone to text Alec and update

him on what I've learned. My pulse races as I realize I've got a text
waiting for me from Izzy.

My Wife

> Can you meet me later? Alana's Coffee Shop,
> 3pm.

She wants to meet me? That's a good thing, right? For the first
time in days, I feel a sliver of hope. I check the time and breathe a
sigh of relief that I've still got an hour before she wants to meet,
giving me time to head home and shower before I meet her. I send
a quick message to Alec before replying to her.

> Of course, I'll see you soon.

I head to my car and my father calls as I'm driving home. I press
accept on the dash and his voice filters through the speakers.

"Luca." He sounds resigned, as though he doesn't want to be
making the call. For fuck's sake, what's happened now?

"What's up, Dad?"

"Damo just called me," he blurts, and my hands tighten on the
steering wheel. Damo is one of our men, the one who I tasked to
watch over Izzy.

"What's wrong? What happened? Is she okay?" I ask and he
sighs in return. "She's fine, son... he didn't want to be the one to
call you, he figured the news would be best coming from me."

I swallow the lump in my throat. Is she with someone else? Has
she met someone? I don't think I'd be able to stop myself from
killing him. No, Izzy wouldn't fucking do that, I know that now.
There's no way in fuck she's seeing someone else.

"Just say it, Dad. What's going on?"

"She visited Alaric Dean at his office this morning, I'm sorry."

Alaric Dean? That name sounds familiar...I feel like I've heard the name before...and then it hits me—Blank Astor Dean law. He's a fucking divorce attorney. She's filed for divorce; she really did it. Fuck, that's why she wants to meet me.

That spark of hope I felt only moments ago fades to dread. I've already begged her on my knees, I've tried giving her space, I really don't think there's anything else that can save us. She was the best thing that ever happened to me, and I set our relationship on fire, burning us both and leaving us to be nothing but a pile of ashes.

I clear my throat and murmur, "It's fine, I knew it was coming, I just didn't want to accept it. I'm meeting her in an hour, I need to go, Dad. I'll call you later." I end the call before he can reply and drive home in a daze, how I make it in one piece I don't know. All I know is my wife really is leaving me, I won't fight it, that will only hurt her more. I've hurt her enough as it is.

I always knew she deserved the world, I just failed to give it to her.

After I quickly shower and change my clothes, I head back down to my car. I'm going to end up being thirty minutes early, but I can't just sit at home and spiral. Deciding it would be easier to just walk, I abandon the car with the valet and start walking the few blocks towards the coffee shop.

My breathing picks up the closer I get, my thoughts firing rapidly.

I lost her.

I fucking lost her.

I thought the worst of her. How the hell could I ever think she would betray me?

She's my fucking lifeline, and now I'm going to have to spend the rest of my life knowing I blew up my entire world.

I pause for a second on the sidewalk and force myself to inhale. *Fuck,* I'm losing my damn mind. How am I supposed to hold onto my sanity, knowing that she's out there, living her life without me? I pull my cell from my pocket and dial Marco.

"Yeah?" he answers on the first ring.

"I need you to promise me something," I murmur.

"Are you okay, man? Dad told me about Izzy visiting the lawyer's office."

"I don't think I'll ever be okay, but you need to promise me that you'll force me to let her go. Have men watch over her and make sure she's okay, but don't let anyone report it to me unless something happens. And I mean something *bad* Marco. Do not *ever* tell me if she's with another man because I'll end up losing my goddamn mind and going on a killing spree. Promise me you'll do that," I whisper, my heart breaking at the thought of her falling in love with someone else, sharing what we shared. "I'm on my way to meet her now and it's fucking killing me, man. This hurts more than taking a bullet," I sigh while I continue walking.

"Are you sure you're really willing to give her up?"

"I'm only hurting her more the more I try to fix things. If this is what she wants, then I'll give it to her. I once said I'd give her the world, it just turns out that world doesn't include me," I say before hanging up as I reach the entrance to the coffee shop. I can see Izzy is already seated at one of the tables through the windows. I breathe a sigh of relief when I see the place is mostly empty, I really didn't want to do this with the place full of people.

I steel myself for what's to come before opening the door and walking inside. Izzy's head snaps up as soon as she hears the bell chime and stands from her chair as I make my way over to her.

"Luca," she whispers, and the way she says my name threatens to bring me to my knees. She sounds so fucking sad, so *broken*.

I did that, I broke her, destroying myself and ruining our future in the process.

"*Mia regina*," I murmur back to her and go to wrap my arms around her, but I stop myself before I do. I don't have the right to touch her anymore, I don't have any rights at all. She must notice my intention because she steps towards me and wraps her arms around my waist. I tense for a moment—taken by surprise at the gesture—before wrapping my arms tightly around her, cradling her head to my chest and pressing a kiss into her hair.

Christ, I've missed her so goddamn much.

I let go and step back before I can get too comfortable, not wanting to cross any lines or push her boundaries. I pull her chair out for her and wait for her to sit before rounding the table to sit down—but before I do, she kicks out the chair that's next to her and motions for me to sit there rather than opposite her.

My pulse skyrockets at the thought of being close to her. It sounds ridiculous, but I'll take all I can fucking get.

"I need to talk to you," she says as I take a seat.

"I know why we're here, Iz," I blurt before taking a deep breath. "We've had guards on you." I throw my hands up in a surrender gesture when I see her stony expression before explaining. "Not for any other reason than to make sure you're safe. I made a mistake before, baby, and you got hurt. I didn't want anything happening to you, it's hard to live with myself as it is, I couldn't cope if something else happened." She nods in understanding and reaches for my hand, giving me a reassuring squeeze and I honestly wish she wouldn't. As much as I love being around her, this is fucking killing me.

"I know where you went this morning, Iz. I know why we're here," I sigh as I rub my thumb across the back of her hand.

"*Jesus* Luca, yes, I went to visit a divorce attorney but it's not what—" She's cut off as a woman approaches our table looking disheveled and Izzy peers up at the woman intruding with her brows wrinkled in the adorable way she always does.

"You." She points at Izzy, fire blazing in her eyes and Izzy tenses and sends me a questioning glance. I shake my head, equally as confused as she is.

"Can I help you?" I ask but she doesn't spare me a glance, continuing to glare at my wife.

"You're the reason he's gone," she hisses before pulling a gun from the pocket of her coat. "You're the reason I have to live without him!" the woman wails, and everything happens in slow motion.

The mystery woman aims her gun at Izzy, and I know a split second before that she's going to pull the trigger, I don't even think—normally I'd be going for my own gun, ready to end the bitch—I shove Izzy down and throw myself over her as she fires. The few people around us scream in terror but I'm too busy checking Izzy over, my heart in my throat as I check that she wasn't injured.

It's only when I confirm she's fine that I feel myself becoming dizzy, a pain in my stomach rendering me immobile.

"Luca!" Izzy screams and I know she's realized at the same time as me. She rolls me over, pulling the gun from my waistband and firing a shot at the mystery woman before leaning over me and using a cloth to try and stop the bleeding. I don't need to see what she's doing to know it's not doing much.

"Luca... just hold on, okay? Someone's calling for an ambulance, w-we'll get you some help, okay? Don't... don't leave me," she sobs, and it breaks my fucking heart.

I reach up and try to wipe the tears that are streaming down her beautiful face but I'm too weak, my visions blurring as the seconds tick by and my arm flops back down. "I got to love you, Izzy, it's okay baby. You'll be okay," I croak.

"I love you, Luca, you're not fucking dying on me, *please*." Izzy's pleas are the last thing I hear as the fight drains from me and I close my eyes, at peace with the fact I took the bullet that was meant for my wife.

CHAPTER FORTY-SEVEN

Izzy

"**I** got to love you, Izzy. It's okay, baby. You'll be okay," Luca says on a broken whisper and my world crashes down around me. I can't lose him.

I can't take the peace that washes over his face.

He thinks he's dying. He *can't* die on me.

I can't do this life without him.

"I love you, Luca, you're *not* fucking dying on me, *please*," I sob as he closes his eyes and I push down harder on his wound, trying to stop the never-ending stream of blood escaping him. "I can't lose you, open your eyes Luca."

My cries fall on deaf ears as he passes out from blood loss. I thought I knew pain; I thought I knew loss, but *nothing* could ever prepare me for the fucking hole in my heart as the other half of me lies unconscious and bleeding on the floor.

"The EMT's are here, ma'am," one of the waitresses says to me but I don't acknowledge her, focusing on Luca instead. Everything passes in a blur as the EMT's arrive, they have to force me out of the way so they can secure Luca on a stretcher and load him into the back of an ambulance, one of the staff members passes me my bag as I climb in the back beside him, and I realize I need to call the family.

I pull up my father-in-law's contact and dial.

"Hello?" He answers instantly and I whimper, unable to find my voice and say the words aloud.

"Sweetheart? Are you okay? What's going on?" he asks, his voice a deep rumble—concern evident in his tone.

"You need to meet us at the hospital," I cry as the paramedic continues working to stop Luca's bleeding while I keep a tight grip on his hand as if he's my lifeline. Hell, he *is* my fucking lifeline.

"What happened?"

"Luca... h-he was shot," I whisper and my voice breaks as a sob tears its way up from my fucking soul.

"We'll meet you there, we're on our way, Izzy. You're not alone."

If only that was true.

F ive hours.

Five fucking hours Luca has been in surgery, and we still haven't had any updates.

Five hours I've been sitting on the floor of the waiting room, arms wrapped around my legs as I cry into them, praying to a lord that I don't believe in to bring him back to me.

Five hours of Enzo pacing the room and threatening every hospital staff member that he'll gut them if Luca doesn't make it out alive.

Five hours of Salvatore murmuring to himself in the corner.

Five hours of Marco stood as still as a statue beside me, as if he's afraid to let me out of his sight. He's as stoic as ever, but I can tell he's worried by the way he keeps clenching and unclenching his fists. I think he's attached himself to me because Luca would kill him if he didn't keep watch over me.

"Romano family?" a voice announces, and my head snaps up so fast I probably gave myself whiplash.

We all stand and turn to the doctor who's standing in front of us. I can't tell from his facial expression whether it's good news or bad news. There's not an ounce of emotion on his face as he glances between the three men before his gaze lands on me.

"Mr. Romano was extremely lucky. The bullet didn't hit any major organs, it took some time to locate the source of bleeding, but we managed to patch him up just fine. He's being transferred to the ICU, you should be able to visit him in an hour or so," he says, and we collectively let out a sigh of relief as the tension drains from my shoulders.

"Thank you," I breathe before taking a seat in one of the chairs and hanging my head, letting myself take a relaxing breath for the first time in hours.

I see two pairs of Italian leather shoes step in front of me from my peripheral vision and tilt my head up to see Salvatore and Marco staring down at me.

"Can you come with us please, Izzy? We'd like to talk to you," Salvatore asks, and I swallow before giving him a jerky nod.

I stand and follow as Marco leads us into an empty room adjacent to the waiting room. I'm pretty sure this is the room the staff use when they need to give family members bad news. I take a seat at the table as Marco and Salvatore take a seat opposite me.

Fuck, why do I feel like I'm about to be interrogated?

There's a tense silence as I look between them both before my father-in-law finally speaks up. "We need to apologize to you, Izzy. You've been nothing but loyal to our family since you've joined it, and we should have stood by you rather than against you. We know you're planning on leaving Luca, but we want you to know that you'll always be a part of our family." I give him a tight nod, ready to refute his claims but Marco speaks up before I get the chance.

"I'm sorry I ever doubted you, Izzy. I should have listened to Enzo. I'll be here if you ever need anything, and I won't tell my brother if you ask me not to," he claims, and my lips tip up in a small smile.

"I saw what was on the thumb drive you received, it did seem bad, and I don't blame any of you for coming to the wrong conclusions," I say and shake my head. "I'm not leaving Luca," I announce.

Both of their brows furrow in confusion before Marco says, "You were ready to divorce him this morning."

"Oh, I still plan on divorcing him." I flash him a grin and his brow furrows even further while Salvatore sends me a knowing look and nods at me before standing and rounding the table, he rests his hand on my shoulder and gives me a squeeze before leaving the room. I watch his retreating form until he's out of sight before turning back around and facing Marco who still sits in front of me.

"Whoever she is, Marco, if you ever find her again, hold onto her." His dark brows jump up to his hairline; he clearly wasn't expecting the conversation to go in this direction. "I recognize that look you have when you think no one is watching, I recognize it because it's the same feeling I've felt these past few days. Find her. Fight for her, and don't ever let her go." I reach over and give his hand a gentle squeeze before leaving in the same fashion as Salvatore, leaving him to sit and think about what I've said.

I let Luca's father and brothers visit him first when we're finally allowed to see him, wanting to wait so I can see him alone. And finally—after what seems like hours—they all leave, and I walk towards the door of the room that Luca is in.

I step through the threshold of the room and suck in a sharp breath at the sight of my husband connected to machines, his body covered by the hospital blanket so I can't see his bandages.

He appears so weak, so vulnerable.

He looks nothing at all like the strong, usually put-together, pristine man I'm used to.

I slowly make my way towards him, my pulse skyrocketing the closer I get. There were moments when I really thought I would never see him again.

I thought I'd never see his chest expand as he takes a breath the way it is right now. I thought I'd never hear his voice again, never feel him hold me again.

I thought I'd never hear him murmur that he loves me in my ear at night when he thinks I'm already asleep, never feeling him press those sweet kisses to my forehead or my hair like he always does.

I thought I'd never get to tell him that I forgive him, and that I want a fresh start with him by my side.

I take a seat in the chair placed next to his bed and take his hand in mine, reveling at the feeling of being able to touch him.

"I'm really pissed at you right now," I whisper, my voice cracking as a tear rolls down my face.

"You scared me, Luca, I thought I was going to lose you, I'm not ready to fucking lose you when we've only just begun." I bring his hand to my lips and press a gentle kiss to his knuckle.

"You need to wake up so I can be pissed, it's no fun being angry when you're unconscious." I let out a chuckle as I wipe my eyes, I've never cried as much in my fucking life as I have today.

"I love you, Luca, till death do us part. I vow to you that'll never change."

I lean forward, resting my head on our joint hands and inhaling.

Finally, for the first time in over a week, I'm able to breathe his air without pain and sorrow surrounding us. I'd love nothing more than to curl up at his side right now and sleep—I haven't had a good night's sleep since I shared our bed with him.

But instead, I spent the night staring at my husband, willing him with my mind to wake up.

Enzo comes to check on me in the morning, bringing me a bag full of clothes and a fresh coffee.

"I can stay while you go home and change, Iz," he murmurs as he wraps his arms around me in a brotherly hug which is a welcome distraction.

"I'm not leaving this hospital without him Enzo."

He rolls his eyes before muttering, "Stubborn as always."

I shake my head and allow a small smile to grace my lips before I turn my attention back to Luca, he still hasn't woken up. It's been fifteen hours, and he still hasn't woken up.

I may have threatened to decapitate a doctor at one point if they didn't wake him up, but apparently there's nothing they can do but wait, so instead I called Salvatore and asked him to find the country's best doctors to look over his charts.

What good is it being a terrifying Mafia Don if you can't manipulate and coerce people?

CHAPTER FORTY-EIGHT

Luca

I can hear a murmuring voice on the edge of the darkness, a siren's song begging me to come closer and never let go, it's the voice of an angel, *my angel. My queen.*

I don't know how long I lay in the abyss; I can hear voices around me but I'm unable to make out the words. Is this death? Am I subjected to a hell of being able to hear the voices of those I love, but never understating their words, never seeing their faces—only a dark pit of nothing?

I'd give anything to see Izzy one last time. To see the smile that lights up her whole face. To see that mischievous glint that she gets in her eyes. To hear her laugh. To hold her at night as she sleeps on my chest. To feel her lips against mine. To hear her voice in my ear as she whispers she loves me.

I know I'll never get that though. I traded my life for hers, and I'd do it again in a heartbeat to know she'd be okay, that she'll live a full life.

That woman was my sole reason for living, for breathing, for existing. It's only fitting that I'd die before she had the chance to leave.

She'll be okay. She'll grieve, my family will take care of her, and she'll move on. She'll be happy in a life without me, in a world in which I no longer exist.

There's an incessant buzzing noise near my ear that makes me want to reach out and fucking throw something to get it to stop. This isn't like the dark place I was previously; this is painful. My abdomen aches and there's a heavy weight on my arm.

I find the strength to open my eyes and I blink a few times as I'm hit by light.

Holy fuck, I'm not dead.

How the fuck am I alive?

I glance around me and see I'm in a hospital room, covered by ratty bed linens that I'd much rather burn than be lying under.

I peer down to see a blonde head of curls resting on top of my arm, sleeping peacefully as she sits in the chair next to me.

She's okay, I remind myself. *She's right here, you saved her from being hurt.*

"It's about time you woke up." My head turns to my right to see Marco sitting in a chair like Izzy's on my other side. I reach my hand over to run my fingers through her hair, needing to feel as much of her while I can—she'll no doubt leave once she knows I'm awake and well.

"Don't wake her up, you've been here for four days, and this is the first time she's allowed herself to sleep," Marco murmurs and I turn to him again.

"Four days? Fuck. Why didn't she sleep at home? Or Enzo's apartment I suppose," I say, my voice is scratchy as fuck. Of course, Marco picks up on it and brings a cup of water to my lips, helping me to take a sip since my mouth is dry as hell.

"Have you met her? She's refused to leave the hospital. She says the only way she's leaving is if you do too," he says and lets out a breathy laugh. I can imagine them both arguing, and *of course*, my stubborn as fuck wife would get her own way.

My brother stands and leaves the room as I focus my attention back on Izzy, only for him to return a moment later with a doctor in tow, who proceeds to quietly ask me question after question—no doubt Marco informed him not to wake my girl or he wouldn't like the consequences—before flashing his light in my eyes and checking the bandages around my wound before they both finally get the fuck out to leave me to stare down in awe at the gorgeous woman who's still sleeping on my arm.

I sift through the memories of what happened in the coffee shop.

Me sitting down with Izzy.

She was about to ask me for a divorce.

A random woman pointing a gun at my wife.

Who the fuck was she?

The mystery woman shooting me.

Izzy shooting her.

Izzy's cries as I laid on the floor bleeding out. Fuck, I can't imagine how hard that must have been for her, if it was me in her position, I'd have lost my goddamn fucking mind.

I close my eyes and mindlessly continue playing with her hair as I try to figure out who the woman was and why in the goddamn hell, she tried to kill the most precious being on earth.

Was she on her own? Was she part of an organization? Was it a lone attack? Will Izzy have anyone else coming to look for her? Is she safe? I can't deal with another threat to her life right now, I can barely take a drink on my own so how the fuck am I going to protect her? My mind is spinning out thinking of a hundred different scenarios as I hear the door click open and my eyes pop open to see Enzo quietly step inside the room.

"It's about fucking time; you know she threatened a doc with a knife because you wouldn't wake up?" he says and gestures towards Izzy. "She was losing her shit man, and that's sayin' something coming from me." He strolls over and takes the seat next to me where Marco sat before.

"Who was the woman and why the fuck was she after her?"

"I had Alec go through the security footage and identify her. Seems like she was Alessi's girlfriend or some shit like that, and blamed Izzy for his death," he whispers, and I let out a breath of relief that it wasn't Mafia related. Thank fuck for that, I don't fancy any more wars right now.

"Once she wakes up and sees I'm good, I'll send her back to yours to rest, let her stay with you until she figures out what she wants to do. I don't know if she'll go back to Chicago or stay in the city."

Enzo chest vibrates with a silent chuckle before he murmurs, "She's not going anywhere man, that girl loves the fuck outta you."

His words give me a spark of hope that I quickly push away, I don't think I have the strength to hope for her to stay only to watch her walk away.

We sit in silence for a while and I close my eyes, thankful to be alive and that the bullet didn't do too much damage.

The doc explained that I'll be here for a few more days, but things are looking good. It'll take me some time to get back to my full strength, and it'll be fucking hard to get around at first, but with some physical therapy and hard work I should get back to my full physical strength in a couple of months.

My body can heal all it likes, but I don't think my heart ever will. Not with the blonde bombshell of a woman still sleeping at my side not in my life anymore.

But she's alive, and that's all that will ever matter to me. Her health, safety and happiness are my priority, and I'll happily die a hundred times over, walk through fucking fire and take every bullet that fires her way to maintain that. I'll break my own heart to heal hers.

CHAPTER FORTY-NINE

Izzy

My neck aches as I wake and I replay the last few days in my mind, the pain and fucking worry I've felt are like nothing I've ever known.

A hand glides through my hair and my brows furrow at the movement. *What the hell?*

My head snaps up and my eyes widen as I make eye contact with Luca.

"You're awake," I breathe and tears instantly well in my eyes.

"Yeah baby, I'm awake," he chuckles and wipes my cheek with his thumb as a tear falls down my face. The gesture is so sweet, so tender, so *him*, that I can't help but let out a sob as I let relief fill my pores—he's finally fucking awake.

"I'm so fucking pissed at you," I cry and slap his hand before he can wipe more of my tears. "You get yourself shot and then don't wake up for days. *Fucking days.* Are trying to make me lose my mind, Luca? Are you trying to punish me? Why would you do that to me, huh?"

Rather than seeming reprimanded, he barks out a laugh and shakes his head. "Fuck, I missed you, Iz," he says in awe as he stares at me, eyes full of wonder. I must look like shit considering I haven't left this goddamn hospital once since we arrived, I couldn't bear to be away from him for longer than a quick trip to the bathroom.

"How are you feeling? Are you okay? Should I get a doctor? Have they checked you over? Why the fuck are you just lying awake when you should be getting examined? Why the hell didn't you wake me up? How long have you been awake? Do you need anyt—"

"Jesus, *fuck*. Take a breath, baby. I'm fine. Just breathe, I'm okay," he interrupts and squeezes my hand. "I've been awake for two hours; I've been checked over and I'm alright. I didn't wake you because Marco told me you hadn't slept in four days. What the hell, Izzy? Why didn't you go home and sleep?" he says with a scowl.

"Like fuck was I just leaving you here!" I yell and stand before pacing beside his bed. "What if you needed me? What if something happened? What if you woke up and I wasn't here?"

"Honestly? I thought you'd see I was awake and then get the hell out of here, I didn't think you cared that much," he murmurs and the vulnerable look he sends me fucking guts me.

"Are you insane!?" I wail and stop my pacing; the man is so fucking irritating. "Why the hell would I just leave?"

"You were about to ask me to sign divorce papers before I got shot, Izzy. I wouldn't blame you for leaving," he says with a sigh and I shake my head at him, the asshole.

"You're right, Luca. I was about to ask you to sign the papers," I say and reach for my bag at the side of the bed and pull out the documents and a pen. I throw them both on the bed and give him a pointed look.

He appears physically pained as he picks up the pen and flips through the pages, signing where he needs to sign.

"It's done," he whispers and hands them back to me. I take them and put them back in my bag before I approach him. I grab his face with both of my hands, using my thumbs to caress his stubbled cheeks before I bring my lips to his.

He freezes for a second before he returns the kiss. It's slow and languid, filled with pain and so much love that my heart swells before he pulls away.

"Don't break my heart like this please Izzy, just leave. I can't have you in the same room as me knowing I can't have all of you."

"I'm not going anywhere, asshole," I mutter as I take a seat and rest my forehead against his.

"Please," he begs, and I sigh in frustration.

"I told you; I'm not going *anywhere*. I don't want an arranged marriage, Luca. I want—"

"I get it Izzy, okay? I don't need you to give me all of the reasons I fucked up and lost you. I hate myself for it as it is. I destroyed us both and it's killing me." I pull away to stare down at him and he closes his eyes and tips his head back into the pillow. "I can't watch you go Izzy, please just leave. I can't do this, I can't watch the woman I love more than anything in this fucked up world walk away, so please just leave now before I lose my goddamn mind."

"Are you going to keep interrupting me, or can you let me speak?" I ask and he gives me a barely perceptible nod.

"As I was saying, I don't want an arranged marriage. I want *you*. I want to wake up with my head buried in your chest every morning, I want evening dinners on the couch watching crappy tv, I want your laughs and your dramatic arguments, I want your punishments and your love. I want to go to sleep every night after you've fucked me into a coma wrapped up in your arms. I want your forehead kisses and stolen glances throughout the day. I want your annoyingly overprotective texts every ten minutes when I leave the house without you. I want *you*." He just stares at me slack jawed, in disbelief and shakes his head.

"I don't get it, you've just had me sign divorce papers," he whispers.

"Because I want to do it right, I want to have a real marriage, not one of obligation. I want a wedding where I'll walk myself down the aisle and give myself to you in front of our family and friends. I want to stand on the beach at your family's island—where we can be closer to your mother—and vow to spend the rest of my life loving you, and in return I want you to vow to me that you'll never let anything get in the way of *us* again. Vow to love me for the rest of our lives, vow to grow old with me, Luca," I plead, and a tear rolls down his cheek. I lean over and kiss it away as he whispers against my ear, "I haven't lost you?"

"Never." I bring my lips back to his and this time he doesn't hesitate; he pours two weeks of tension and heartbreak into me, and I pour all my love into him in return.

"I love you so fucking much," he murmurs against my lips, and I pull back and smile at him.

"I love you too."

"Get the fuck in here," he says while he pulls back the covers and I shake my head, but he just glares at me.

"I don't want to hurt you."

"The only thing hurting right now is me not holding you. Please just get on the damn bed and fucking cuddle with me, woman."

I roll my eyes before carefully climbing into the bed next to him, taking extra care not to jostle him or touch his wound. I place my head on his chest—thankful to hear his heart beating—as he places a kiss on my head and brings his hand up to play with my hair.

"I'm so fucking sorry, Iz. For everything."

"I know, just don't do it again," I mumble as I fight to stay awake.

"Never, baby. And I'll never let you go. I missed you so much."

"I missed you too. Enzo is fucking annoying when your around him all the time." His chest vibrates as he chuckles beneath me.

"Come home, I need you back home with me."

"There's nowhere else I'd rather be."

He presses a kiss into my hair, and I hear his breathing change as he falls asleep. For the first time in what feels like forever, I fall asleep peacefully, with him wrapped around me.

CHAPTER FIFTY

Luca

I've been in this goddamn hospital for three fucking weeks. Three weeks that could have been better spent at home with my girl, but instead I've been stuck in this shithole room, staring at the same four walls until my physical therapist collects me to get me up on my feet.

It's hard—a *lot* harder than I expected—to get back up on my feet. Even though the bullet missed any major organs, it still fucked my body up and I've spent the last three weeks killing myself every day to be able to do things for myself.

The first few days were the worst, I was fully unable to get out of bed, they even had me using a fucking catheter because I couldn't get up to take a piss. Ridiculous, and utterly fucking *humiliating*. I'm the underboss of the New York Mafia—goddamn heir to the throne—I should be able to take a damn leak without a tube's assistance.

The best part was when on the day I woke up, a nurse attempted to give me a bed bath, the nurse in question hadn't been one of my regular nurses, because Izzy lost her shit. Apparently—while I was still unconscious—she had refused to let another woman touch me and opted to do it herself. So, when the sweet, sixty-year-old nurse came and offered her assistance, she flew off the fucking handle and started threatening the poor old lady.

The woman is *insane.*

But she's mine, she agreed to stay, so she can act like a fucking lunatic all she likes as long as she does it with me by her side. I love her special brand of crazy, sometimes I forget how utterly unhinged she is until she goes ahead and threatens to slit the neck of a woman twice my age.

Fuck, I love her.

Since that day, Izzy has been my full-time nurse, and I've loved it. Not just her taking care of me, but just being around her. I honestly thought I was losing her, but then of course she goes and does what's least expected of her and asks for a divorce so that she can be with me for *me.*

I thought it was ridiculous at first, but after I thought it over, I realized that she's fucking brilliant. I don't want us to ever have to think back on us being in an arranged marriage or a business deal. I want to make her my wife because I love the shit out of her, not out of family obligation.

I'm sat watching her now as she gathers everything in the hospital room, I'm finally getting the fuck out of here and she's been flustered all morning. I didn't think it was possible for Izzy to be flustered, but she's been flapping around all morning, trying to make sure everything is perfect and "just right for you to come home to" she said.

I don't know what the hell she's worrying about, I don't give a fuck what happens as long as we're together.

I watch as the woman I'm obsessed with crouches down to look under the bed. "Baby, what in the ever-loving *fuck* are you doing?" I ask but it falls on deaf ears as she continues rummaging around.

"Izzy?" I bark and her head finally snaps up.

"What's wrong? Are you okay? Maybe we should stay here a few more days," she mutters the last sentence, and I can't help but roll my eyes as she stands and rounds the bed, but rather than coming to me, the infuriating woman starts digging through our bags.

"Like fuck are we staying here any longer. What the hell are you searching for?"

"I just want to make sure we don't forget anything." She nibbles on her bottom lip in a rare of act of vulnerability and *fuck me*, she's adorable.

"C'mere, baby," I murmur and motion for her to step between my legs from where I'm perched on the side of the bed. She takes a tentative step forward, but I grab her hand and pull her to me.

Once she's nestled between my legs, I release her hand and tuck a stray piece of hair behind her ear before looping my arms around her neck. She steps closer into me and burrows her head in my chest and mumbles, "I'm scared."

"What are you scared of, *mia regina*?" I whisper against her hair, and she sighs before pulling back to peer up at me.

"It feels safe here, if something happens then there's plenty of doctors around to help you."

So, she's worried about me? This I can deal with.

"One of our family doctors just moved into our building on the floor beneath ours. Would you feel better if I gave you his number?

That way you can always reach someone, but nothing is going to happen, Iz. I've been cleared to go." I don't tell her about the fact I moved him in the first month she had her period because I was stressing out over her being in pain—I really don't think she'd appreciate that.

"You're right, I just... I don't know, I just don't want to lose you, I guess."

"I'm not going anywhere, baby," I whisper and pull her back to me as I tip my head down, capturing her lips with mine and we exchange a slow and tender kiss, but I tear myself away before my control snaps and I take the kiss deeper.

Somehow, I don't think she'll let me fuck her on a hospital bed where anyone could just walk in.

It's a damn shame too, considering it's been nearly six weeks since I've been inside her.

"I love you, Iz," I say and rest my forehead against hers.

"I love you too."

The elevator opens into our apartment, and I breathe a sigh of relief.

Home.

We're finally fucking home.

I follow Izzy as she saunters in and heads straight towards the bags that I had one of our men drop off ahead of us. I stand still for a moment in the threshold of the kitchen, taking in the view. I never thought I'd ever see her inside our home again, I thought I'd either have to sell the place or burn it to the ground in attempt to free myself of the pain that came when I didn't have her with me.

I take three quick strides to reach her and swallow up the space between us as I spin her around and push her backwards into the kitchen island with my body.

"What are you—" she starts but I press my mouth to hers in a hungry kiss to silence her. I bite her bottom lip and she lets out a mewl that has my cock throbbing against my zipper.

"I need you, baby," I groan into her mouth, and she whimpers before giving me a jerky nod in reply.

Thank fucking God.

I take her hand and all but drag her towards the bedroom, I'd usually just go ahead and fuck her on the kitchen counter, but this feels like a big moment for us, and I'll be damned if I don't get to worship her in our bed like the queen she is—plus she'd probably strangle me if I pulled a stitch while not playing it safe.

Once we reach the bedroom, I let go of her hand and bring my lips back to hers, teasing my tongue against hers and she returns it by kissing me with everything she has, as though it's the last ever time she'll get to kiss me, as though she can't fucking breathe without me, as if she's savoring every moment—I know because I feel the exact same way.

"Christ, I've missed you, Izzy," I pant into her mouth before I pull away to stare down at her. She's a fucking vision, the most breathtaking woman to ever exist.

"You said you were sorry for everything right?" she asks, and I nod as she starts to lift my shirt over my head. I help her shrug it off and reach to help her with hers, but she bats my hand away before I can.

"Tsk, tsk, tsk, not quite yet, *amore mio.* You're going to strip, lay down on that bed, and wait for your punishment." She arches a brow as I stand and stare at her.

Well, fuck.

This is *not* how I expected this to go, but I do as she says anyway. I'll do anything she fucking wants for the rest of my goddamn life just to keep her by my side.

CHAPTER FIFTY-ONE

Izzy

I didn't plan on punishing Luca for everything that happened, but at that moment, I felt like this would be good for both of us. This will help him let go of some of his guilt and it will help me take back some of my control. Win, win, right?

I watch as Luca lowers himself onto the bed, his movements are still stiff with his injury—another reason for me to be in control, the last thing I want is for him to hurt himself. I'm just being a good wife... or ex-wife? Girlfriend? Fiancé? I'm not really sure since I haven't gotten my ring back from him.

He lays in the middle of the bed, and I take in every beautiful naked inch of him. He's so hard that it must be painful, he's already leaking pre cum and we haven't even gotten started yet. His eyes haven't left mine since he took his position, silently waiting for me to move, waiting for instruction.

Such a good boy.

I slowly pull my sweater over my head, leaving me standing in yoga pants and a sports bra. Luca's eyes widen and his nostrils flare as he takes me in, but he remains still. Once I see he's not making a move to get up, I continue undressing, taking my clothes off slowly to torture him further and he curses under his breath once I slide my panties down my legs, leaving myself completely nude for him to ogle.

I walk over to the dresser and pick out one of his ties before I make my way over to the bed. I climb on the end and crawl up towards him before carefully straddling his waist and taking his arms. I tie the tie around his wrists and secure it to the headboard like he did to me all those weeks ago. He can easily get himself free, it's more of a test to see if he'll let go of his control for me.

"Mmm, you look delicious, laid here at my mercy, your body begging for release," I murmur as I bend down and run my tongue across his neck before lifting up to grin down at him and he squirms underneath me.

"Fuck, you're killing me, baby," he groans, and I climb up his body until I'm hovering above his head, giving him an up-close view of what he wants so badly.

"Do you have any idea how much I got myself off thinking of you while we were apart?" I skim my fingers down my body. I pinch both of my nipples and let out a breathy moan before sliding my hand down further until I reach my clit. I pinch my bud between my fingers and tip my head back as I let the zap of pleasure run through me.

"Fuck. You're drenched, Iz. You're dripping on my chin. Give me a taste baby."

I shake my head and side two fingers inside, coating my fingers in my juices and pulling them out for him to see.

He tips his head up, wanting a taste, but I return my fingers to where they were, slowly pumping them in and out. He can hear

how wet I am each time my fingers move in and out and I want
nothing more than to crawl back down him and impale myself on
his dick, but I keep going, wanting to torture him further.

I use my thumb to circle my clit as I continue fucking myself
with my fingers, the rhythm increasing as I bring myself closer to
the edge until I'm falling over the cliff of insanity and screaming
out my release as Luca pants beneath me.

"Jesus fucking Christ. Holy fuck. I've never seen anything so
fucking sexy in all my life. *Please, Izzy.* I need you to fuck me, or
let me go so I can fuck you into the mattress," he begs, and I grin
down as him before crawling back down the bed until I'm nestled
between his legs.

I take his length in my hand, and he lets out a whimper—yes, he
fucking *whimpers*—before I circle my tongue around his tip and
glide my tongue down to his base, I use my free hand to cradle
his balls and repeat the process of teasing him until he's a pleading
mess.

"I'm begging you, baby, please make me come," he groans, and
I take pity on him, sliding his cock inside my mouth and sucking.

"Fuck, yes," he moans and shifts his hips up in an attempt to
fuck my mouth.

I pull back and glare at him, silently ordering him to remain still
before I take him back inside my mouth. I slide down his length,
letting him hit the back of my throat. I slowly fuck him with my
mouth, keeping a torturous pace until I feel him swell inside me
right before he announces, "I'm going to come." I quickly pull
back and let go of him.

"You're not allowed to come until I tell you to, understand?" I bark and he closes his eyes and takes a deep breath before reopening them.

"Yeah, baby. I understand."

"Good boy," I grin at him and lower my head back down, restarting the process of teasing his length with my tongue as he pleads with me to let him come. I'm not sure how long we stay like that—repeating the torturous pace of my lapping at his tip and swiping my tongue up and down his length before taking him in my mouth and bringing him to the brink of orgasm before pulling back and repeating the same—until I'm convinced Luca has been punished enough, he's a whimpering, begging mess and I'm fucking soaked, so turned on I'm pretty sure I'll orgasm as soon as I slide myself onto him.

"Think you've been punished enough?"

"Jesus fucking Christ, Izzy, please let me come. I swear, I'll never doubt you again," he pleads, and I believe him.

I lift and maneuver myself until I'm straddling him and bend down to capture his lips with mine in a hungry kiss before I line up his dick with my entrance and slam myself down on him until he fills me.

"Fuuuuuck," he groans, and I gasp for air. I lift up to do the same again, it only takes three times until I'm falling off the edge and my walls are squeezing him as I moan his name so loud, I'm pretty sure everyone in the building can hear.

"Fuck, baby, let me go," he grunts, and I reach up to undo the tie from the headboard.

As soon as his hands are free, he grabs hold of my hips and flips me over before grabbing my legs and throwing them over his shoulders. He keeps his promise and fucks me into the mattress, his movements are unhinged, completely feral, and I'm absolutely here for it as he thrusts into me like a man possessed.

"One more, baby, I need to feel you shatter around me once more before I fill you with my cum," he groans and reaches for my clit before pinching it once, twice, three times, and I'm crying out as waves of pleasure run through me and my vision blackens as I spiral through an orgasm so intense, I become dizzy. His movements become choppy and stilted as he groans my name and pulses inside of me, coating my walls with his release.

Luca leans down and captures my lips with his in a tender kiss, before resting his forehead against mine. It's only then that I realize he's just fucked me like an animal while injured.

"Luca, your stitches—"

"Are fine," he interrupts. "I love you so fucking much, Izzy."

"I love you, too. Always, *amore mio*."

EPILOGUE - THREE MONTHS LATER

Luca

I look out over the few faces I see seated in front of me on the beach. This time around, we opted to only have our close friends and family here rather than make a big circus for our wedding.

In turn, the only people here are my father, Marco, Enzo with the object of his obsession—Robyn and Alec. Izzy spoke to my father and brothers and asked if they'd be okay if we held our wedding here on the island my dad bought for Ma. They all immediately agreed, of course they did, they all love Izzy—probably more than they do me—and would do anything to make her happy. She wanted us to get married here because she thought it would be good to honor my mother, and because it's in the exact same spot as I got down on one knee and proposed to her.

Turns out my wife is rather sentimental; I can say for certain I never expected the psychotic woman I met on our wedding day to become my whole world. I thought she was unhinged—and she certainly is—but I fucking love how hard she loves, how much she cares, how much she wants to help people and make a difference in this godforsaken world.

I watch as Izzy comes out of the house and makes her way towards me. Unlike last time, she's not decked out in a full wedding gown but rather a white jumpsuit thing that is absolutely her. The front dips down between her breasts and gives me a view of her cleavage, a goddamn dream, and I never want to wake up. She slowly makes her way towards me, carrying a bouquet of red roses that match her lipstick perfectly. I can't take it any longer, it's been three hours since I've had her in my arms and that's three hours too fucking long.

I take off into a run towards her and swing her up into my arms, making everyone around us laugh before making my way back to the front and setting her down on her feet beside me.

"Impatient as always," she mutters, and I give her my best winning smile.

"You look amazing, baby."

The officiant clears his throat and begins the ceremony. His voice buzzes in the back of my mind as I continue to stare at the woman in front of me, she's everything I never knew I needed, wanted, desired. When I was told I'd be getting married, I drank myself into a stupor while burying my head in the sand. Little did I know then that it would be the best thing to ever happen to me. I can't imagine my life without this woman in it. Without her by my side, I wouldn't be the man I am today. I'd be a shell of myself, unable to go on.

"Luca! Your vows," Izzy whispers and gives me a chastising glare and I realize that I completely tuned out while staring at her. Oops.

"Right," I say and clear my throat.

"Izzy, you came into my life at a time when I needed you, and not because of a deal or business, but because I needed your light to brighten up my world. I needed your smile to make me feel alive. I know I've made mistakes in the past, and I know I'll probably make more, but I vow to love you, always. I vow to take care of you for the rest of our lives, to protect you, to give you the freedom you need and want and to stand by your side through everything. I vow to believe in you, in us. I'll spend the rest of my life showing you just how much of a queen you are. Even on the days when you drive me insane, I'll be right by your side showing you just how much I love you. In sickness, in health, in good times and bad. Forever, till death do us part."

Tears stream down her face as I finish, and I use my thumbs to wipe them from her cheeks. Even when crying, she's still the most beautiful woman in the world.

"Luca, you blasted your way into my life and tipped my whole world upside down. You came in and changed everything, and I couldn't be more thankful. You've supported me, carried me when I needed you to, and brought me a whole new family that I didn't know I needed." She trembles as she clasps my hands with hers. "You mixed up my whole life and added color to an otherwise dull and gray existence. Thank you for giving me a kaleidoscope of colors. I promise to stand by your side, to be your support system and your home. I vow to take care of you, the way you do me. I vow to fight by your side, loving you in a way that no one else ever will. I'll always be yours, in good times and in bad, in sickness and in health, forever and always. Until death do us part."

S. WILSON

My lips descend on hers as soon as she finishes speaking and I can hear Enzo let out a whoop. I internally roll my eyes as I hear the officiant mutter something under his breath before announcing, "I now pronounce you Mr. and Mrs. Romano."

Fucking finally, it's been three months of torture not being able to refer to her as my wife but having to use *fiancé* instead.

I pull back and grin down at her and she gives me my favorite smile of hers. I'm one lucky asshole to be gifted that smile for the rest of my life and I make an unspoken vow to keep that smile on her face every single day for the rest of my existence.

"*Ti amo, mia regina,*" I whisper against her hair as I pull her into my chest.

"*Sempre, amore mio.*"

The End.

BOOKS BY S. WILSON

The Romano Empire

Vow to Me
Read Izzy and Luca's book here:
https://mybook.to/hL04

Run to Me:
Read Robyn and Enzo's book here:
https://mybook.to/EgvgU

Lie to Me:
Read Sloane and Marco's book here:
https://mybook.to/2nAB

ABOUT THE AUTHOR

S. Wilson is an author from the UK who enjoys writing dark, spicy books featuring morally gray men and the women they fall for. When she's not writing, you can find her at home spending time with her daughter, reading and supporting other indie authors.

For exclusive insights and news before everyone else, join S. Wilson's readers group- S. Wilson's Little Warriors. You can find us here: https://www.facebook.com/groups/8785376824852063/

You can also keep up to date by following on social media.

@authorswilson on Instagram: https://www.instagram.com/authorswilson/

@authorswilson on TikTok: https://www.tiktok.com/@swilsonauthor

Don't forget to follow S. Wilson on Amazon to get notified about her latest releases!

ACKNOWLEDGEMENTS

Okay, so... I guess I wrote a book? Firstly, I want to thank anyone who's made it this far. Thank you so much for taking a chance on reading my book! I'm so incredibly grateful to each and every one of you.

Thank you to my beta readers, ARC readers, the bookstagram community, my AMS chat girls (I love you both) and everyone else who had helped me. Thank you for your support, for answering my hundreds of questions and just overall being amazing.

And a special thanks to Stacey for re-editing my baby for me, you're amazing. THANK YOU.

Made in the USA
Coppell, TX
08 March 2025

46825005R00184